Tree
People

for Leslie,
"May your waters
never cease."

M

Tree People

An Ecological Thriller

M. St. Croix

MCP

Mill City Press, Inc.
2301 Lucien Way #415
Maitland, FL 32751
407.339.4217
www.millcitypress.net

© 2018 by M. St. Croix

Cover art by Claire Whitehead (clairespaintings.etsy.com)

Printed in the United States of America

ISBN-13: 978-1-54562-242-1

To Don and Betsy

1.
They're making it sound like a hoax

A clack-clack on glass stirred Jim Cassaway from a restless sleep, blinking at a circle of harsh light.

"Move it!" boomed a voice, as the beam of a flashlight streaked across Jim's face and scanned the interior of his '98 Honda beater, hesitating here and there at scattered books, a bag of clothes.

Jim untucked his knees and sat up in the back seat. His pillow flopped onto the floor as puzzle pieces of reality sluggishly aligned:

Uniform.

Presidio security.

Got to go. Find another spot.

He stumbled from the car, a slim, fair-haired feather of a man.

"Can I ask a question?"

Strutting to the company vehicle, the burly security guard didn't bother looking back. "Somebody called."

Jim slipped on his sneakers wondering how a 'somebody' could see the car tucked back under a row of cypress smothered in the fog? X-ray vision?

This was Jim's fourth night since being evicted from his studio apartment in the Marina District after the owner tripled the rent. Silicon Valley salaries had skyrocketed rents all over the Bay Area sending long standing tenants out, and out-raged. After a slew of advance warnings, June 1st came with a yellow sheet taped to his door: TWO WEEK'S NOTICE. June 15th arrived and the locks were changed. So much for living in the Now with scant attention on tomorrow's thundering certitude.

The headlights chewed through the fog to Fort Point at the base of the Golden Gate Bridge. Jim parked, checked the time on his cell phone: 5:35 am.

This wasn't his first experience on the street, but it needed to be the last. He'd read somewhere that if you've been homeless by the time you're twenty-four, there's a good chance you'll be homeless at forty-eight. He could have crashed at a friend's place. Still might. But the last thing he wanted was to look like a charity case.

This changes nothing was his attitude.

Jim wasn't ready to reconsider his calling as a documentary filmmaker. He'd known it since waking from a near-death experience in his teens. Now, at 23, he already had a full-length documentary under his belt entitled, *Why Is There Anything?* The heady existential film earned praise from a couple critics at the San Francisco Film Festival. High expectations followed, but projects were slow in coming. He did land some freelance work at *News Bang*, a video-driven online news source, but the work was spotty. Not near enough to pay the rent.

He pulled a wool blanket from the car, draped it around his shoulders and stood at the edge of the bay gazing at a formless wall of fog. At his feet, water slopped against an embankment of rocks, while high overhead a torrent of caffeinated commuters poured into the city across the bridge. As he pictured them in their cars, an idea bubbled up: make a film of rush hour people at a dead stop for one minute. Catch them on the street, heading into buildings: titans of finance, anesthesiologists. Have each one stand still for a solid sixty seconds. How would they act? Could they last? Call it, *Wait a Minute…* or, *Freeze*.

Worth pitching to News Bang?

No, not edgy enough.

Out of the surge of traffic Jim isolated the snore of a foghorn. Soothed by its solemn tone he strolled along the walkway that rimmed the bay forcing himself to sequence a to-do list for the day: Straighten out car. Shower at the Y. Charge phone and tablet at Yang's coffee shop. Check in with Wiley at News Bang for possible work.

What else? Sell some books. Get a quart of motor oil. And don't forget the one o'clock meeting with Omar at Spartan Limo about working as a weekend driver. He pays cash, no address required.

Jim shuffled back to his car, pondering why life had to be an all-consuming money hunt. What he wanted was time, to contemplate, to question things. He was a walking questionnaire. Gomez, his cameraman friend, called him an askaholic.

As Jim approached his car he noticed a soft light glowing inside. His cellphone. Recognizing the number, he palmed it off the seat.

"Christy?"

"Jim! Did I wake you?"

"No." He shut the car door and backed up a couple steps. "I've been up. How are…"

"You're not going to believe this! Have you seen the Charlie Tanner video?"

Leave it to Christy Jones to bypass small talk.

"Tanner…" Jim tripped on broken pavement. The blanket slipped off his shoulders.

"You've got to see this, it's mind-blowing. The trees are…"

Nothing like: *'When can we get together again.'*

Jim had interviewed the famed activist for a *News Bang* video in April. They'd met a couple times since and he chose to believe it was leading to something until it all stopped. Repeated calls went nowhere. Two weeks passed since he'd heard from her. Not that he wanted Christy to see him living out of his car.

"I've been trying to reach you," Jim interrupted.

"Sorry, I was, well, that's something else, but you've been on my mind, a lot. Listen…" Christy tore into a story about people morphing into trees. A story so over-the-top bizarre Jim's sleep-deprived brain couldn't keep up. He listened to random bits, figuring he'd fill in the blanks later.

"I'm not following. Can we grab a coffee and…"?

"Can't," she said, "I'm making arrangements to leave today so I can help out with the protest, the 'Last Stand Protest,' and I want to hire you to film it all."

Jim's heart rate jacked. The torrent of bridge traffic hushed in his ears. He turned his head to the east, to the blush of sunrise buried in the fog behind the Berkeley hills where Christy lived.

"Shoot a protest?"

"It's just part of the bigger thing— the metamorphosis."

Jim gathered up his blanket and draped it around his shoulders. "When is it again?"

"This weekend."

Too soon, he thought. How am I going to book Gomez or another shooter that quick?

"And where is this happening?"

"The redwoods, up north. Oh, tell me you can do it."

Christy was breathing fast into her cordless phone. Jim could hear noises in the background, acoustical shifts like she was walking through rooms, moving things. He pictured her in the attic apartment where he'd interviewed her for the Earth Day piece among posters, banners, and protest signs.

"Sorry about the short notice," Christy said. "Do you know the Safeway by the Marina Green?"

"Yeah, it's right near where I used to..." Jim balked.

"I'll pick you up there around 11."

"This morning?"

"It's a long drive."

No way. Jim shook his head. Too much too soon. Why didn't she call to set this up weeks ago?

"They're making it sound like a hoax. Somebody's Bigfoot prank. But make no mistake, it's real as rock. People are morphing into trees and you're the one to break the news to the world. This is bigger than big. It changes life as we know it... Jim?"

Jim had shut his ears, thinking it through. Slim chance Wiley at News Bang would be receptive to covering a demonstration. Then again, I could pitch it to him as a follow up to Christy's Earth Day interview.

"Jim?!"

"I'm here, seeing how to work it."

"Great. Work it out. I'll look for you in the Safeway lot at 11. If you're not there... no, you *must* be there. I want to see you. Got to go. Need to make my last goodbyes."

Jim was about to say, 'I want to see you too', when Christy came back with, "I'd love you to be there with me. We'll make history together." And clicked off.

Synapses fired: shoot a protest, redwoods, Tanner video—whatever that's about. Wait, we didn't talk about my fee. She can barely pay her bills. And where are we going stay, a tent?

Hey! He caught himself. It's work, a job! And it's Christy Jones!

He stretched the blanket wide. Words he once read blew across his memory— *There's no such thing as an insignificant opportunity.*

No, there's not.

He flapped the blanket like wings.

So how to make it happen?

Call Gomez.

Jim tossed the blanket in the back seat. He didn't need to change clothes, he'd slept in his uniform: white cotton shirt, khaki pants, tan photographer's vest.

He punched Gomez's number.

He's going to hate me for calling him so early, but…

"T'sup?"

"Gomes? Hey, I just got a call about a project."

"Can't talk now, I'm shooting a live home birth."

"A what? Where? I'll come to you."

2.
You have a court date, remember?

Christy Jones set the cordless phone on the bedside table. *He'll come. Jim will find a way.*

She went to the closet and lifted a long red silk scarf off a hook. The mirror on the door reflected her tall, toned frame, clothed only in sports bra and boxer shorts, her cinnamon hair brushed skull-tight in a ponytail.

If Jim can't shoot the documentary, at least he'll meet me at Safeway. Then I can explain why I didn't return his calls.

She felt some solace in that. But as she tossed the scarf on the bed the whiplash of events over the past ten days came rioting back, pitting rage against grief.

Don't! She stamped her foot. *Never give them the satisfaction of losing it. Not now. Not ever.*

Christy had been dodging a meltdown ever since coming home from work to find her beloved dog hanging lifeless from a tree in the yard. A scare tactic? No, worse. An execution plotted to incite her wrath and revenge. Which it did, thanks to the complicity of a friend who urged her on, saying: "*You know who was behind it, Christy. And I know how you can retaliate. I can get you inside.*"

And into Ingot Industry's corporate building she went the next night, punching the security codes she'd been given, laying her dead dog on the desk of Richard Hersh— the forest killer, her soul nemesis. The place eerily silent. All too easy. Until, taking the corridor back to the front lobby, she found herself engulfed in smoke, and waiting outside, police and fire trucks at the ready, as if rehearsed.

Betrayed, entrapped, and arrested for arson.

With friends like that...

To relieve the fist in her stomach, Christy gulped a bubble of air and belched. She turned back to the closet, rifled through hangers, her body trembling.

Settle... settle. Everything happens for a reason, right?

She pulled a puffball jacket from a hanger and smushed it into its compression sack.

What else...? Her brain stuttered.

Christy hadn't slept much since the horror of her dog's murder, her ensuing arrest, and days later, when the impossible happened— someone sent a wacky video, Charlie Tanner's video, and the axis of her world flipped.

She tucked the compression sack into a faded blue backpack. What else?

Headlamp...

Topo map...

She dug in a drawer. Move it girl, you have work to do because hallelujah, a miracle is afoot.

A miracle, indeed. At least in her mind. The Tanner video gave Christy a ray of hope.

Over the past year there had been scattered accounts of people grafting themselves inside the trunks of redwood trees. Gross, preposterous stories, swiftly dismissed. Then the video came showing Charlie Tanner sitting naked inside the hollow of a tree as wiggly tendrils lifted from the ground, seemingly knitting his hands and feet to the tree's inner bark.

Sheer lunacy. Just Charlie having a bit of fun. A bullshit stunt rigged to look real with computer animation. Nobody could convince her otherwise.

Except one.

'The John' Albers, a dear and venerated guardian of the forest, who phoned her, exuberant: *"It's really happening, Christy! You must come see!"*

Nature had intervened and finally given Christy and other activists the end-all act of resistance. One that, for her, could not have come at a more fateful time. There'd be no jury trial. No incarceration. No coming back.

Everything happens for a reason.

She crammed a map into the front pocket of the backpack, zipped it closed and grabbed the cordless phone. More calls to make. She tapped the numbers and waited for the message to finish on the other end.

"Hey-hey guys, it's me, I know it's early but I'm leaving today and wanted to get your take on the Charlie Tanner video I forwarded and…" she paused. Someone at the door, knuckle-rapping in two sets of two. "… and if you're going."

Christy dropped the phone on the bed, snatched a pillow and held it to her chest as she headed for the door. Through the eyehole she saw her father's pointy white goatee. She undid the chains and deadbolt.

Roland entered glum-faced, a tablet tucked under one arm. "Tell me you've made coffee and why I'm here at the crack of dawn."

She gave him a lengthy hug.

"You okay?" he asked. "No, you're not, of course you're not. How can you be," he answered his own question and drew back from the embrace. "This about your arraignment?"

"Not really." Christy turned, flicked a streaking tear from her cheek. "Be right back."

Roland made his way to the kitchen. Something was different about the place. It was quiet for one. Eerie. No music. No sleepovers. And it was picked up. Books on shelves. Counters clear. He set his tablet on the round, unsteady table in the kitchen nook, bent down, found the folded patch of cardboard on the floor and wedged it under a wooden leg. With the table stabilized, he looked out the third-story window.

"Looks like your paparazzi found a parking spot." He'd noticed the suspicious-looking Ford Taurus parked along Swift Street when he arrived. A slouched figure vaping at the wheel.

Christy didn't respond. Roland could hear her talking to someone on the phone. Her voice sounded strained. He moved a small duffel bag off a cane chair, dropped it on the floor and sat. Tacked to the wall above his head hung a poster, curling at the corners—a black and white photo of Yosemite Valley with a quote:

> *"I only went out for a walk and finally concluded*
> *to stay out 'til sundown, for going out, I found,*
> *was really going in.*
>
> *John Muir*

Christy came into the kitchen, dressed in shorts and cotton hoodie. "Nobody's buying it," she muttered, setting the phone on the table.

Roland depressed the power button on his tablet. "Not buying what?"

"N-nothing." Christy stifled what she was about to say. Roland would commit her to a psych ward if he heard her intentions. She left the kitchen, only to return with a fanny pack she stuffed into the duffel.

"What are you doing?" Roland asked.

Christy sucked in a breath and belched the word, "Packing."

Roland chuckled, momentarily amused. As a young girl, Christy had stomach problems. Her homemade remedy was to gulp air into her throat and belch. It relieved the cramps. Talking while she burped evolved over the years to the point where she could disgorge an entire sentence.

"Packing for what, prison?"

"The Last Stand."

"That protest up north? You have a court date, remember?"

Christy filled a hot pot with water from the tap. "This is Friday, and that's…"

"Tuesday. My point." Roland stiffened.

"So I should just stop everything? That's what you're saying?"

"You can't just run off. These are formidable allegations, not some parking ticket."

Christy flicked the power switch on the hot pot, then faced him fingering quotes in the air. "And what happened to your: 'Never stop fighting for what gives life its life.'"

"This is different. Sure, you've been arrested before, but nothing like this. You could be locked up for a year, maybe more. How does that fight for life?"

She lifted a ceramic cup from a cabinet, thumped it down on the counter and walked out of the kitchen.

Roland stepped to the window. The black Taurus still idling at the curb. He shook his head. "Could they be any more obvious?"

Water burbled in the pot.

Christy returned to the kitchen in hiking boots. She leaned her backpack against the refrigerator door.

"I understand why you want to get away," Roland said. "But now is not the time."

Christy wasn't listening as she poured hot water through the coffee grounds.

"We need to get ahead of this." Roland sat back down.

Christy set a steamy cup of Italian roast on the table in front of her father. On the side of the cup was a quote from planet Earth in fat black letters: "Wake Up & Wake Down."

"I only wish you'd have called me before you…"

"Before I what? They killed Mercy!" Christy clenched, flashing on the horror of finding her golden retriever swaying by a noose from a eucalyptus. The trunk of the tree lashed by its fighting claws.

"Yes, they did, or someone did. And your dog's death, wretched and unspeakable as it is, will be lost in the smoke of an arson indictment."

"It was a trap!"

"And convincing them of that…" Roland held up, drew in a calming breath, took a sip of coffee. "Anyway, we'll get into it all this afternoon."

"No-no, I can't meet with your lawyer buddy. I'm leaving."

"Listen, if it wasn't for my lawyer buddy you'd be in custody right now, or shackled with one of those ankle bracelets." Roland punched his password on the tablet.

"So *you* meet with him. I have to go. We're shooting a documentary about the protest and…"

"What documentary?"

"I hired a guy."

"You, who?

"Jim Cassaway. He interviewed me back in April for an Earth Day story on News Bang."

The cordless phone jingled.

"I need to take this." Christy seized the phone and dashed out of the kitchen.

Roland took a swig of coffee. "News Bang…" He typed the words into the search engine. As he waited, he noticed a white letter envelope on the table with a list of names under the hand-printed heading: GOODBYES. Four of the names were crossed off.

"You're not telling me something." Roland listened for her. "Hey? Are you skipping town?"

3.
There are three kinds of woman

Headphones clapped around his neck, Hector Gomez pressed a fingertip to his lips as he led Jim into the kitchen of an upscale Sausalito home. A spacious iceberg of stainless steel appliances and china white cabinets. The sterile kitchen could double as a lab for autopsies.

The marble island where Gomez had set up recording gear was a junk fest of Red Bull empties, a half-eaten bowl of M&M's, Dorito bags and licorice wrappers, some strewn on the floor among crumb litter. The video monitor displayed a quad of camera angles all focused on a pregnant woman squirming and panting on her back, fingers clawing and carving the bed sheet into mountains and valleys.

As Gomez plugged the headphones into his digital recorder he explained how he'd been hired to record the birth, how he pre-set wireless button cameras and mics in the master bedroom down the hall. Even though the woman giving birth refused to have video or photos taken of the delivery, her husband had covertly gone ahead without her consent.

"How'd you get this gig?" Jim asked.

Gomez ignored the question. He handed the headphones to Jim. "Have a listen on the big ears."

Jim winced. "Sounds like someone's choking her to death." He lifted the headphones off and looked at the monitor, forgetting why he came. He'd never seen a birth before. "How long does it last?"

"What, labor?" Gomez slid a rope of red licorice from a bag. "No telling. Could be …"

"Agh! I can't! I can't do this!" The woman's clipped screams reverberated from the headphones in Jim's hands.

"… a while," Gomez said.

In one of the video frames, the nurse, a composed, penguin-shaped man in blue scrubs, stood at the foot of the bed coaching the woman, who bucked and cringed, gritting her teeth and snorting out her nose.

Gomez snapped off a bite of licorice. "I guess it's nice doing it at home. Ballsy, for sure, what with all the complications that can go south."

"What complications?"

Gomez shook his head. "Nah, don't want to jinx it. Besides, whatever happens, that nurse dude will handle it. He's a saint."

In the upper right frame, the male nurse nudged the husband aside to speak to the woman up close. Jim could tell her energy was flagging by her hooded eyelids and swollen frown. He put the headphones back on as the nurse leaned to within a foot from the woman's face.

"Look at me now… I need you to listen to me and to me only." His voice was kind, yet firm.

"Hurts like hell!" Teeth clamped, the woman poured her pain at the man.

"Yes, it does," affirmed the nurse, swabbing gleams of sweat from the woman's forehead with tissue. "And now it's time to push with everything you have. Your baby is coming home. Say it, say it to yourself: my baby is coming home."

She mouthed the words and exhaled.

"He's really good," Gomez said.

Jim watched, transfixed on the nurse, until Gomez poked him with an elbow. "So what's this project you got?"

"Oh, right!" Jim lifted off the headphones. "I got a call about a shoot up north. Are you free this weekend?"

"Who called?"

"Remember Christy Jones? One of the activists we interviewed back in April?"

Gomez groaned. "How could I forget."

"She really liked that piece and we hooked up a couple times since and now she…"

"You 'hooked up'?"

"I know, me and a tree hugger. But like they say, even opposites can attract."

"Or make war."

"We'd have to leave today."

"No way, man. I gotta help my uncle hang drywall."

"Then could you lend me a camera and…."

"My gear?" Gomez's shoulders slumped. "You know I don't let it out of my sight." True. Gomez coveted his video equipment, but it was worth one more shot.

"Just a travel package: a camera, extra batteries, a couple mics. Oh, and the laptop with the editing software."

Gomez shook his head and turned his eyes to the monitor. "All back Monday. Promise."

"What are you shooting?"

"A protest rally. Come on Gomes, I need mobility. We'll be way out camping in the woods somewhere."

"You and that woman?" Gomez thrust his face at Jim and raised a finger. "Now you make me nervous."

"Your gear will be fine."

"No, not that. It's her. She's got you under a spell. I saw it when you interviewed her. Your eyes big as tortillas." Gomez shot a sideways glance at the monitor and abruptly whisked the headphones out of Jim's hands.

In the upper left frame, the nurse moved to the end of the bed, his arms extending under the sheet between the woman's legs.

"Here we go," Gomez said. "You watching?"

"Is that what I think it is?"

'Yeah, the baby's head." Gomez fingered his soul patch. "It's crowning."

Jim's throat cinched in gag reflex at the sight. He forced an inhale through his nostrils. The image on the screen looked repugnant, a mucous-streaked dome bulging between white thighs like some ogre burrowing out its hollow.

"Yo… Cass-way, you getting sick?"

"Huh?" Jim blew out a nauseated breath.

"You look pale as smoke."

"Gotta go," Jim mumbled as he fled the kitchen, slipped on his shoes, and exited the front door to the wails of a newborn.

"So now what?" Jim stood outside the heaven-pillared house in the fog, pondering his next move. His only option was to stop by the *News Bang* office and see if Wiley would back the project, or at least lend him gear for the shoot.

He started down the driveway.

"It's a girl!" Gomez rushed from the door. He waved Jim over to his minivan, pulled out a Sony camera in its hard-shell case.

Jim's mouth awed open. "Wow, you, really?"

"I figure you're in the woods and this is a good camera in low light. Can you handle it?"

"Absolutely!" Jim knew its basic operation.

Gomez set out a canvas satchel with batteries, charger, memory cards. "Back to me by Monday or else you die."

The loan covered most of Jim's needs, but he still lacked wireless mics, a transmitter, and a laptop for editing.

"What changed your mind? How can I repay you?"

"Stop the questions. I have to get back inside. But listen to me. I'm going to say this because I care the best for you, even if you get sick at the sight of a woman giving birth, which would *not* happen if she was someone you loved."

"I didn't get sick, I…"

"Shh… listen, there are three kinds of woman."

"Only three?"

Gomez held up three sausage-fat fingers. "Solamente tres. Y esa mujer, *that woman*, she's none of the three."

"I get that. Christy's different. I've never met anyone like her. She's like this radiant, incandescent light."

"Radiant?" Gomez scrunched his nose. He scanned the street before lowering his voice. "She's a fucking incineradora."

"In-cin-er-a-what?"

"Incinerator. An inferno. You get too close, she will burn you to ash."

4.
Did you have him checked out?

Roland Jones sipped coffee in Christy's kitchen nook as he watched the Earth Day interview with his daughter on his tablet.

"Environment, environment," Christy railed on the screen, "I stopped using that word. It's shapeless and touchless. There's no *there* there." She opened her palms. "Call it what it is: the planet. The mother that bred us and feeds us. The one these soul-less corporations like Ingot Industries and NorCal are genetically tampering, raping and re-jiggering into a Hallmark billboard that says, 'Progress is our pledge to all people.' Blech. Makes you wish they go to hell. Trouble is, they're taking us all there with them."

"Great job slamming Ingot and NorCal Lumber," Roland called out. "I'm sure the prosecutors will find a prominent use for this in court."

Christy returned to the kitchen, crossed off two names on the envelope and stuck it in her back pocket.

Roland tossed his hands in the air. "And now you're going up north to face off with NorCal and pour more gas on the fire."

"Where's the once proud father? Where's the: My daughter doesn't cower or crack under pressure?"

"He's cowering and cracking in fear for his daughter's life, that's where he is. You should lay low, feeling lucky to be out and about and not behind bars right now." Roland exhaled a tired groan. He knew his daughter had set her mind, unstoppable as a comet. "And no interviews for a while. News Bang, talk about an offensive site."

"Present for you." Christy set a ring of keys on the table in front of her father. "You can stay here while I'm gone."

"Thanks for the offer, but no thanks."

"You always say 'no' first."

"No, I don't."

Christy placed her hand on his shoulder, "This is why I asked you to come this morning. I know what's happening."

For more than a year Roland had been living in a friend's RV, parked in the driveway of their Piedmont home. Recently the neighbors signed a petition to have him removed. Being a naturalist educator for grammar schools, he'd been seen hauling boxes, cages and plastic tubs in and out of the RV with all manner of questionable critters and materials living and dead—whale bones, coyote skulls, dead bats, live toads, grasshoppers and earthworms.

"Take them." She pushed the keys into her father's hand. "The shelves are stocked. You can wash your clothes. All I ask is that you water the plants."

"Okay, one condition," he replied without emotion. "You're back here by Monday noon. We need you prepped and daisy fresh. I know how these protests heat up. Don't get dragged off to that Arcata holding tank. If you're not in court the judge will nail you for contempt and then the Anti-Christy demons will chew you up like a power lunch."

Christy snapped the closures on her duffel bag. She was ready to go, but not ready to say goodbye to her father. She laid the red scarf out on the table and began folding it into a long, flat band.

"Oh god, here comes the warrior headband." Roland looked back at the tablet, a frozen image of Christy in the same chair he was sitting in. "So, this guy who interviewed you… Castaway?"

"Cassaway. He put me in a zone. I've never felt so free and at ease in an interview before."

"And he's producing the documentary for who? News Bang?"

"No, for me." Christy wound the scarf around her forehead and tied it in the back.

"Did you have him checked out?"

"Dad!"

"Being cautious here." Roland stood and went over to the window. The black Taurus still parked down at the curb.

Christy strapped on her backpack. It was time. Give nothing away. Just hug and go.

Roland enclosed her in his arms. "Can't say I didn't try."

She picked up her duffel. "Love you much."

He trailed her out the door. "And how do I reach my cell-phone-phobic daughter if I need to remind her to get home in time to face the judge's ruling? Who do I call, Drum?"

"No! Not Drum. Call The John, or Mae. Their numbers are on the refrigerator." Christy descended the stairs and blew her father a farewell kiss.

Roland returned to the kitchen table. He took a slurp of coffee and hit the play button on his tablet to watch the rest of his daughter's interview. He cringed when Christy blistered the name, "Richard Hersh," calling the VP of Ingot Industries "excrement" and "a malignant planet butcher."

"Oh god, she slipped," he said to an empty room. "Damn, she knows better than to make it personal."

Right then everything crystalized: the motive behind the lynching of Christy's dog, the conspiracy, the trap, her arrest.

"Holy shit!" He banged the table with his thighs, spilling coffee as he hurried to the window.

The black Taurus gone.

5.
No spin. No shill. No shit.

Jim crossed the Golden Gate Bridge and drove into North Beach where he parked his car in someone's private driveway, blocking the sidewalk. The reflective sign on the garage door read: NO PARKING, VIOLATORS WILL BE TOWED, but Jim had no time to go hunting for impossible curb space in this city.

Jangly cable car gears vibrated under his feet as he crossed Mason Street, the aroma of roasting coffee beans celebrating the air.

"All the complications..." Gomez's words rung in Jim's ears. He wondered if it was 'complications' that caused his mother's death only days after he was born. Did her complications lead to his hospitalizations? He'd never been given the whole story. He pictured his own birth and the fleshy-messy way he came tunneling out of his mother's warm round womb into this cold, hatchet-edged world.

News Bang commanded the top floor of an old three story Victorian building. The family residence was remodeled in the 70's into business offices, its peeling, pus-colored stucco exterior untouched since. If paint had a color for despair that would be it.

Jim shut his nostrils to the ammonia sting of the antiseptic-sprayed lobby. He would've taken the elevator if it worked. He climbed the worn carpeted stairs, rehearsing his protest pitch. At the third floor, a wave of fatigue plowed through him. He stopped at the pebbled glass door hand-painted with bold, black and red lettering:

THE NEWS BANG NETWORK
No spin. No shill. No shit.

News Bang was an internet news source made notorious for controversial 'hands-on/gloves-off reporting'. The video-driven network was founded and helmed by Bryce Wiley, everybody's sworn enemy. "Nobody likes a rogue radical with a trust fund," one congressman said. Called 'a pulp wikileaks' and 'gotcha porn', anyway you sliced it, Wiley had cut himself a wedge of the new media pie, and reveled in it.

Jim had been freelancing for the network for six months, doing research, copywriting, creating web teasers to pull people to the site. Besides the Earth Day report, he'd done intermittent fieldwork for paltry pay. Still, something is better than nothing.

He listened at the door. All quiet inside as far as he could tell. Most staffers typically didn't drag in until noon. He turned the knob and shoulder-pushed the heavy, jamb-stuck door. It swung in and bumped against a clay pot harboring a derelict jade plant that defied death day after neglectful day.

The third-floor office was a roomy, open layout of workstations scattered among overstuffed chairs, couches, and library tables stacked with magazines and tablets. Hearing Jim enter, reporters Spider Phillips and Vicki Razoukio, sitting side by side at an editing bay, spun in their chairs.

"Hey man, I finally saw your doc." Spider said, peering over thick-rimmed glasses. He turned to Vicki. "Have you seen it?" She shook her head, finger-twirling her jet-black dyed hair, visibly annoyed by the interruption. "It's called…"

"*Why Is There Anything?*" Jim said, adding, "The primal philosopher's mind boggler."

"Right, right." Spider swiveled back to Vicki, "He's going around interviewing philosophy professors and rabbi's, Zen dudes, evangelicals, quantum physics geeks, and asking them why is anything here? Why is there even a here here? Like existence, right? And at the very end, the last person, she's this bag lady on the street, gray and grizzled, pushing a shopping cart with a shaky wheel, and she says straight to camera with a craggy voice: 'Because nothingness got lonely.' Right? Why is there anything? 'Because NOTHINGINESS GOT LONELY.' Rimshot, man. Made all the heady metaphysics and god almighty stuff sound like freakin' gobbledygook."

Vicki creased an impatient smile, re-crossed her legs, wanting to get back to the edit where shadowy shapes hung frozen on a 42" screen.

Jim waited for the 'but' to come, which it did.

"But…" Spider added, "…personally I would've gutted ten minutes. And the music didn't work at all. And I would've locked on that last frame of that woman's face, but hey…"

Jim blinked his leaden eyelids and changed the subject. "So what are you guys editing?"

"It's a sting on a judge," Vicki explained. "Benedict the prick."

On the screen two figures stood beside an idling black limo among dimly lit brick warehouses.

"Wiley set it up. Got an actor to offer the judge a fat wad of cash in exchange for a reduced sentence on some convict."

Spider pointed to a corner of the screen. "You can just make out the undercover parked across the street ready to pounce."

"Cross-fade to San Quentin," Vicki said.

If *News Bang* couldn't uncover a coverup, expose some corporate crime or government corruption, Wiley would apply homemade tactics. Jim continued to question the journalistic ethics, but he'd noodle that when he was hired to produce such a sting.

"Say, have either of you heard about a Tanner video?"

They both shook their heads.

Jim left them and proceeded to a glassed-in corner office at the rear of the space. A faded news clipping gaff-taped to the door read: 'Bryce is like that dog in Wizard of Oz, the curtain-puller, just one difference, this mutt is rabid.'

Inside, Bryce Wiley stood violently shaking an envelope in his hands at a rather affable Friar Tuck of a lawyer Jim had seen a few times before. Seemed like every month a lawsuit was dropped on Wiley's desk.

"Watch your balls," the lawyer said, angling past Jim in the doorway. "He's got the clippers out today."

Wiley's office was a jungle of paper. Newspaper piles and stacks of magazines toppled from couches and tables. Two modest-sized, wall-mounted TV's, turned off most of the time, flanked a gigundus plasma screen center-wall with the *News Bang* website on permanent display. The room's high, double-hung windows overlooking Columbus Avenue were solid blanks of fog, lending an extra dose of gloom to the space.

"They got nothing!" Wiley kicked a waste basket, spewing old mail and Styrofoam cups.

Jim rapped on the door.

"What!" Wiley burned, then saw Jim. "Oh, hey, come on in man."

Wiley dropped behind his desk, ferociously combing his fingers through thick, prematurely graying hair, the light of a goose-neck lamp catching ridges of his moon-pocked cheeks.

He wore his standard black mock tee and black denim pants, his shoulders salted with dandruff.

"Bad news?" Jim said.

"Don't ask," Wiley grunted. "But good you stopped by. I might have something for you. Gimme a moment. Here…" Wiley slid papers around, uncovered a large clam shell loaded with Ghirardelli chocolates. "Help yourself."

"That's okay," Jim declined the offer. "I got something for you, too."

"Yah?"

"A big rally this weekend in the redwoods called, 'The Last Stand.' Serious stuff. Could be a great follow-up to the Earth Day story."

"Trees?" Wiley shrugged.

"It's a protest— confrontation, tear gas, police beatings."

"They're still doing that 'save the trees' thing?"

"Yeah, why?"

"It's so '90's."

"Remember Christy Jones, the activist I interviewed?"

"The one who just got arrested?"

"What? N-no," Jim stuttered, taking a half step back.

"Smell the dead, Cazzway. That Earth Day piece got zip reaction. Strong journalistically, but the abysmal lack of responses put it in the same graveyard with 'The Homeschool Epidemic.'

Jim had prepped for rejection and parried with, "I only ask 'cause I'm shooting the protest anyway and I thought it'd be a good follow-up story, you know, show the activist in action, walking the talk, nose to nose with loggers and cops, straight in the teeth of their rage.

"The teeth of their rage," Wiley mimicked Jim's words with a snarl, then lifted his head. "There was that lumberjack…

what was his thing? Guy was certifiable. Even the Chronicle wouldn't print it. Or did they?"

"So that's a 'no'?"

"Listen, bogus UFO sightings get more air play than protests. Wiley bit into a bagel. "Damn, I'm blocking. I know I saw a clip about it. Some wacko logger."

"So… no?"

"Oh, yeah, no."

Jim was about to ask him if he knew about a Tanner video, but held back. He turned to the big white board on the wall lined with a grid of current *News Bang* stories being developed and produced.

"You said you had something for me?"

"Next week. We need backgrounding on a questionable banker dude."

"How about that one there." Jim pointed to the fourth story down on the board. "Nobody's assigned to that."

"No-no." Wiley wagged a finger. "You're not ready to do any heavy lifting. You need to get your hands bloody before you hunt big game."

Heavy lifting. Jim's skin bristled. Stuck doing scutwork. Fact-checking and writing teaser captions were not going to cut it. He stayed on for the chance to make a ground-breaker, his 'ticket to the world' as he called it, maybe not with *News Bang* but somewhere, and right now this place was the only somewhere around.

"That's it!" Wiley remembered. "The logger murders his wife and he blames it on the trees!"

Jim was out the door, but Wiley hadn't noticed. "We should have a segment called, Wacko of the Week," he said, and started typing.

Refusing to hear another 'No,' Jim decided to borrow first and apologize later. Without turning on the overhead fluorescents, he slipped into the tech room, crab-walking between gray metal erector-set shelves. He nabbed a laptop and stuffed a wireless mic and transmitter into a satchel. Then he tiptoed to the back corner, hooked a monopod under his arm and slunk out the *News Bang* door with neither Spider nor Vicki catching sight.

6.
The most cockamamie thing I ever heard

As Jim sped down Chestnut Street to the Safeway rendezvous, he replayed the wild story Christy rattled off on the phone about people morphing into trees. He repeated her last words out loud: "We'll make history together." What was that? A way to entice me? Doesn't she know I'd jump through hoops to make this happen? If not for the project, then for her?

Jim's attraction to Christy had little to do with her notoriety and everything to do with her physical presence. Dynamic? Magnetic? He couldn't put it in words. Maybe that's what charisma is, someone's inner luminosity, without shadows, a beacon, like a sun.

Whatever it was, she emanated it. He loved her morning glory blue eyes, the gap in her front teeth, her unpretentious manner and blunt, no-nonsense speech. And her stories— like being eight-years old and tree-sitting in a redwood for a month of protest before media pressure forced her down. Or getting suspended from middle school for rallying classmates to boycott the cafeteria's genetically modified food. Jim could listen to Christy for hours. Simply being with her was an adventure.

The tricky part was how to keep his affection from detracting from the work. He needed to make this documentary stop time.

He arrived at the meeting place forty-five minutes early. The fog so thick he could barely see the front of the grocery store. He parked his Civic in the lot where he thought it would go unnoticed for the weekend.

Since he had some time, Jim googled a number of searches on the *News Bang* laptop: redwood trees, California lumber history, protests—any background to prep for the shoot. Maybe find public domain footage that would add dimension to the story. Someone's sound bite to reinforce another's message, or run contrary to their opinion.

YouTube had a few shorts. He clicked on a black and white film showing a hard-hatted man at the base of a gargantuan tree, its girth as big as a bus. The grainy, MOS footage looked to be 16mm. The camera on sticks. The man wielded a chainsaw with a four-foot long cutting blade that chewed into the tree, spitting woodchips out the side. The cut was flat, perpendicular to the trunk, followed by a higher slice canted at a 30-degree angle. The notch in the trunk grew until it reached a certain point. Then the camera was moved back for a wider angle to capture the tree tipping and tilting away in an explosion of spinning debris.

Jim checked the time on his phone—10:39.

He shuttled down the search page and double clicked: *Redwood Moratorium, Arcata Community Center, 1994.* The video began in a packed auditorium. Jim fast-forwarded to a husky man in a windbreaker, standing among rows of people seated on folding chairs.

"You say loss of habitat, we say loss of jobs. You ask for limits, we cut back. But a zero-down moratorium will take away our livelihoods and for that we'll fight you to the end."

"Bet your ass!" another voice blurted, followed by a cacophony of cheers and boos.

"People! We've been down this road too damn many times." The camera panned to a governing official at a lectern, waving his hand to settle the clamor. The video then shifted to a gaunt, gray-bearded man in the audience being handed the microphone.

"All this talk of biomass, timber count, and losing your way of life," the man spoke earnestly, in a slow march. "No one said a word about the extermination of these ancient beings. Your minds are stunted like the stumps out there. The life of this forest goes back to the beginnings of our breath. As their life diminishes, so will ours. With all due respect to activists, plant biologists, forest restorationists, I propose a more thorough healing. I propose that the citizens of Humboldt and Del Norte Counties move away. Close shops, schools, cafes and car dealerships, pack our belongings and leave for a hundred years or so. Then, when our great grandchildren come back, they'll find a vibrant forest and will honor us for our caring… as will the trees."

The raspy voice of a man behind the bearded guy belted out, "That's the most cockamamie thing I ever heard."

"Not happening," Jim said under his breath. He was about to check out a protest video, but stopped when he saw the time on the screen.

10:55.

He put the laptop in his gym bag, grabbed the gear and stepped from the car.

How are we going to find each other in this fog?

Normally, Jim loved the fog. It gave the world a soft focus. Even the most destitute city street took on a forgiving, watercolor wash. But in this case, it made seeing Christy impossible. Add to that, there was no way to reach her. She was one of the nineteen people on the planet who didn't have a cellphone. "I don't want to be looking down all the time," she'd told him.

He moved between the rows of parked cars searching for her green Subaru.

11:05… 11:10…

The more the minutes ticked by the more he felt like love's pathetic fool willing to risk the only job he had, snatching equipment from *News Bang,* only to be stood up. Intoxicated by a woman. Under her spell. Yeah, Gomez psyched it.

Jim couldn't deny he'd slipped off his moral center, impersonating a staff documentary producer to impress her, when in truth he was a glorified grunt.

If she doesn't show up…

Then again, he didn't think she'd show up the second time they met. The day of the labyrinth.

It was a week after the Earth Day piece went online. Christy invited Jim to a Save-the-Sea-Turtles fundraiser at Huntington Park. Didn't see her anywhere in the small crowd gathered at the Fountain of Tortoises. He felt stood up and was turning to leave when she tapped him on the back.

"Some people go to museums, movies and baseball games. Not you," he recalled telling her. "You go to protests and endangered species rallies."

"This is where I live," she said.

"Your passion."

"No passion. Just me."

After the speeches and request for donations, she invited him to a place "near and dear" to her. They walked across the street and through the bronze Renaissance doors of Grace Cathedral. Inside, they removed shoes and silently stepped along the looping pathway of a medieval labyrinth. Jim thought the large inlaid design in the floor was incongruous with the Gothic architecture and Christian theology.

"Let go all desires and aversions as you go in…" Christy whispered at the start. "… when you reach the center, open your heart to the new and unknown, and you'll return to the world more whole."

Later, in the café downstairs, Jim shared how serene she seemed, how unhurried her footfalls in front of him.

"I know," she agreed, "Unlike my typical frenetic state. I just surrender and let it have me as is and I always come out with my dents and cracks somewhat patched up. Some places are medicine."

Jim wanted to tell her where the labyrinth took him, but a better idea came to mind. "Next time, it will be my turn to take you to my medicine place."

11:17…

Jim scanned the entrance to the Safeway lot. No sign of her.

A kid maneuvering a chain of shopping carts stopped and stared suspiciously, as if Jim had just stolen things from somebody's car.

"Enough of this," he said out loud, and crossing an aisle toward his parking spot he heard the slam of a door. Then, out of the fog, a lean figure appeared.

"Jim!"

The shorts, the hiking boots, a crimson headband.

Christy saw the camera case and bags Jim carried and threw her arms around him. "I'm sooo glad," she said, as her Subaru nosed into view. "This is Dodd," she gestured to an iron-jawed, skin-headed man at the wheel of her hatch back. "He's driving us the first leg."

No 'hello' out of Dodd. The man didn't even look at Jim.

"The first leg?"

"It's okay, all our rides are set." Christy took his camera case and laid it in the back.

He ducked into the rear seat, buoyed by her welcome, but unsettled by the hammer-head in the driver's seat.

7.
Meet Mr. Alchemy

"**E**ver been to the redwoods?" Christy asked.

"First time." Jim slid across the back seat to see her better.

"You've lived in the Bay Area all your life and you've never been to redwood country?"

"I've been to Redwood City, does that count?"

Dodd said nothing. He seemed locked down on some serious mood-leveler meds. He stared numb-faced out the windshield, navigating the car through the wool of fog across the Golden Gate Bridge.

Is he part of the project or her boyfriend? Jim wondered, opening the laptop. Do I interview him or throw jealous vibes?

As they sped north on 101, Christy elaborated her fantastical story of people mutating into trees. Jim had heard his share of shape-shifting accounts. An influx of weirdness funnels into the *News Bang* offices daily, everything from werewolves gamboling down Mt. Diablo, to mermaids shedding flippers under Fisherman's Wharf to party. But Christy was not describing shape-shifters. These were trees supposedly inviting people to be grafted to them.

"Nobody's on to this, Jim. Nobody will touch it."

Gee, I wonder why. The thought of people encased in a tree trunk seemed a lame idea for a prank. But Jim gave her some play. This was Christy Jones talking. Unlike the other ecovangelists he interviewed for the Earth Day report, she was by far the most grounded and compassionate. Not to mention the most attractive.

He tapped Christy's words into a file labeled: THE LAST STAND, nodding as she spoke with his best journalist's look of curious detachment.

"Front tires are out of alignment." Dodd came alive.

Christy shrugged.

"It pulls to the right," he said, evidently more interested in the car's condition than people ghoulishly mutating into wood.

Sunlight bloomed as the highway cleared the ceiling of fog. Mt. Tamalpais looming to the left.

"Let me show you..." Christy unzipped her fanny pack and held out a flash drive in her palm. "... it's the Tanner video I told you about."

As Jim slotted the flash drive into the USB port. Christy hurdled over the front seat and squeezed in next to him, her glacier-blue eyes gleaming.

The first image on the screen was the bare white ass of a man holding his jockey shorts at arm's length, saying, "Won't need these no more."

Christy chuckled.

"You know him?" Jim asked.

"Charlie Tanner. Gave up law to become a full-blown activist."

They watched as Tanner tossed his underwear next to a pair of running shoes at the foot of a big tree.

"What's that on his hands?"

"He'll explain."

Tanner stepped out of frame for a moment. The image zoomed in on a dark, cone-shaped cavity in the tree. "My new home." His voice more distant. "Rent free." His hands entered the picture, slightly blurred, coated with a cottony fuzz.

"The spores are already sprouting." He turned his left hand over to show the palm. "Kinda tickles." He brought his right hand up to the lens, and squeezed a raggedy, open-celled sponge between his thumb and forefinger.

"Meet Mr. Alchemy. The catalyst under the old ones," he said. "And what a fun-guy he is. A bit scratchy and delicate as tinder when dry." Tanner compressed the fibrous, milky-colored material until it disintegrated into powder he blew at the lens.

Jim turned to Christy. "Under the old ones?"

She prodded him to keep watching.

Tanner's face filled the frame, a chin bristling with gray stubble. He removed his glasses, revealing weary, red-veined eyes. "Mom…" Tanner's mouth stretched a smile. "…going to join Marianne, Carla Sayers and the other tree people now. Couldn't be happier. Love to you and hugs to all."

Tanner puckered and smooched a kiss, then stooped to enter the hole in the trunk. He sat in the hollow with the bottoms of his feet at the entrance, toes up, swollen with little knob-like growths and patches of the same whitish fur that covered his hands.

"Are you seeing this?" Christy finger-tapped the screen.

"You mean the mini-marshmallows stuck on with white glue?"

Tanner set his glasses aside, pressed his palms and the soles of his feet on the ground. Then the video suddenly sped up.

"Okay, here goes," Christy said.

"What goes?"

"This is the sped-up edited part. Time lapse. Otherwise you'd be watching for hours and hours."

The image stuttered, went black, then brightened.

"It's the next day. Keep watching."

"I'm watching."

"There," she pointed. "You see that?"

It looked like pale white tendrils wiggling out of the flesh on the sides of his feet.

"Tree shoots," Christy said.

"Of course." A tinge of sarcasm in Jim's voice. "And the dark dots?"

"That's blood. In the long version you can hear Charlie talking it through. He says it burns, but the pain is mostly endurable."

"Mostly?"

The scene dimmed. Jim figured the sun had gone behind a tree, or hid itself from the sight of such theatrics.

"Okay now... look there."

Thin fibers appeared to be lifting from the ground, twitching and curling around the man's hands. But Jim pictured something else— accomplices inside the tree puppeteering the carnival act with wires or pipe cleaners.

Then the image tipped. The screen went black.

"What was that?"

"Something knocked over the camera. A bear or raccoon." Christy turned to Jim. "So... what do you think? Unreal, huh."

"Unreal yes, definitely un-real."

A screech broke their attention. It came from the windshield wipers.

"Out of washer fluid," Dodd said.

"Watch it again," Christy urged as she hurdled back into the front seat.

Jim didn't need a rerun. He ejected the flash drive, puzzled at how Christy, or anyone, could believe such silliness. He titled his head, recalling the three times they'd been together— the Earth Day interview, the day of the labyrinth, and the trip to Ocean Beach. Nothing in those get-togethers suggested she was prone to escapist fantasy. A bit fanatical perhaps, intense as a bullet train, but gullible? No. Unless something's… but he didn't want to go there.

Out the window. dry blonde hills shuttled past, studded with live oaks. Here we go, Jim said to himself. He'd never traveled this far away from the city. He rubbed the flash drive between his thumb and forefinger like a worry bead, then reclined deeper into the seat and closed his eyes.

They were north of Ukiah when Christy turned and asked, "Hey-hey, did you watch it again?"

Jim yawned, told her he'd seen a lot of clever tricks and computer-generated imagery. And, as touched-up videos go, it wasn't bad. But Gomez, his cameraman friend could've made a more credible version with basic software.

"Nature is re-tooling humans," Christy said, "It's like a cross pollination, only in this case, it's to keep the forest alive. Loggers are not going to take down a tree if there's a human body grafted inside. No one would allow that."

Jim stared blankly.

"You wanted a ground-breaking story, right?"

"And the protest?" Jim asked, his fingers resting on the laptop's keys.

"The last big stand of old growth redwoods in the world is about to be destroyed."

Do I dare ask? "And there are people in them? Like this guy?" Jim lifted the flash drive in his fingers.

"He's one."

"Let me get this straight. You're saying the logging industry will not cut down any more redwood trees because…"

"They're desperate to keep the public from knowing about people like Charlie Tanner…"

"Who have grafted their bodies…?"

"Yes."

Christy gazed out the window as the car descended a hill.

"Well, as publicity stunts go I guess...."

"I never expected you to believe it. Question everything, that's your motto, right? But do you trust me?"

Loaded question.

"I'm here aren't I?"

"And I'm happy you are so you can see for yourself and tell the world."

Christy's confident smile was troubling. But Jim played through, asking, "Have you personally witnessed one of these tree mutations firsthand?

"No," she said. "But my contacts are infallible."

"And who might they be?"

"What, reveal my sources? Isn't that taboo number one for a journalist?"

"I mean, are they with a particular group like Earthfirst or ...?"

"They dance along the fringes, nameless. Their eyes are the wind."

"Poetic," Jim responded. "Will I be meeting any of them, or have they all turned into trees?"

Christy tapped Dodd's shoulder. "It's after the stoplight on the right." She turned back to Jim, "They'll be at the protest."

Jim hadn't noticed they were coming into a town. A sign on the side of the road read:

WILLITS

Gateway to the Redwoods

Looked like an old hippie town. Rustic. Bead shops and long hairs. Street corners with brightly painted garbage cans.

"What happens here?" Jim asked.

"We meet a friend who'll drive us to where we'll be staying."

Jim offered the flash drive back to Christy.

"Keep it," she said. "A gift. Your ticket to the world."

8.
This runt is our ringleader?

"**T**his runt is our ringleader?" Chief Dixon scowled upon seeing the squat fifty-six-year old man descend the stairs of the Gulfstream corporate jet.

Argus Beldare didn't personify the commanding presence depicted in the emails sent to Dixon. Not by a long shot. The man appeared hunch-backed, or perhaps he padded the shoulders of his overcoat with day-old bagels. Dixon couldn't tell. Maybe he was missing a neck.

Following Beldare down the steps onto the tarmac of the Arcata-Eureka airport came Richard Hersh, West Coast VP of Ingot Industries, a multi-national corporation that owned a diverse family of companies, one of which was NorCal Lumber.

Hersh waved a hi-sign to the two men at the foot of the stairs—Glenn Dixon, the Special Enforcement Police Chief for Humboldt and Del Norte Counties, and Curt Hardin, a NorCal Lumber Tactical Officer. Hardin had sat with Hersh on a number of roll-up-your-sleeves 'muscle huddles' over the years, mostly those dealing with save-the-redwoods groups. This was Dixon's first face time with Hersh, who looked exactly like the cologne-smelling snake he'd pictured the suit to be.

Hersh introduced Beldare as the brains who performed damage control on a situation Ingot faced the previous year.

At 6'4, Dixon towered over Beldare, who seemed disinterested, looking west of the tarmac to the froth of Pacific Ocean surf with dark, unblinking eyes. In the short man's hands Dixon spied a spiral student's notebook fastened to a clipboard, and a faded green hardbound book abraded at the corners.

"Mr. Beldare has earned a reputation as a master crisis manager to intractable problems, and seeing how…" Hersh stopped mid-sentence, his attention abruptly drawn to the jet's mobile stairway where a woman stepped leisurely down, a cellphone pressed to one ear. "Ah, here she comes."

Seeing her, Hardin's lips fell slack. He lowered his mirrored shades as she sauntered toward them. A sleek, starlet's body with maple-brown hair done up in a casual swirl.

"This is Dee Rotter, our Field Operative."

'Major babe' would be Hardin's term. Thirty, if a day over, and fire-hot. She made everyone around her look like used cars.

Dixon tipped his big, white Stetson hat to her. No question, in his eyes Dee was quite fetching. As for Beldare, having sized up the woman on the flight, he'd concluded that beneath the alluring exterior lived a cold-blooded reptile with barbed wire DNA.

"Dee is here on special assignment for us." Hersh smiled. "And who knows, there may come a situation where your paths intersect."

"Gentlemen," she said, slipping the smartphone in her pantsuit pocket.

"Now," Hersh continued, "I understand you've put Mr. Beldare's initial plans into action."

"They're happening." Hardin grinned.

"Excellent." Hersh gestured to Beldare. "This man has an uncanny strategic mind. Please carry out his directives with the same attention you'd give a four-star general. Unfortunately, I can't stay for the bash. I'm giving a speech at a conference of mucky-mucks. Are there any questions?"

No one said a word. A baggage carrier came speedily rolling toward them.

"So then," Hersh concluded, "The next time we meet I'll be rewarding you generously for your heroic work."

Dee forced a smile. Hardin reached for her hand to shake. "Can we drop you off somewhere?"

"Thanks for the offer," she said, dismissing the extended hand. "My ride will be here shortly."

"Maybe we'll see each other again."

Dee gave an impassive, "Anything's possible." Her phone hummed. "Excuse me." She lifted it to her ear.

Hersh gripped Beldare's upper arm, "Do your magic. Speed and skill."

The clutch of people broke up.

"Those are mine." Beldare pointed out two vintage leather suitcases on the carrier. The only other baggage was a backpack and a duffel bag.

Dixon hefted Beldare's suitcases off the cart, begrudgingly. Not one to smolder, he didn't enjoy relinquishing control to an unknown entity.

As Beldare walked toward the Humvee, he overheard Dee say to Hersh, "That was them. She's on her way."

"What'd I tell you," he replied, adding, "Time to get into costume."

"Secrets," Beldare murmured under his breath. He knew nothing of Dee Rotter's assignment, and that didn't sit right with him. As he waited in the Humvee, he sized up Curt Hardin: NorCal Lumber's high-level alpha dog. As for Dixon, he surmised the police department here was in bed with the Lumber company.

Over the years, the Welsh-born, partially Harvard-educated crisis consultant had been hired to handle a number of cover-ups, mop-ups, and fuck-ups. All of them four-alarm urgent. Some required coercive action: blackmail, bribery. Whoever controlled the story won.

But this job struck Beldare as an odd duck. Given the years of mass protests and countless arrests, what made it any different? Jail the trespassers, start your engines, and commence timber cutting. Why call for his services? When he broached that question to Hersh, the man gave him a vague, "extenuating circumstances" answer.

No, Beldare wasn't being given the whole story. Not by half. But like most of his clients, the prevailing company ethos was to bare little flesh. The less they disclosed to him about peripheral affairs, the sharper his focus on what he was hired to expedite.

"Three, four days. Five days max," he muttered to himself.

"Woo! What a fox!" Hardin exclaimed, seating himself shotgun. He turned to Beldare in the back seat. "What was it like flying with her?"

"We didn't speak."

"No way. Damn." Hardin scanned the runway for Dee. "She sure lifted my lever."

Once Dixon loaded his body behind the wheel, Beldare opened his spiral notebook and unfolded a topographical map, which he neatly spread across his lap.

"Now, to confirm a couple things…"

"Shoot," Hardin said, as Dixon steered the Humvee toward the airport exit.

"First, the roadblocks are in place."

"Affirmative," Dixon said. "They're solid on the two main arteries—Highway 101, north and south, and 299 from the east."

"And the Rough Riders?"

9.
Who's Rolf?

J im stood on the Willits sidewalk in front of the Sunflower Co-Op. Through the Subaru's passenger window, he watched Christy pluck a piece of paper from the glove compartment, sign her name on the back, and hand it to Dodd.

"And here's an extra key," she said.

Dodd took the key, pulled a fat, rubber-banded envelope from his blue nylon jacket, and pressed it into Christy's hand. She tucked it behind her belt and stepped from the car.

"I don't see Rosco," she said, looking up the street.

Dodd sprang the engine.

"Wait!" Christy tapped the glass. Dodd resisted, or zoned oblivious. He put the gear in drive. She yanked open the door. "Hang on a frickin' minute. You can't just leave us here." She shook her head in a huff and turned to Jim. "I'll stay and keep an eye out." She slipped off the rubber band, opened Dodd's envelope, peeled off two twenty's and asked Jim to buy some food from the co-op. "Easy food. Picnic food. I'll watch our stuff."

Did she just sell her car to that guy? Jim wondered as he entered the store. How do we get back to the city? He lifted a green hand basket from a stack and wandered the aisles. *Picnic... picnic.* The raucous music thumping from store speakers added to Jim's mental agitation in how to handle Christy's delusion about the bogus Tanner video.

If that's the impetus behind shooting a documentary then what?

Then it's a big waste of time, that's what.

He set a sourdough baguette in the basket, scolding himself for being seduced into chasing a preposterous story.

Then turn it around. What else can you make out of it? Jim challenged himself as he searched for cheese. Scenarios shuttled by like boxcars. Why not reframe it? Make the story about the art of creating a hoax, or exposing one. Not exactly a groundbreaker, but Wiley might even go for that at News Bang.

He tossed a box of granola bars into the basket, and veering down aisle nine to the cheese section, he heard a whistle. He checked his phone and read the text:

> Where the F R U?

No!

It was Omar at Spartan Limo, the no-frills limousine service. Jim spaced-out his job meeting. He thought of calling, but instead typed a reply:

> Something came up.
>
> Apologies - can we
>
> reschedule for monday?

The response was immediate:

> don't bother
>
> filled opening

I just blew the limo job! And for what?

A young woman bumped him in the aisle, hamster-cute, with a drape of pumpkin-colored hair falling off half her head. The other half exposed a scalp tattoo obscured by stubble.

"You and Jones are being followed," she mumbled. "Meet me at the Skunk line."

"The what?"

"Out the back, down the street." She hurried off.

Skunk Line?

When he emerged from the co-op wheeling an empty shopping cart, Christy was standing alone on the sidewalk, her Subaru nowhere to be seen.

"Don't look around, just listen to me." Jim went on to describe what just occurred.

Christy didn't flinch.

"I'm serious," he said. "You're not surprised?"

"Fill you in later." Christy figured it was about her arrest—Hersh's people making sure she wasn't fleeing the country to evade trial. But she didn't let on.

They loaded their luggage in the cart, rolled it into the co-op and out the back.

"That guy Dodd... he just took off?" Jim asked as they walked the four blocks to the Skunk Line railroad station.

"Uh-huh," she said, glancing at Jim's feet.

"A friend?"

"My zombie mechanic."

"None of my business, but did you just sell your car to him?"

Christy paused, then said, "Should've told you to wear hiking shoes."

Jim looked down at his knock-about Converse sneakers, then to her high-ankle, tractor-treaded boots.

As they crossed the street to the train station, the flatulent rumble of a cracked muffler flooded their ears. A blood red Camaro crept past, its hood bungee-corded to the front bumper. The car burned a U-turn in the middle of the street.

"That's her." Jim spotted the orange hair.

The Camaro pulled up next to Christy and stopped, it's engine idling bullishly. The driver cracked the window.

"Get in."

Christy stared hard at her. "Who are you?"

"There's been some changes."

"Where's Rosco?"

"The pigs set up a road block out of Garberville. Rosco went ahead to manage another route, so I'm taking you."

"But I don't know you."

"Well I've seen plenty of you before, honey. Oh, here." The woman handed Christy a folded piece of paper. "From Rosco."

The paper was a map. Christy examined the wiggly road lines, X's, and circled words.

"They moved the checkpoint." She hoisted her backpack off the asphalt, stuffed the map in her pocket and turned to Jim. "It's okay, we're going with her."

As Christy opened the trunk, she recalled meeting the woman once before. *Tracy, right. Crazy Tracy.*

Jim loaded their gear into the trunk and crammed himself, camera case and laptop into the back seat of the gas guzzler.

Tracy asked, "Who's the cloud in khaki's?"

"He's a filmmaker."

Jim caught her eyes in the rear view. "How are you doing, my name is…"

"Don't wanna know," she cut him off.

Christy took another look at the map. Changes alright. Because of the roadblock they'd be taking fire roads.

"How far can you drive us?"

"I think I can get you to the checkpoint but I'll need money for gas."

Christy slapped a twenty in Tracy's hand. They roared off.

"Roadblocks, huh." Christy twisted in her seat to speak to Jim in the back. "You hear that? Now why would the police be blocking the highways?"

Jim could think of several reasons: a raging forest fire, an overturned truck spilling airborne toxins.

Tracy checked the side mirror. "Oh shit! Get your heads down!"

Jim and Christy slunk in their seats.

"And stay down."

Tracy hung a hard right, drove a long block and ducked into a rodeo park where she whipped an immediate U-turn and stopped under the shadow of some trees, watching the road.

"Don't think they spotted us."

"What kind of car?" Christy said.

"Big badass black car. And don't tell me why they're tailing you. Better I know nothing."

After a minute, Tracy pulled out, made two turns, and after a long slow stretch, flattened the gas pedal.

"I think I lost them."

Jim and Christy sat up and looked around. They were back on the highway, ripping the air at 90 miles an hour.

"The car looks like crap, but it's got more horse power than the Kentucky Derby." Tracy lit a cigarette and blew the smoke toward the chink in her window with most of it buffeting to the back seat. That and the smell of exhaust eeking in from somewhere made riding in the backseat nauseating.

"Can you lower your window more?" Jim said.

"It's busted." Tracy continued sharing the latest news with Christy.

"Could you speak up?" With the wind and engine noise their words were gibberish.

"She said they're not telling people why they closed the highway. They're only allowing locals to get through." Christy checked the highway in her side mirror. "And that Rolf broke away from home detention."

"Who's Rolf?" Jim asked, staring at a dark car a quarter mile back that appeared to be gaining on them.

"A logger accused of killing his wife," Christy shouted. He's on the drive I gave you."

Jim opened his laptop and stuck the Tanner-labeled flash drive into the USB port.

"Find the file: Zetzer."

Jim clicked on it. A KIEM News Channel logo sprang up, followed by a short video report showing a brawly man being perp-walked in handcuffs from a house trailer to an idling patrol car. The news camera pushed in on his sag-eyed face spouting muffled words.

"So you're saying what? The guy didn't kill his wife? That she went into the woods and turned into a tree?"

"He swears by the story."

Jim wondered if it was the same guy Wiley mentioned earlier at News Bang— 'the wacko logger.'

"They put him under house arrest," Tracy continued. "Confined to his trailer with an ankle restraint. But he busted free. Dude better watch out, they got a manhunt on him."

"What did you say?"

"I said they're going to burn him at the stake!"

"Who's they?" Jim asked.

"NorCal and the cops!"

Rosco's map directed them off the highway onto a narrow, gritty road that wound northwest through hilly terrain.

Jim checked to see if any vehicles made the turn, but road dust clouded the Camaro's rear window. He shut the lid on the laptop and wilted back in the seat.

"Hey, I'm getting dizzy back here from exhaust leaking in."

Christy cranked her window down. It only deafened their banter.

After a bumpy, corrugated mile, Jim succumbed to the fumes and drifted into a delirium haze.

10.
They don't like the name 'rough riders'

From the Arcata-Eureka airport Chief Dixon drove south along the Redwood Highway.

"We've got four patrols, two to three men in each unit," Hardin said, responding to Beldare's question about 'rough riders.'"

Beldare scanned the topo map, taking in the expanse, number of isolated roads and mountainous terrain.

"Are they NorCal workers?"

"Nah, these are freelancers who've assisted us on occasion. Could be one or two ex-loggers in there, but none currently employed by NorCal or the timber industry. Most of them wouldn't touch this kind of guerrilla action for no amount of coin. Got families and all that."

Beldare's eyes studied the Arcata storefronts they passed.

Ace Hardware…

Liquor Land…

Hardin went on. "Yeah, so looking at the map you got there, we split Humboldt and Del Norte Counties into quadrants: they're patrolling every back road, fire road, lumber road and ATV track that wends and winds…"

"How long have they been active?"

"Started two nights ago." Hardin said. "And, by the way, they don't like the name 'rough riders.' One unit goes by

'Masked Marauders.' Another is the 'Humboldt Volunteers,' after the group that slaughtered the Wiyot Indians back in the 1800's."

"Whatever they call themselves is irrelevant," Beldare said. "What is important is that they sustain a public perception of being ruthless vigilantes. A throw back to your wild west, only in this case their task is to perpetrate terror in the hearts and minds of those coming to demonstrate."

An RV dealership…

Armageddon Ammo…

They drove a couple blocks without a word. Then Hardin asked, "What gave you that vigilante idea?"

"Simple deduction. To limit the number of protestors, you need to challenge access. And what would communicate a media-proof reason for blocking major roadways? Not a forest fire you can see from the air. A toxic spill is too localized. And with a contagion, there'd be quarantine complications and it would bring the CDC down your throats. No, it needed to have a visceral impact that strikes the fear center in people's brains. The threat of rampant, violent attacks by bands of roaming vigilantes achieves this, does it not?"

"You got that right."

"To another point: how many homicidal tree huggers have you ever met?"

"A few would love to have my head on a pole." Hardin said.

"But the majority are pacifists committed to peaceful pro-testing; they eat, drink and preach non-violence. No chance of them suddenly goose-stepping with automatic weapons."

"Unlikely," Hardin said.

"At least not in our short time frame. So, given those elements, this 'idea' delivered the most traction. Not to mention the added image value it offers."

Dixon eyed Beldare through the rearview mirror awaiting the punchline. Hardin couldn't wait, he swung around in his seat, "Which is?"

"Chasing down vigilantes puts the police force in a favorable light. The grateful public will hail them once again as protectors of public safety. I understand they could use a bit of badge polishing."

Dixon and Hardin couldn't argue with Beldare's strategy. But that didn't mean they had to kowtow to the man.

"I see a coffee place up here on the right," Beldare pointed. "Would you mind if…"

"We can do that." Dixon veered into the small lot adjoining Joe's Joe.

Hardin said he'd fetch the drinks.

"Nothing for me," Dixon said.

"A cup of black tea, thanks," Beldare reached into his overcoat pocket.

"No-no, I got it." Hardin waved him off. "Here, check out this story, just below the fold." Hardin handed Beldare the Eureka Journal and left.

All was quiet for a moment in the Humvee.

"I gotta hit the john." Dixon lurched his hulk out from behind the wheel but he didn't go far. He yanked open the passenger door. He wanted the ringleader's complete attention. Beldare didn't flinch or look up from reading the article reporting an unprovoked assault along a forest road.

Dixon cleared his throat. "Gonna give you some slack, Mr. Beldare. But just so you know, I don't like taking orders from nobody, not some bigwig wise-ass from Ingot Industries, and definitely not some newcomer who's got no fuckin' experience digging in my backyard. So, should your brainy scheme go off to skinners, it'll be your head, not mine.

11.
How bad?

"Hey, there you are. Didn't think I'd get through."

"Who's this?" Hardin mashed the cellphone to his ear.

"Big Foot."

"Hang on." Hardin stepped away from the coffee shop counter and the siren of an expresso machine. "Who?"

"You know, the Humboldt Volunteers." Big Foot stood in the center of a dry, back country road, finger-scratching the eyehole of his flesh-colored ski mask. The rolling landscape around him was tufted with small trees, open to the sky, having been logged years before.

"What's up?"

"We ambushed a couple cars." Big Foot pivoted and faced the two vehicles, doors out, parked helter-skelter, four bloodied bodies crumpled in various postures along the shoulders of the road. Two more masked men stood over them, one shouldering a Louisville Slugger, the other tapping his shoe with a #3 wood.

"Where abouts?"

"Lumber road south of Crescent City ten miles give-er-take. Just need to know how bad."

"How bad...?"

"Yeah, how bad you want these dudes beaten up?" Big Foot bent his right leg at the knee, set the heel of his boot on his truck's front bumper, it's license plate concealed by duct tape.

"What's their present condition?"

"The works - cracked ribs, broken nose, hematomas head to foot.

"Good enough. Snap some photos."

"You got it."

"Oh, and tell'em to go back and warn their friends to stay home."

12.
Look again

Tracy ping-ponged her head left and right looking for a fork or widening of the fire road to U-turn the Camaro around. But there was none to be seen. After more than a mile of searching, she planted her pink croc on the brake pedal and announced, "Far as I go."

A plume of dust spooled up from the rear tires, alighting on the car in a thin, uniform veil. Christy waited for it to settle before stepping out.

"End of the line, sleepyhead."

Jim's eyes peeked through pained lids, "Are we there?"

"Not exactly. We hoof it from here."

They grabbed their stuff and stood by as Tracy wheeled the Camaro back and forth to point it in the direction they'd come. Jim tried to guide her, but Tracy ignored his coaching. Ultimately, she straightened out and the car grumbled off.

"Did I do something to offend her?" Jim asked.

"Not you personally, just men in general, and you happen to be one." Christy strapped on her backpack. "She told me she's been trying to take a man-cation, but has yet to find an enjoyable place with no men. When I wished her luck she said, 'I know, they're everywhere, like gravity.'"

The Camaro disappeared and the quiet of the place sunk in around their ears in a deepening hush.

"You look hung over."

"Got a headache from the exhaust fumes."

"Walking will help. Here…" Christy handed him a thermos.

Jim took a swallow, the pounding at the back of his head unrelenting. The water was cool and tasted tart.

"It's got electrolytes and some pickle juice." Christy unfolded a topo map, comparing it to Rosco's hand-drawn directions.

"How far away are we?" Jim asked.

"Five, maybe six miles. Plenty of time to reach the checkpoint and catch our next ride."

Under a layer of powder, stenciled by the tread of tires, the road was ribbed and rock hard. Scraggily bushes flanked it, with occasional scrub oaks. For Jim, having never been out in the wild, it was a walk into the unknown. No buildings, street signs or stoplights, just an empty lane of dirt meandering through back country.

Christy described the area as once being a lush redwood forest before being logged in the 80's. She set a swift pace which Jim matched stride for stride. The road led north, scribbling around the hilly contours of the land. Other than an occasional chirp of a towhee or stirrings from a covey of quail in the undergrowth, the only sound was the tramp of their footfalls.

Jim felt glad to be alone with Christy at last, yet at the same time, unsettled. Here he was, on foot miles from anywhere, with a woman whose impulse in taking the trip came straight out of Fantasyland.

"How's that headache?" Christy asked.

"Still throbbing."

"Ever pinch your pressure points?" Christy stopped in her tracks. "Like this…" She pushed her right thumb into her left hand at the apex of the webbing between thumb and index finger and rubbed the spot in a circular motion.

Jim tried it.

"Is it sore?" she asked.

"It is."

"You constipated?"

"Not really, in fact I…" He blushed, obviously embarrassed.

"Got to go? Well there's no restroom for miles, but there's a toilet everywhere you look. Need some TP?"

Jim scanned the landscape with lost eyes. "I… okay, yeah."

"You've never taken a crap outdoors before."

"I've peed. And I vomited in Golden Gate Park when I was 14, does that count? Haven't had alcohol since."

Christy shook her head as she pulled out a scrunched roll of toilet paper from her pack and handed it to him. "You don't drink or do drugs, don't smoke, don't swear. You're a one-off." She handed him a plastic poop shovel. "Watch out for poison oak."

Jim knew of poison oak, but not how to identify the plant. Christy walked along the edge of the fire road until she spotted the bush. "Right there. Three leaves. Shiny. Nature's way of keeping people out of the wild. Don't even brush your clothes against it. I had it once so bad I got blood poisoning."

Jim didn't have to go far to be hidden from sight. After he finished his business he returned the toilet roll and asked, "How would you feel about me shooting a short interview with you while there's still good light?"

"As long as we can keep walking."

Jim handed Christy his gear satchel to carry, opened the camera case and pulled out Gomez's camera. He mounted a compact shotgun mic to the camera for better audio, attached the monopod to the underbelly of the housing and planted the pole in his vest pocket to help stabilize it.

"Okay, camera's on. Now… I've been meaning to ask you the question you side-stepped last April."

"And that is?"

"What was it that first inspired you as a kid to become such a hyper-activist?"

Christy cocked her head. Jim felt it too. A tremor underfoot. Earthquake, was Jim's first thought, until he heard the growl of an engine.

"Move!" Christy waved him off the road seconds before a flatbed truck stormed around a bend, hauling what to Jim looked like two monstrous Danish pastries made of wood.

"Poachers!" Christy shouted, her face livid red as the truck tore past. She dashed into the middle of the road, shaking her fist, her body vanishing in the wake of its billowing dust.

Jim spun in place, protecting the camera lens with his hand.

When the dust settled, he found her slumped over, as if stabbed in the gut.

"Hey?" he said, but held up asking what that was all about.

Christy straightened, looked down the road and said, "They sneak in and cut off redwood burls. It's barbaric." She sucked in a mouthful of air and belched, "Fuckers."

Although it sounded like the possessed girl in *The Exorcist*, Jim found Christy's belch talk oddly endearing.

She patted the dust off her arms. They walked on.

"Whenever you feel like it, we can start again," Jim said, giving her time to cool.

Christy let out an audible exhale. "On second thought, I'd rather talk about something other than myself."

"Let me get out in front of you." Jim back-peddled ahead of her a few steps and hit the record button. "Rolling." He stared into the viewfinder as he toe-heeled up the road. "Tell me if I'm going to bump into a tree or a poison oak bush."

Christy stared straight into the lens. "What I want to say is how we're really good at honoring people. We hand out statuettes to actors and athletes, pin medals on war heroes, but we've overlooked the truly great ones. I'm talking about the ones that created a home for us to exist on this planet— like the forests, 'cause without them there wouldn't be any athletes or heroes. Hell, there wouldn't be an *us*."

Christy took a deep breath. She eyed the sun sinking toward the ridge of the coastal range. "So why is it we've failed to give accolades to the redwood trees? Why no trophies to them? What I'm trying to say, or propose, is a Hall of Fame for the life-bearers. *These* are the fucking champions of the world." Christy threw up her hands. "Whoops, sorry. You can bleep that, right?"

Jim took his eyes away from the viewfinder.

"Something wrong?" Christy asked.

"No." Jim shut off the camera and reset the lens cap. "Never heard it put that way." He set the camera in its case and slung it over his shoulder.

They walked on in silence, passing in and out of shadows cast by taller stands of trees. At one point the nerve-rattling thwop-thwop of a helicopter invaded the stillness. Christy watched the chopper approach from the south before slanting off to the east.

"They must be looking for people morphing into trees," Jim grinned.

"So says the self-proclaimed free thinker. Well, Mr. Questioner, let me ask you a question, do you believe Nature has a mind?"

Jim pondered it as they walked. He liked the question. What is the nature of Nature? Is it capable of thought? "All I can say is it's a force that seeks to live. To evolve and adapt to changes, and that takes consciousness."

"Which is what the forest is doing, seeking a way to survive extermination."

Jim shrugged. "I guess you could call me an experientialist."

"Meaning?"

"Meaning information does not equate to actual experience. You can tell me something you firmly believe in, but until I experience it I won't accept it as real."

"Experientialist…"

"Right. And here's where things can get enslaving, when people impose their beliefs on others to convert, before they've been able to experience it for themselves. Why is that? I mean if you feel whole and happy in a belief, isn't that enough? Why seek reinforcements?"

"Maybe my belief will help others. What's good for me is good for you."

"And does your belief allow others to think differently? Can there be multiple beliefs, even multiple realities?"

"Ahh." Christy looked ahead. "Now we're getting into it."

Jim thought she was responding to his comment, only to realize it was about the grove of redwoods they were entering. The sky-high trees stood along a lazy rivulet that broadened into a pool. The air under their canopy gave off a rich, earthy smell. A kingfisher darted across their eyes in a flash of blue.

"You can't cross the same stream twice," Jim quoted Heraclitus as he tiptoed through the cool water feeling how hiking boots would definitely be the footwear of choice, if he owned a pair.

"This is a good place," Christy murmured to herself, then called out, "Okay experientialist, you want to know what inspired me to be what you call a hyper-activist?" She strode through the shallow water toward him. "I have an answer you can experience. But you'll need to put all your stuff down."

"What are you going to do?"

"I'm not going to do anything. You are. First, empty your mind. Empty, empty, empty. Not one single thought— brain blank. And close your eyes."

"Is this one of those tests of trust?"

"Not really, you'll see. But first you're not to see."

"Shutting my eyes is easy. Shutting off my curiosity impossible."

"Okay, now imagine yourself as if you've been dropped into your body. Can you do that?"

"Not sure what…"

"No peeking! So what are you going to do?"

"Drop into my body."

"Right, when you open your eyes everything you'll see will be the inside of your body. You ready?"

"Let's do it."

Christy quietly stepped behind Jim so she wouldn't be the first thing he saw.

"Now, open your eyes and look around the inside of your body."

Jim's eyelids lifted. She was not there. He turned until he saw her. "There you are."

"And what do you see?"

"Besides you, some big trees, the hills…"

"Look again."

Jim scanned the area. "I don't know what to look for."

"Look again. Nothing changed?"

The exercise wasn't working. But Christy wasn't going to give up. After all, she'd never walked anyone through visualizing the world this way. In fact, it came as a surprise when, at seven years old, she realized no one shared her view of things. Fear of ridicule and wanting to fit in forced her to keep it to herself. But with Jim, this kind-hearted soul, she felt free to experiment.

"Let's try it one more time," she said. "Here," Christy untied her red scarf and wrapped it around Jim's eyes. She rotated his body. "I'm turning you so you face the stream, not me."

"Just point me at the piñata."

"This time, when you're ready, lift the scarf. As you look around, consider everything outside your body as being the inside of your body."

The first thing Jim saw was a cluster of redwood trees along the stream with shafts of sunlight splintering though the fretwork of their limbs.

"I'm... inside my body," he whispered to himself. He took a couple steps toward the bank. Christy remained behind, silent.

The kingfisher flew back. Jim followed the belted bird with his eyes as it landed on a branch above the pool. The sight made his body twitch. Then, taking in the larger surroundings, the wooded slopes and sky, his lips parted. It felt like his feet had sunk up to his ankles in the ground. "Whoa..." He waved his hand across the landscape. "So... everything out there is inside?"

"There is no out there. There's no outside. These trees, the water, this light... this is your inside world."

"Inside... outside." Jim took it all in. Something had shifted alright, like changing camera lenses, only bodily. The landscape became more alive and more intimate at the same time. Christy had shown him a new reality. One he felt with a caring and wonder more acute than ever.

Christy could see Jim had touched something. "Kinda changes your feelings about the great outdoors when it's the inside of your greater body."

He pivoted on his heels and faced her. "And this is how you see everything?"

"When I'm away from the city, yes. It hurts to take in the world when you're confronted with concrete, traffic and power lines."

"I get that." Jim scanned the limitless blue of the sky. The sun crowning the range of the hills to the west.

"We need to keep moving. But see if you can sustain it for a while."

Jim handed back her red scarf. "Well, I'll say this, I'm glad you're inside my body."

Hearing that, Christy shone a full smile.

13.
Bunchers?

"**B**am!" Hardin mimicked the shoulder-kick of an invisible rifle. He and Beldare stood on the deck of a lodge overlooking a sea of redwoods and a straw-colored clearing in the valley below. Hardin was reenacting the time he shot a twelve-point elk from that spot on the deck. The same elk whose head Beldare saw mounted above the mantle of the lodge's stone fireplace.

Built in the 1960's, the NorCal lodge stood on top of the coastal range eleven miles east of Eureka. It was constructed out of redwood logs with notched ends, traditional chinker style. Hardin guided Beldare on a tour of the guest rooms and through the kitchen, where he popped a Budweiser before striding out the patio doors onto the deck.

"So what sort of corporate scams have you been hired to deal with?" Hardin asked. "I take it you do more than sledge hammer hard drives."

"I'm not at liberty to disclose."

"Ah, come on. I won't tell."

Beldare found Hardin's loose, cocky demeanor repulsive. The NorCal tactical officer looked to be mid-to-late thirties, an eraser-pink face and narrow slits for eyes, as if he peered at the world through Venetian blinds.

"Use your darkest imagination and dig down from there." Beldare said as he headed back inside to the long, rectangular dining room turned command center. He stepped up to a swipe board, dug a dry erase marker out of the trough, and began printing a bulleted action plan for discussion.

Outside the lodge, Dixon paced, talking on his cell phone, kicking bits of gravel off the driveway with his handcrafted cowboy boots.

Hardin stepped to a high table, pressed a couple keys on a laptop computer. A green aerial image lit up on a wide projection screen.

"Alright. Take a look. This here heavily wooded parcel is called North Fork Forest. It's approximately 18 square miles. The aerial's a few years old." Hardin zoomed in and circled an area with a red laser pointer. "It doesn't show the spur cut in there."

"The site of the demonstration."

"Yeah, it's a short road that's gated with a turnaround for vehicles."

"Which you need cleared of protestors by Monday morning so you can bring in your timber cutting equipment."

"Actually, most of the machinery is already parked there—a couple of feller-bunchers, dozers, harvesters, haulers and whatnot."

"Bunchers?"

"Yeah, yeah… hang on, I'll show ya."

Hardin pulled up a video file.

"Right there… ya see? It's a mega-machine, kinda like a big backhoe with a long hydraulic arm, only the rig's got a massive, high-power saw blade with chunky teeth spinning at 1800 RPM's."

The video went to a close-up of the horizontal blade slicing into a tree trunk just above the ground.

"After the saw cuts the trunk, then the operator grabs the tree in the collector arms… like so. Cut and load."

Dixon entered, set his Stetson on a table, stroked his buzz cut hair and stood quiet, stoically so. He looked ex-military to Beldare: rebar backbone, box jaw, and pressed long-sleeve shirt, its collar stiff as tin.

"We're walking through Stage Two," Beldare informed the chief. "And now that you're here I have a question for you both: How many people did you foresee coming to the demonstration before you knew we'd be deploying vigilantes?"

"My guesstimate? Five, six thousand," Hardin said. "Maybe more. You never know about these things. It's on a Sunday. This is June."

"And given the barricades, the menacing media reports, how have your projections changed?"

"There are basically two types of protestors," Hardin explained. "First off, you got your fanatics who are welded to the cause. Nothing stops them no matter how long it takes or what shit you throw at them—head bashing, tazing, incarceration."

"And the second?"

"Weekend warriors. They'll carry signs, but it's not the end-all, be-all. They enjoy the camaraderie, but are less likely to go the long haul. They got jobs, dogs to feed, and won't sacrifice creature comforts for getting bloodied and dumped in the cage."

"And..." Beldare cut to the chase. "...should Stage One succeed?"

"The roadblocks are not much of a deterrent," Hardin said. "More like an annoyance. The real stopper's a fear for their lives. So when a bunch of bloody encounters with vigilantes repeatedly hit the news and internet, it should reduce the numbers, maybe by as much as a third."

"Too many," Beldare noted.

"You don't know these people," Dixon said. "They're clever and highly motivated. If they have to hike in overland, or drop out of the sky by jet packs, they'll find a way to be there. And they will not budge."

"All the more reason to inundate the media with images of beatings and savaged bodies. Even some fake fatalities if need be. Perception conquers reality. We have to own and control the story."

"We own it." Hardin demanded.

"Then let's go over the protest." Beldare kept his eyes locked on Dixon. "I propose a time-release response. We allow their gate action to gather a head of steam without incident or intrusion. Let them feel empowered, even complacent. Then…" Beldare wrung his hands. "…we send in the masked marauders."

"A surprise attack," Hardin beamed.

"I can get behind that," Dixon agreed. "But nothing severe. Strictly black and blue bludgeoning to disperse the crowd."

"And into this melee, the cavalry comes to save the day," Beldare curled a Cheshire cat grin.

"Da da da dut duh-da!" Hardin bugled.

"All right." Dixon couldn't stop nodding. "We chase out the vigilantes, then clear the rest. Dress a few wounds. Even help evacuate the protestors safely. Granted, there'll still be skirmishes and arrests, but all under the auspices of harm reduction."

"Excellent." Beldare applauded Dixon, pleased that he now had the chief's assured cooperation.

"Then we flesh out the squatters," Hardin said.

"The ones you claim to have an enclave somewhere in the North Fork region."

"An *enclave*, yeah." Hardin chirped at the word.

"And how do you know there's an encampment around there?"

"Oh, it's there. We know." Hardin took a chug of beer. "Just don't know where, exactly."

"Do you have an informant embedded with these people...? Well?"

After a pause, Hardin confessed, "We got one."

"When can I meet this person?"

"Never."

"Set up a meet, tonight."

"Not gonna happen." Hardin shook his head.

Two things Beldare found tiresome in his profession: the word 'no', and the see-saw disloyalty of paid informants.

"He demands complete anonymity." Hardin explained.

"They all do," Beldare countered.

"No worries, man. He's all mine."

14.
Well if it isn't Jones of Arc

"There's movement. Somebody down there."

"How many?"

"Hang on," Drum said, dialing the focus on a pair of binoculars.

Drum and Rosco stood in the fire road at the top of the coastal ridge, the sunset melting down their backs. Others hunkered nearby, eager to get moving.

"Two… on foot."

"Is Christy one of them?"

Drum studied their approach. "Looks like her. Walks like her."

"Told you she'd be coming."

"Don't recognize the dude with her."

"Okay, let's saddle up," Rosco called to a man sitting on an ice chest, cleaning wire-rimmed glasses with a chamois.

Drum lowered the binoculars and called to the others who were facing west. "Hey, load up guys, we may finally be leaving."

Rosco lifted the cooler off the ground and set it in the bed of his Toyota pickup. The others slid open the side door of Drum's yellow van and crammed their bodies inside among backpacks and camping gear.

Drum lifted the binoculars to his eyes again. He wanted to get a bead on this stranger walking with Christy Jones.

71

Neither Jim nor Christy saw the men standing on the western ridge. After walking for more than five miles Jim's legs were Jell-O. Though the blisters burned his feet with every step, he didn't let on. Christy, however, was becoming worried that Rosco would give up waiting after nightfall. But talking helped deflect her doubts.

"All the time organizing people, rallies, marches, I had to stop. I saw myself becoming someone I didn't like, edgy and militant. Having to resolve internal disputes and maintain some semblance of solidarity with strong personalities— talk about a headache. We may call them affinity groups, but not everyone agrees on how to stop the genocide of old growth forests. You're juggling the gamut, from fundraising, pushing documents through legislation, to gate actions and ecotage."

"What's that?"

"Environmental sabotage. Mucking up the works. Disabling equipment, power outages… not something I condone."

"Is that why you're being followed?"

"No, that, well, I trespassed. They hung my dog from a tree. Thought it would shut me up."

"The golden retriever?"

"Yeah, Mercy. They broke into my loft and lynched her."

"Oh god no," Jim swooned.

"Like my father says, 'You know you're making headway when you start getting death threats."

"So… you…"

"So, I took Mercy's carcass, noose and all, and dumped them on the Ingot VP's desk along with a photo of her hanging from the tree in the yard and a note that read, 'You killed my dog, you piece of shit coward."

Jim nodded. Of course she would do that.

"But I was blind-sided by a close friend who'd gotten me into the VP's office. She turned out to be a paid stooge." Christy gulped a ball of air and belched, "So fuck me."

Jim had a question, but she continued.

"And then, knowing I was there, somebody set fire to some waste baskets with bogus papers in them. A minute later, police and fire engines arrive, so fast it was freaky. Even the judge saw something wonky in that. Anyway, they arrested me for arson and destroying high-value intellectual property." Christy stopped walking. "Hang on. I think this is the culvert." She studied the landmarks on Rosco's map. "We can't be too far."

As they hiked up a hillside Jim's eyes traced the road to the top and caught sight of a figure silhouetted against the sky. "There's someone up there."

"That's them!" She waved.

Jim felt relieved. One last climb and he could rest his legs and flaming feet.

"Now, they may ask you a series of questions. That's why they call it a checkpoint. Strangers are scrutinized. Call it cautious paranoia, but over the years infiltrators have undermined our efforts. In fact, wherever we go, be alert to whoever you meet. You may be talking to a lumber industry… oh shit." Christy groaned. She recognized Drum standing on top of the hill.

"What?" Jim asked, seeing Christy's shoulders slump and her teeth bite her lip. "What just happened?"

"I… nothing." She knew she might run into her ex-boyfriend at some point, just not at this checkpoint."

"You look like something just sucked out your blood."

"No, it's…" Christy drew in a breath and let out a long snore. "Nothing that a couple Pisco sours couldn't help."

"Ever hear of the American philosopher, William James?" Jim didn't wait for an answer. "He once said the best weapon against stress is our ability to choose one thought over another. So…" Jim flicked his index finger at Christy's head. "Maybe you've got another thought in there?"

A smile lifted her face. She clasped her fingers around Jim's upper arm. "You're a gift, Jim Cassaway."

Cresting the hill, they came upon a pickup truck and a van parked at an intersection of fire roads. Three men stared at them.

"Well if isn't Jones of Arc, come to save the world."

"Hey, Drum," Christy responded without a hint of warmth.

The bear of a man had a full black beard and long hair drawn back in a bun through a hand-carved wooden ring.

Jim sensed some personal history— intimate, unresolved— between her and the swarthy guy.

"We should have left an hour ago, but Rosco insisted you'd be coming," Drum said.

Rosco gave Christy a hug. He'd heard about her arrest, but didn't mention it. When the time was right he'd ask her why she thought Ingot was the culprit? He could name a number of people who could've killed her dog. Christy had a knack for attracting hostility. Truth-talking women do that. "We almost gave up on you," he said. "What happened?"

"Tracy dumped us off six miles back. I think the rough road frightened her. So what's with the roadblocks?"

"Who knows," Rosco said. "But most everybody's driving up tomorrow, and I'll be here to show them the back way."

Jim set the camera case, gear satchel and gym bag on the dirt, then stretched his back, releasing the stiffness in his shoulder blades.

"This is my friend, Jim Cassaway," Christy smiled at him. "He came up from the city with me."

"Name's Ross. But they call me Rosco." The man came striding over, suspenders spread taut across a wine barrel body, a skullcap on his head. "Good to meet you."

Drum looked visibly annoyed by Christy's friend, and ignored him. Another man walked over.

"I remember you," Christy smiled, "From the last time I came up. You're the botanical scientist."

"Plant biologist," he corrected in a monotone.

"UC Davis, right?"

"Good memory. That was two years ago."

Jim heard Christy say "UC Davis," and took it as the man's name rather than associating him with the University of California at Davis. The biologist had a pale, bovine face with a high forehead flat as a marquee. He gave Jim a bored and bothered dip of his head as he pushed his glasses up the bridge of his nose.

"Leon, Joni and Isaac are in the van," Rosco said. "Another carload left an hour ago."

"Can we go now?" Drum grumbled. "It's about to get dark real fast." He marched over to his yellow van and pulled open the rear doors. Christy followed and stuffed their gear inside.

Jim sat on a log, untied his shoes and gingerly peeled off socks. Pus oozed from ruptured blisters.

"Oof. Hurts just looking at it," Rosco declared. "But I can fix you up. Follow me to my clinic."

Jim hopped on one leg to the Toyota pickup where he sat on the tailgate as Rosco dug into the glove compartment.

"All out of moleskin, but this outta help for the time being." Rosco handed him some white bandage tape.

Drum shut the rear doors of his van.

"I see you got the banana slug running again," Christy said, averting Drum's eyes. She didn't let on how surprised she was to see him taking an active role with the protest.

He tipped his head toward Jim. "Who's the milquetoast?"

"Don't start. You got nothing on him," Christy said.

"Yeah, so what's his story?"

"Jim's a documentary producer I hired to capture it all and show the world. Do you know where they are?"

"Who?"

"The tree people, the Charlie Tanner thing."

"That? Hell, nobody would tell me squat. Said I had to have an advocate. Everybody's got to have an advocate. Fuck'em. Wouldn't even tell me where the action camp is."

Christy shook her head. "Wow, they're seriously guarding it."

"It's bullshit."

"No, The John said..."

"The John's gone bonkers. You mean that Tanner prank is why you brought this guy?" He didn't wait for Christy's answer, he called out, "We're going!" Then turned back to her. "You're with me up front."

"What? No." She bent her thumb toward Jim at the pickup. "We're together."

"I need you on the map with this..." He handed Christy a walkie-talkie.

"You know the way, you drove here."

"Yeah, but it's not for me. It's to help navigate them in the dark. Now come on."

"I'll go get Jim."

"No room, we're full up." Drum tugged her by the elbow.

"Shit." Christy broke free and hustled back to Jim who was applying bandage tape to his heel.

"They want me to ride shotgun in the van and handle the walkie-talkie."

"He can ride with me and botany here," Rosco said.

Christy hunkered to Jim's eye-level. "You'll be fine with Rosco. Here…" She stuck the folded map in the pocket of his vest. "Just in case we get separated."

It all happened too fast. Before Jim could wrap his head around being split up, Drum's yellow van disappeared with Christy and his gear.

UC Davis took the passenger seat in Rosco's pickup. There wasn't room for another person in the cab unless Jim wanted to squeeze between them on top of the console. The only place left was in the truck bed with backpacks, duffel bags, camping supplies and stuff. After shifting things around Jim laid his body down, cradling Gomez's camera to his chest like a sacred relic.

15.
Jeez Louise, looks like a garage sale

Riding in the bed of a truck wasn't what Jim anticipated. Nothing was. The whole thing felt disjointed. And the thought of risking his part time job to chase a joke kept hounding him. But what do you do— waylaid in the boonies with night sinking in? He dashed any remaining expectations about the trip and resigned himself to whatever lay ahead, however chaotic or discouraging.

Be grateful for the little things: my headache is gone and I'm breathing real air this time and not carbon monoxide fumes.

Rosco slid open the window between the cab and the truck bed. "Hey back there, just a head's up, the suspension sucks, the brake pads are almost bald and it's going to get bumpy. So you might want to hang on to the side rail."

Bumpy was an understatement. Every time the truck hit a rut or a rock in the road, Jim's head slammed into the cab wall and all the gear would levitate. One of the items was a sleeping bag in a stuff sack. Jim slumped down and wedged it behind his head to cushion the concussive blows.

Night darkened to utter blackness. At times the overhead forest canopy would part and reveal the heavens, sizzling with stars. Awed by the vault of constellations, Jim vowed that when he got back to the city he'd study celestial charts so he could identify the luminaries on sight.

After half an hour of random bouncing, the fire road became a hard, ribbed crust that never smoothed out. At fifteen miles per hour, the constant juddering got old fast. Finally, after maneuvering countless switchbacks, roller-coasting steep slopes and ravines, splashing through creek beds, the truck rattled to a stop. The two vehicles sat idling. Christy got out of the van and came back to talk to Rosco.

"We're about to cross 101. Lights off till we're into the forest on the other side. And follow close. If the highway patrol shows up, you're on your own."

"Got it."

Christy checked on Jim in the truck bed. "Hey, you miss me?"

"Actually, yes."

She set her hand on his shoulder, "Not much farther."

"Make sure no one sits on my gear in there."

"I warned them."

"Christy, we're going," Drum announced.

The two vehicles pulled away, accelerating as they cut across the dimly lit highway to another back road posted with a yellow sign: RESTRICTED USE, NO TRESPASSING.

Jim sat up on his knees and stretched his neck.

"How's it going back there?" Rosco asked.

"Fine if you like being tenderized."

Rosco chuckled.

"Say, I got a question…" Jim had lined up a series of questions to ask Rosco, including: What moved him to activism? What this Last Stand protest means to him? Is he aware of the weird story going around about people mutating into trees? And if so, has he witnessed it? Then he'd follow with questions about Drum, the guy's background, his relationship to

Christy. But before he could get a word out, Rosco hollered, "Uh-oh!" and pumped the brakes. Jim latched onto the rail as the pickup screeched to a gyrating halt inches from rear-ending the van.

"Sorry," Rosco called back. "Like I said, the brake pads are thin as paint."

They were at a fork in the road. Jim could hear Christy's voice on the walkie-talkie telling Rosco to stay right.

"Got it," he said, and shut the slider.

They thumped along. Jim's cell phone read: 9:57 pm. He noticed the battery display was low and it hit him— in his haste, he forgot to pack the charger. "Oh, great!" he blurted. But another sound, like a surge of thunder, smothered his outcry.

"Hey!" He knocked on the glass.

The slider opened. "What's up?"

"Anyone you know following us?"

"Nobody I know."

"Look again," Jim said, ducking his head for Rosco to see.

A blaze of headlights and roof mounted spots burst out of the darkness from a fast-moving tow truck, bucking the furrowed road and bearing down on them.

Jim kept his body prone on the bed, out of the tow truck's blinding lights.

Rosco called the van on his walkie-talkie. "Mayday guys. We got some assholes on our tail and they're coming up fast."

A shotgun blast blew a side-view mirror off. "What the fuck!" Another blast peppered the tailgate. "Keep your head down back there," Rosco hollered.

Drum hit the gas and the van sped off, pelting Rosco's windshield with road grit.

Rosco stamped the pedal to the floor, but his ancient pickup was no match for the bigger truck's power. Lights swelled as it bore closer, tagging the pickup's bumper, horn blaring. Jim could make out voices from the tow truck's cab, shouts and gusts of laughter.

Who are these guys? Jim reached for the rail just as the beast slammed into them, somersaulting bags and gear.

"Motherfuckers!" Rosco cranked the wheel to the right, riding the soft shoulder only to be rammed again by the tow truck's bull bar, sending his Toyota into a tail spin he couldn't control. His pickup careened off road, tipped down an embankment, skidded and slammed head-on into a tree with a deadening WHUMP!

The collision trampolined Jim and all the camping gear into the air. He hit the spongy forest ground on his back, and lay there, stunned, the air knocked out, fighting to draw a breath into his lungs.

Dust motes and twigs swirled in the headlights of the attackers. The tow truck had stopped. Its vibrating engine droned in the stillness.

Jim gasped. His back a plank, his legs stone numb. Christy's pocketed poop shovel dug into his butt cheek. As fits of breath returned, he heard faint groans from the wreck. Gaining back oxygen, he sighed in relief, feeling the weight of the camera case resting on his chest intact, its strap still slung round his neck.

Two men stepped out of the idling tow truck. The driver, lean and long-legged, wearing a backwards feed cap, stayed by the vehicle. The other, a short bump of a man on bowed legs, strutted to the side of the road shouldering a shotgun and making a hacking sound as if clearing an obstruction from his throat.

Jim stretched his neck so he could get a better look at the two men as they passed through the high beams— faceless, phantom-like.

They're wearing masks.

Not a good sign.

The driver stepped on the running board and rotated a door-mounted spotlight until it shone on Rosco's wreck, the front end cratered against the tree trunk, doors winged out, camping gear strewn all over the ground.

"Now that's one totaled Toyoter," Shotgun said, stumbling down the bank and checking out the license plate: Bob Turley's Toyota San Leandro. "Not from around here now are ya?" He knocked on the roof. "Hel-looo!" He peered inside the cab, then turned his face into the spot, gave a shake of his head. "Must'a jumped!"

A rustle in the near trees tweaked his attention. Shotgun jammed the weapon into his shoulder, pointing the barrel toward the sound. "Shine that light over there."

The driver swiveled the spot into the forest. "You run on home now and don't come back. Consider yourself lucky. Trespassing's a violation of the law, and we're The Enforcers."

This is not about trespassing, Jim said to himself. These guys mean trouble. He lowered his head as blood started to burn back, filling the veins in his arms and legs, making the skin itch. He worked his fingers, clawed the ground litter, his torso still deadened with shock.

Seeing only a clump of ferns, the Driver swung the spotlight back to the area around the crash.

"Jeez Louise, looks like a garage sale." Shotgun inspected the camping gear on the ground. "Anybody need an ice chest?"

"Leave it for now," Driver called out. "Let's go. We can still catch the ones ahead."

"Hang on, I gotta take a leak." Shotgun said.

Jim was about to urge his body upright when Shotgun stepped out of the spotlight. In no time he heard the man's throat-runting and the crump-crump of his boots stepping his way.

Don't move. Don't breathe.

Then came the unmistakable sound of a zipper being tugged, followed by the stream of urine wetting the cuff of Jim's pant leg and running down over his sneaker.

Shotgun couldn't see Jim in the darkness, but as he finished, he sensed a presence nearby. He twitched back a half step, a little spooked and curious at the same time. Tentatively, he reached out a hand to touch whatever was there in front of him.

"Hey!" Driver hollered from the road. "We got a live one here."

Shotgun shook off and zipped up, leaving Jim in a mix of relief and humiliation.

Driver beamed the spotlight to the ground where a body crawled along the edge of the road.

Rosco, busted up, dragging his legs.

Shotgun stepped up. "Where you off to mister, taking these back roads all sneaky like?"

Rosco winced and spat. He rolled onto his back, squinting at the imposing silhouette above him. "What's with the masks? Too ugly to show your face?"

Driver appeared at Shotgun's side. "Leave him." He tapped Shotgun on the arm and headed back to the truck. "Come on. We're done."

"You gonna ditch me out here alone with a broken foot."

"Yeah, we got more of you to hunt down."

"Kunkle, let's boogie!" Driver said, climbing into the rig.

"Shut the fuck, you idiot!" Shotgun railed, furious at hearing his name called out.

"Kunkle, huh?" Rosco said. "I don't know what you look like, but I got your name now and that's all I need to track down your ass."

"You got nothin'." Shotgun walked away.

"Know what you are, Kunkle? You're the skuzz that floats on the sewage of time. Ee-yah!" Rosco clenched his teeth. "You hearing me, you hemorrhoid-sucking maggot?"

Kunkle kicked up road dirt, pivoted in the headlights, and marched back to Rosco's body.

Rosco kept it up, attempting to delay their pursuit of the van. "Yeah, you're beyond an asshole, Kunkle. An asshole has a function. You're more worthless than that. You're like the waste of waste. Yeah, if shit could shit you'd be it."

Kunkle lowered the weapon to Rosco's lips. "You don't clamp your mouth right now, I'm going to blow it off your face."

Rosco didn't flinch. "You think that's going to stop me? You're way wrong. I'll come after you from the dead, Kunkle. From the *dead*. My ghost will spook you twenty-four seven…"

Driver revved the engine. "We're leaving now!"

"Crazy ass bastard." Kunkle backed away, turned and stamped through the high beams to the tow truck.

Rosco spooked his name, "Kun-kle… Kun-kle…"

Kunkle opened the passenger door and yelled at Driver, "You gave that dude my name, you shithead!"

The door slammed shut on muffled words.

Brmm-brmmm. Driver gunned the engine. Then he rolled the truck alongside Rosco's body and stopped.

The two men got out.

Jim stood on rigid stilts, waffling: run or record it. He wished he could do both. No telling how far into bad these men were going to go.

As he undid the clips on the camera case, he heard one of them say something about "giving you a tow," but couldn't see what they were doing. He stiff-stepped up the incline, the camera on his shoulder. Before he reached the road, doors slammed and the truck barreled off, spurting rocks behind its tires.

"Roscooo?" Jim howled.

No reply.

He shuffled along the roadside in the dark, feeling his way. "Rosco! Where are you?"

"Hey!" A voice called out.

"Rosco?"

"No! Ober here! I'm hurd!"

It was UC Davis shouting from the woods.

"Can't see where you are." Jim kneeled on the ground, returning the camera to its case.

"Hang on!" UC hollered.

Jim tread slowly along the edge of the road toward the voice. A pinprick of light wobbled in the distant trees behind the wreck.

"Ober here."

Jim found UC Davis lying prone behind a tree, ten yards from the pickup, wiggling a cellphone in his hand.

"My lep knee id hurd. Tore domding when I dumped."

"I don't understand a word you're saying."

"I bid my tongue," UC explained.

"You bit your tongue."

"Yeth."

Jim helped UC upright. They staggered out of the trees led by the light on UC's phone.

"You said you jumped?"

"Ad da lath thecond.

"At the last second."

"Yeth. He pumped the brakth. We thaw the three. He hollered, "Dump!" I dumped and landed on my knee."

"Could've been worse. You could have done a header through the windshield."

"Or gotten thot." UC winced. "Who were thoth atholth?"

"Don't know. They wore ski-masks."

When the two got to the pickup, Jim lowered the tailgate. "You rest here," he said, then hollered, "Rosco!"

Nothing.

Jim called again.

Only silence responded.

"I'll go look for him." Jim said.

"Therth a flathlite in my pack in the thruck."

Jim combed the roadside with the Maglite. When he returned, he found UC with his cargo pants rumpled around his ankles, inspecting his swollen knee.

Jim set a hiking boot on the tailgate. "That's all I found."

"Hith boot? Did day dake him wid dem?"

Jim didn't answer. He stared up the dark road hoping Christy was far and safe away from the brutes.

UC rubbed his knee and shook his head. "Madneth... madneth."

16.
What the hell were
you thinking?

Richard Hersh stepped out onto the third-floor balcony of the Hotel del Coronado in San Diego where outdoor spots lit the sandy beach below. He'd just closed a call with Argus Beldare debriefing the day's strategy meeting with Dixon and Hardin. The sound of the nearby surf might as well have been rush hour traffic. It didn't matter to him. What mattered was making this entire redwood situation go away. And that meant more than Beldare's penchant for 'owning and controlling the story.' Screw that. He wanted the whole thing vaporized permanently and undetectable as air.

That and the Christy Jones problem. He could still hear the trenchant voice of Ingot's CEO pounding on him: "What the hell were you thinking?"

The man who supervised the multi-national rarely phoned. Yet less than an hour ago he called Hersh to bust his balls. Yes, lynching the dog should never have happened. Turning the tables on that bitch, although seamlessly executed, nonetheless could raise another ugly welt on Ingot's already cankerous image. And yes, having it go to a jury trial would prolong the mess. The worst of it was, Hersh had no one to blame but his own reckless judgment.

No, the worst of it was it ruined his moment.

He'd dreamt about this day. Worked his tail off to stand before a gathering of American business executives delivering a speech he called, *The Critical Little's to Making It Big*, based on the book he co-authored.

Ever since he was partners in a Phoenix turn-around business that consulted with faltering companies, applied boiler-plate tactics to boost their numbers, fired the creative types and kept the robo-ployees, he'd fantasized about being in such an esteemed position, recognized by his peers, center stage at a lectern, waves of applause pummeling his ears.

No, he may not be the conference's keynote speaker, but with a blitz of self-promotion he'd be the man next year.

Yet here he stood, foundering on the eve of making it to the big show, shaken by the CEO's corrosive words, pacing the balcony, grubbing for positives. The temptation to tell the man the deadly measures he was taking to make sure there was not going to be a trial still clung tight to his throat like a bow tie.

Good he hadn't.

As he inflated a chest-full of sea air, the image of his father's face came to mind. Yes, his father would've been proud. Not about the divorces and estranged daughter, but about his achievements, his wealth, carving a name, his father's name, in the treacherous business world.

Hersh went back inside the suite, poured another Dewar's. He popped two pain pills in his mouth and returned to the balcony.

One more call to make. He needed to find out how close his field operative was to executing her mission.

17.
Whack him in the junk

"Here we go…" said the Masked Marauder wagging a bull whip.

"If he gets out of the car, whack him in the junk," said another.

"No worries, I'll scare'em off."

Three men stood in the darkness next to their ATV's that blocked the backwoods road. The six side-by-side headlights lit up an idling car that had shuddered to a stop.

The driver squinted out his window. "Hey there, do you mind letting us pass?" Hearing nothing, he stepped from the vehicle, unable to see the men's faces. "The police barricaded 299. We're trying to get around it."

"Nobody's going through here dude. It's a dead end."

"No, it's not." The driver shook his head.

"It is for you."

"This some joke?" The driver moved toward them, one hand vizoring his eyes to dim the burn of the beams. "What's your deal?"

"Don't come no closer," growled the man tightening his calluses around the leather-braided handle of the whip.

"You don't own this road."

CRACK! A burst of road dust splashed on the driver's boots. He recoiled, "What the hell?"

"That's a warning."

"Yeah, get back in your wussy car and go home."

The driver didn't move. A passenger got out. Female. "What's going on?"

"They won't let us through."

"Why not?"

"Don't know. Bunch of losers got nothing better to do." The driver stepped toward the ATV's. "Look guys, you may get your kicks blocking cars, and that's all cool, but this is the only detour we can take to get to…"

The eight-foot bull whip floated back and in a split second the thong unfurled, a whisp, slicing the night air, snap-jolting its popper threads in the driver's crotch.

Stung! the driver flopped to his knees, whimpering, rocking back and forth.

"Woo!" The men hooted.

"Holy shit!" The woman hissed. "What'd you do!" She hurried to the driver. "You okay?"

He spat and groaned.

"Motherfuggers!" she shouted back. "You're going down for this! We're getting the cops on your ass!" She leaned over to help the driver up.

WHAP! The whip bit into the back of her neck, slicing the skin.

Her shrieks sang out only so far before being swallowed by the watching stands of towering trees.

18.
He's always been a loner, now he's just alone

"**R**arff! Rarff!"
A dog barked as Christy slid open the side door of the van. "Okay everybody, grab your stuff, we're here."

They'd parked in a pool of light that spilled from the porch of a rustic board and batten house tucked under the roof of the forest.

"Rarff! Rarff!"

Christy pulled out her duffel and backpack, set them on the ground and listened for Rosco's truck.

Nothing.

A screen door croaked and a standard poodle bounded out of the house to greet her.

"Barley, Barley!" Christy kneeled to be tongue–lashed by the ecstatic dog.

"Is that you, Christy?" The hoarse voice of a woman sounded as she stepped falteringly out onto the porch in a bathrobe, working a cane.

"Hi Mae," Christy appeared from the back of the van.

"What a sight. Come here girl and gimme a crunch."

Christy unloaded Jim's luggage, stepped onto the porch where Mae pulled her into a firm embrace.

"Someone told me you were in jail," Mae beamed, smelling of wood smoke. "And I said, that's my Christy, thumbing her nose at authority."

"I'm setting these guys up in Cabin Three." Drum flung-shut the van door.

"That's fine, it's tidy." Mae waved a welcome hand to the other riders who followed Drum down a path behind the main house, lugging bags and backpacks.

"This all of you now?"

"No, some others were behind us, with Rosco, but we lost them." Christy turned on the porch to listen again.

Still no sound.

"Nothing to worry yourself. Rosco knows this place. Come, you need to catch me up on all your shenanigans. How long has it been?"

"Two years." Christy opened the screen door for Mae and Barley.

Except for a thin film of dust coating everything, little had changed since she'd last visited. The same woodland paintings and sketches hung on the walls. The visitor's sign-in book still sat on a podium below a placard: SANCTUARY STATION. To her right, the river rock fireplace and the comfy, timeworn seating area crowded by a swaled couch, a dog-clawed love seat, Mae's easy chair, and a disorderly shelf where guests left paperbacks, videocassettes and DVD's over the years.

Christy could almost hear the late nights she and others conspired to end the cutting of trees. Wild ideas, like infusing the coastal fog with a hypnotic gas that tempted lumbermen to abandon their chainsaws and seek other jobs.

Mae shuffled in, bleary-eyed, her hair a gray helmet of steel wool. The woman's condition had deteriorated since Christy last saw her.

When Christy was thirteen, a couple years after her mother moved out, Mae became a summer-time replacement mom, as she was to many young tree huggers. Mae didn't show favoritism for any of them, but everybody knew she adored Christy, the firebrand, the most.

"Our computer's down," Mae said. "I think we got hacked. My son disagrees. Any-who, we can't email or do that social-netting, so instead we're talking to people. How about that, actually making meaningful sounds with our mouths. Some folks even stop by and share the latest gossip face to face. It's back to basics in the backwoods. Can I get you anything?"

"No, don't bother."

Mae eased her plumpish, pear-shaped body down on her recliner. Christy worked the lever, lifting the woman's sixty-six-year old legs onto the foot rest. Then she pushed an ottoman up close, all the while petting Barley, which revived the grief of losing her own dog.

Drum stomped into the house, saw them sitting there. "I'll take that." He pointed to the walkie-talkie clutched in Christy's right hand.

"No-no, I need it." Christy pressed the unit to her chest. "I may be going back."

"Pfft!" Drum scoffed. "Suit yourself." And marched into the kitchen.

"Going back where, dear? You just got here." Mae said.

"We heard a mayday from Rosco's truck. Sounded like they were being chased by somebody. Drum floored it. We lost contact with them." Christy gestured toward the kitchen, softening her voice. "I pleaded with him to stop or at least go back and check on them. He refused. So we fought the rest of the way here."

"He still has a thing for you."

"Don't go there."

"I know. What's over's over. Accept the things I cannot change and… and I forget the rest."

"All we ever did was fight."

She leaned over to Christy. "He can be a bit over-bearing."

"You took the words…" Christy checked the owl-faced clock on the wall above the front door. Time clipping by. She trusted her instincts, and right now her alarm bells were clanging hysterically.

Mae noticed Christy's hand scrubbing Barley's back.

"I tried to have him trained as a service dog but they told me he was too old and set in his ways, like me.

"And how have you been?"

"Oh, some days good, some not so good. They don't know if it's multiple sclerosis or single sclerosis."

Christy gave a quizzical look.

"That was a joke, dear. No, my life has become a circus of tests and checkups. And to think how I hated doctors before all this. Do you know Bev the shaman?"

"Beverly, yeah."

"Or is it sha-woman? Anyway, she looked me over. Said she'd be back with something, a potion, I imagine. Ha! Can't wait to spring that on the medical staff."

"It's not fair."

Mae shrugged. "Life's a pickle."

Christy was about to ask if Mae would be going to the protest when Drum came back into the room.

"If you don't need anything more Mom, I'm going to go. I'll check in with you tomorrow."

"Thanks no, dear, I'm fine. Goodnight now."

The room went quiet. They heard him thump the luggage on the porch, the van's motor start up and purr away.

"He's changed," Mae confided. "He's always been a loner, but now he's just alone."

"Does he still teach survival skills and tracking and all that?"

"No-no. Everything went down the crapper when that girl broke off their engagement after sucking him dry. Left him holding a lot of debt. Of course, the bank wouldn't even look at him sideways. Had to take loans from people. The wrong people."

Christy nodded. She'd heard the rumors. Mae didn't mention the drinking, gambling, and pills. Didn't need to. The grapevine spat that news for all to hear. Drum had slid over the edge, and those once close left him faster than spent money. Christy was about to say how surprised she was to see him carpooling protestors when Mae pointed to the mantle.

"Oh, I just remembered, a letter was left for you. The John dropped it off."

Mae was referring to the elder, veteran activist known as 'The John,' a moniker he'd been given to distinguish him from every other John in the world.

Mae's eyes followed Christy as she crossed the room to the fireplace. "And now there's all this hogwash about people mutating into trees. What idiot came up with that nonsense? Makes us all look ridiculous."

Christy kept mum, stuffed the letter unread in her back pocket, and returned to the window, the dog at her heels.

No sounds or movement outside.

"Are they here?"

"Something's wrong." Christy said, her heart racing.

"They'll come. Can't say how many times I've been lost in the maze of back roads."

"Well, I feel lost waiting here and not knowing. I really need to go and see if they're okay. My friend is with them."

"Someone I know?"

"No, a new friend."

Mae sensed this friend was the reason for her unease. "And what's your new friend's name?"

"Jim." Christy turned. "He's like no one I've ever met. I mean, he's deep, like a mystic, and he listens."

"No man listens."

"You'd like him, Mae. He's got kind eyes, and a strong Nordic nose, y'know, heroic, and when he smiles it's like a sunrise."

"Oh my, now you've got me wanting to meet this young man."

"And he's never been out in the woods. He's never even been out of the Bay Area."

"But he's with Rosco."

"Can I borrow your Jeep?" Christy sat down again on the ottoman next to Mae, her hand on the arm of the chair. "I'll just go a few miles and come right back."

Mae patted her hand. "Never seen you quite like this."

"Can't get him out of my mind."

"And have you told him how you feel?"

Christy shook her head.

Mae's eyes goggled large. "Well get on it!" She pounded her cane on the hardwood floor. "You think men can read minds? Far from it. They're numbskulls. You have to tell them to their face."

Christy blinked hard, taken aback.

"You must tell him how you feel 'cause when your heart can't reach your voice, your throat clogs up like a toilet and what comes out of your mouth is just crap!"

"Okay-okay." Christy said, wondering how she could get up the nerve to outright do it.

"What does he think of you?"

Christy gazed at the window. "He probably hates me for leaving him out there."

19.
Dead!

Rosco's truck was dead. Not a whimper from the ignition. As for Rosco himself, other than his hiking boot, Jim and UC Davis didn't have a clue. Conjecture led UC to believe or hope the tow truck thugs drove the man's busted body to the nearest hospital. Jim didn't share that view. But where else could he be unless passed out in a ditch?

Jim found an ace bandage in Rosco's first aid kit and wrapped UC's knee while the plant biologist clicked his tongue, working to restore its facility to make 's' sounds.

Looking over the map Christy had given Jim, they decided to keep heading north and try to reach the circled X on the map with the words: BASE CAMP, which looked to be still a few miles away.

They inventoried the camping gear littered about the ground, prioritizing what they needed to bring, and what Jim could carry, given UC's bum knee.

"The tarp will come in handy in cazze of rain," UC said.

"What else?

"Food, from the cooler. And I muzz take my laboratory. Zee the big Pelican there next to the cooler?" UC pointed to a silver, hard shell case. "Can't leave without my injecton… inject-zzion toolz."

"Injection tools?"

Jim lifted the case to feel the weight of it. *No way*. He didn't want to lug forty pounds around.

"It rollzz." UC pointed out.

The unit had plastic wheels attached to one end which might roll easily on sidewalk, but not across a rugged backwoods road.

"Oh, and where izz my intrument bag?"

Jim shook his head. "I can only take so much. Besides, we need to travel light."

"They're going to come back, and when they do, they'll pick through all thizz and pilfer my toolz." UC's tongue was coming around.

"We can hide them and come back later."

"You willing to hide your camera?"

"It's not mine. And if I don't get it back I'm dead meat."

"And without toolz I can't do my job."

A daypack with the instrument bag was all UC could handle. Jim shouldered Rosco's large backpack. It held a sleeping bag, trail mix, jerky, two water bottles, and Rosco's boot. He strapped the roll of tarp under the backpack's flap. In one hand, he carried the video camera. In his other hand he rolled UC's lab equipment case.

The two headed up the road on alert to any sounds, especially those resembling an oncoming tow truck. Jim called out Rosco's name as they walked to no avail. UC manned the flashlight and worked his tongue around his mouth, making ticking sounds. The flashlight's beam revealed the contour of the fire road six feet ahead of them but made the periphery disappear into an abyss.

After about a hundred yards UC stopped, grabbed his left knee and screamed, "Aw shit!"

"Your speech is back." Jim stood the Pelican case up for UC to use as a resting seat.

After UC's pain subsided, Jim tapped the case with his shoe and asked, "What's this laboratory of yours do?"

"The curious filmmaker. Well, I'll tell you. A few years ago, an experimental study was conducted with the roots of redwood trees."

"Wait!" Hearing something Jim hushed him.

They listened for a few seconds.

Jim called, "Rosco?"

But there was nothing.

"Anyway..," UC continued as they walked on, "…the theory behind the study suggested that trees transfer sustenance to one another, such as nutrients, through the network of their root systems. The experiment involved injecting a natural dye into a root at the foot of a tree, and after some time elapsed, tap the root system of a neighbor tree to see if the dye passed on. Not only did the theory prove out, the dye was discovered in roots fifty feet away. Two years ago, I took the study farther, and found that after a month, the dye turned up in roots of trees more than a hundred feet away. A bit more diluted mind you, but nonetheless, irrefutably transferred."

The road dipped and curved through dense forest. Jim thought about what UC was describing and how such a transference could be happening right there under his feet, passing from root to root like veins circulating blood throughout the body.

"I submitted a paper detailing my findings with a plethora of charts and scientific data, enough to make your head spin, and hopefully satisfy the gods of science to autograph a sizable grant for me to continue my study."

"And?"

"Haven't heard zip."

They walked in silence for a while, making slow headway.

"So you're going ahead with the study on this trip?" Jim asked.

"Not exactly. I got a call. They said, in their cryptic words, "Something was happening," and would I consider doing the same injection study on a grove of trees in a particular parcel of forest, only this time extending the scope of the transference to the limit of its reach. They didn't indicate where. And they guaranteed me they'd order enough lab tubing for the test."

Jim thought of Christy's wild mutation story but rejected bringing it up.

Wingbeats slapped the air above their heads. The two held up.

"What's that?"

"Not an owl. Most likely bats." UC shone the light around. "Only other creature flying low around this forest at night.

They moved on.

Jim asked if UC was going to the protest.

"No. But I am going to the base camp where a lot of the protestors convene. A man known as 'The John' will take me to the parcel. It's all very secretive, unusually so. But the incentive is good. Just hope they've got the one-eighth inch clear tubing I requested, otherwise…"

The Maglite dimmed. UC rapped it with his hand. It brightened again illuminating a bulge in the road a few feet in front of them.

"Rosco?" Jim crouched over the motionless body. "Hey-hey, you okay?"

Rosco was far from okay. He'd been dragged by the tow truck for nearly half a mile. His body a mangled heap of shattered bones and torn muscle. A nylon rope, tethered to an ankle, had come loose from the truck's bumper and lay curlicued in the road.

UC Davis panned the flashlight beam over Rosco's buckled legs, the pants shredded and streaked with dirty blood. Although the man's suspenders were still intact, his t-shirt was in tatters, a busted rib bone jutted out the skin of his chest.

"Dead! He's dead!" The reality sent a tremor ratcheting up Jim's spine.

"What? Those men dragged him… and killed him?!" UC stumbled, aghast, disbelieving what he was seeing. "No!" He swept the light up the torso once more, this time fixing on the man's face, one eye open, vacant, the other eyeball missing, its socket caked with road dust. Rosco's skull cap was gone. The top of his head crushed-in, a broken melon, brains like melted cheese curds burbling through a crack in the skull.

That did it. UC staggered in a drunken circle before doubling over to spew a flume of vomit.

Jim left his camera and the lab luggage there on the road and shuffled away. The only way he knew to calm his body was to imagine ocean swells rhythmically lifting and gently subsiding with his breath. Even so, it took everything he had to fend off gutting a launch.

After UC was done hacking and spitting, Jim uttered. "Got to call 911."

"Yeah, I would, but there's no service out here."

Still queasy, Jim ambled back to the body in the road. "We've got to do something."

"You could video it. Or I could for that matter."

Jim shook his head. "We better not. I doubt he'd want his family and friends to see him like this on the internet."

"Good point.

Jim exhaled a shell-shocked sigh. "Aw, God, how could they do this? I mean, how could anybody do *this*!"

"We should bury him. Can't leave him out, the critters will gnaw him to the bone."

20.
This is Christy, over

"**R**osco?" Christy worked the walkie-talkie as she maneuvered Mae's Jeep down a bumpy back road, headlights fluttering up and down. "This is Christy, over."

No response.

She knew she needed to be close to make a clear connection. The walkie-talkie makers claimed a fifteen-mile range, which they must have tested in a Nevada desert and not with thick forest and hills in the way.

"Hello! Talk to me!"

Christy wasn't sure she was on the same fire road Drum took and now wished she'd made note of landmarks on their way to Mae's. She pressed her chest into the steering wheel as if sheer will power would make Rosco's pickup manifest in the high beams.

"Where are you!"

She felt distressed, culpable. If anything bad happened to Jim she would not be able to forgive herself. She brought this thing on. She'd coaxed him into coming, "It's my turn," she said, advancing the leap-frog game they started.

A week after she'd taken Jim to walk the labyrinth, he said it was his turn and invited her to come to his medicine place. She played along, joining him at Ocean Beach on a breezy May afternoon. The day of the sand dollars. As the tide slid ropes of foam across their bare feet, Jim shared his story of how the ocean there saved his life.

"They couldn't figure me out. There I was, a spindly fifteen-year old, fading away. They thought something was shutting down my immune system, a pathogen. Had me in a clean room draped in plastic. I lay there in two worlds, floating between the dead and the living. And one night, for a minute, I died.

"My aunt, who'd seen me through a lot of health problems, could no longer afford me. The medical debt was tearing her up so bad she made me a ward of the state. I can still hear her sobs in the hall outside the hospital room, leaving me there, feeling like a burden to her and to the world.

"Luckily, my night nurse, Miko, made me her pet project. A bit unorthodox, but with some inventive paperwork she took me home, fed me bubbling pots of stink soup and gag-me teas. She had an apartment on Balboa, few blocks from here. She'd bring me to this beach before her shift, out in the sun, Vitamin D, fresh air. I lay in the sand while people jogged by me, running dogs, riding skim boards.

"One afternoon Miko walked me to the water's edge to stick my feet in the surf. Then, each day a little farther, to my ankles, to my knees. I'd lay in the shallow tide and let the waves wash over my body. Little by little I'd go out deeper, back-floating, rolling in the swells. Sometimes getting battered. This surf can get mean and rough.

"Turns out my formative brain was not developing in a natural way. Miko told me the tides inside me were out of sync and submerging my body in the ocean for long periods of time helped bring about a healthier neurological rhythm."

Christy remembered asking him what death felt like. "Hard to describe," he said. But a little later, they spotted sand dollars floating in on the waves. More than a hundred bone-white discs drifted toward the shore on the high tide. Each shell embossed like a medallion with a radial, five-petal flower.

The memory filled Christy's senses as she drove— the tingling joy of wading waist-deep in the cold surf, palming the porous shells, gathering them in her arms like a harvest.

"This is what death felt like," Jim said. "Like these sand dollars, floating... weightless in full sun."

"Shit!" She pounded the brakes. The road hit a dead end.

Mae was right, they all look the same at night. She wheeled the Jeep around and started back to the fork she'd taken.

What if instead of going to Mae's, Rosco went straight to the base camp? The probability eased her mind. She let out an audible sigh. I'll check there in the morning, if they're not at Mae's when I get back.

She pulled the walkie-talkie to her lips. "Hey, I can't hear you, but if you can hear me, I'll be at Mae Drummond's place, over and out."

A fizzy sound came back.

"Hello?"

Broken chatter. Somebody there.

"Rosco? That you?" She cut the engine and listened, plunged in darkness. "Talk to me dammit!"

"Howdy there!"

Howdy there? "Rosco! Where are you?"

"Out and about. Who might I be talking to?" Kunkle fiddled with the tuning on the tow truck's CB radio.

"This..." She hesitated. A shiver rippling up her spine. She let it pass. "This is Christy... who's this?"

"Well hi there Christy. Had a funky reception there, but now I gotcha loud and clear."

Not Rosco. "I'm... trying to reach a friend..."

Christy saw headlights flicker between trees in the distance. She rubbed her thumb along the edge of the walkie-talkie.

"You in trouble? Maybe we can help. You gotta be close by."

She didn't answer. She watched the vehicle slow as it came to the fork in the road ahead and stop there.

"Lost you," Kunkle called out. The truck idling. "You disappeared on us, darlin'."

Christy felt for the knob on the walkie-talkie and clicked off.

21.
They're called goosepens

The legs of two black-tail deer froze suddenly in the pre-dawn forest. Before them stood a strange structure made from a tarp draped over a slanted, fallen branch of a tree. The lead deer lifted a front leg and thumped its hoof, tamping the ground. The object did not move. Still, something didn't feel safe about it, and the pungent, sweat gland odor of two-leggeds struck a tone of caution. The deer changed course, angling away from their normal path before descending among dew-drenched ferns to their water pool in the lower valley.

A short while later, Jim woke, chilled, needing to pee. He stepped feebly out from under the tarp in the half-light. The damp forest quiet as sleep. His feet stung from busted blisters, his legs stiff and sore from dragging UC's equipment case. But his physical discomfort could not compare with the recurring horror of seeing Rosco's mutilated body.

Jim had mummy-wrapped the man's corpse with a section of the tarp. Then he dug a shallow grave in the soft earth off the side of the road with Christy's poop shovel. He planted a thick redwood branch on the hump of dirt, and topped the branch with Rosco's hiking boot to flag the site.

Standing at the makeshift grave, Jim wondered if Rosco had family. "Did you know him?" he asked UC.

"As much as you can know someone on a five-hour drive. I met him once before. So when I was informed about the road-block, and how I could leave my car in Willits and catch a ride with him, I agreed. What I can relate is that the man was a jokester with a formidable flatulence talent. Thank your lucky stars you weren't cooped up in the cab next to his stinkers."

"Well I know one thing,' Jim said. "He made those tow truck guys think he was alone."

"He did?"

Jim dipped his head to the mound of dirt at their feet. "I heard you, Rosco. Heard you protect us while you laid there in pain and I won't forget it."

After the burial, the two moved in stunned silence for about half a mile before UC's inflamed knee crapped out. They bivouacked off the road under the trees, unzipped the goose down sleeping bag wide for a blanket. Jim slept intermittently, at times awoken by UC's groans and stabs of pain, as well as strange crunching and titterings in the nearby woods. Silence exaggerated every sound. And every sound had eyes.

When Jim returned to their tarp tent after peeing, UC was sitting up rubbing his bad knee which had locked up.

Judging by Rosco's crudely sketched map, they figured if they went off road through the forest due west, they'd come to the highway. Once there they could call police and get UC to a clinic. As it was, even if there was cell phone reception, they'd be hard pressed to give clear directions to their location in these woods.

Taking down the tarp, a vague memory surfaced in Jim's mind of feeling the ground quake during the night. Could have been those murderers in the tow truck driving back to look for Rosco's body.

UC hadn't heard a thing.

For all Jim knew, it may have been Christy and that guy in that van searching for them.

With UC's knee re-wrapped, they tramped on looking like battle-worn refugees. The good news was they were crossing through an open forest with enough space between trees and vegetation to move freely with few obstacles. When they rested, every hundred feet to so, Jim would ask UC questions about the redwoods. Anything to help take his mind off Rosco's death and gather information for the documentary.

He learned how the redwoods go back millions of years and were instrumental in creating atmosphere for the planet. "The very oxygen you respire."

Jim thought about recording an interview with UC, but not knowing when he would retrieve his gear, he decided to conserve the camera's remaining battery life.

When they stopped by one tree to give UC a rest, Jim asked, "Can you tell how old this one is?"

"I could venture a guesstimate, judging by its girth. But in actual years, I would need to see its annular rings. This one is perhaps two or three hundred years old."

Jim fingered the trunk's thick, shaggy bark, springy to the touch.

"There's still a few standing that are a couple thousand years old." UC went on. "And their root systems can stay alive a thousand years beyond that."

"Wow."

At one stop Jim noticed a cavity at the base of a massive redwood. It reminded him of Christy's video— the hole in the tree Charlie Tanner entered.

"They're called goosepens," UC explained. "They're a hollowed-out section you find at the foot of many trees. You see, redwoods carry so much water in them, they're flame-resistant. When a fire sweeps through the forest their trunks get charred, and their base is carved out like a canoe, but the trees live on. Redwoods also carry a lot of tannic acid. That makes them bug-proof, which is the reason the tree is such a valued building material."

"Got it," Jim said, and decided to go ahead and take the leap. He asked UC if it would be possible for a living human being to become grafted into a standing tree.

UC stopped to adjust the fork-ended branch he'd been using as a crutch. "I just heard about such a stunt."

"Yeah? What do you know about it?"

"Pfft, another silly ploy to draw more people to the protest they're staging. Make a bigger media splash. I remember, way back, they conducted a naked tree-hugging day. Made quite a sight. All these people along the roadside, their arms wrapped around tree trunks with their bare asses sticking out, white as marshmallows. But, to your question..." UC blurred off a lengthy, speculative description of how such a mutation could ever occur.

"A plant or tree has a narrow range of geometric forms. To undergo such a mutation, the rigidity of humanoid cell walls would have to stiffen up. The cells would enlarge and then divide. No longer would you have soft flesh and skin, and the parts that are flexible, such as the joints, would harden as well."

Jim's brain sputtered as the man went on and on, belting out words like 'chloroplasts', and 'cambium layer,' as if Jim knew what they meant. The only thing Jim noted UC saying was: "Oh it would be messy, the absorption, no question, but as you know, animal cells are only bound by membranes that can be twisted and contorted."

UC thought about it for a while as he carefully stretched his injured leg.

"Now, just for grins, let's expand on your question: Could redwood trees carry some previously undiscovered trans-mutational agent capable of inter-mingling species? I can't say yes. I can't say no. Just because I'm in science's pocket doesn't mean I dismiss realities that may exist outside my comprehension. I mean, nobody believed me there were albino redwoods growing in Mendocino County, three feet tall, pure white, devoid of chlorophyll, until I brought one to the lab. Or for that matter, think about antennas for a minute. Twist some coat hangers together and abracadabra, you've got picture. How's that not magic. Get my point?"

They continued hiking until they came upon a disturbing shift in topography— *up*.

"I don't know if I can do this," UC said.

"Maybe we should have stayed on the fire road."

"No-no, we're too far along." UC let out a strained breath. "I'll just need to stop more often.'

The two climbed the rise through redwoods and ferns, evading poison oak bushes, with many breathers along the way. On a shelf below the crest of the hill Jim posed the idea of the biologist doing the outside-inside visualization Christy had shown him.

"A what?"

"A different way of looking at the world."

"What do I need to ingest?"

"No, it's a visualization. All you have to do is first close your eyes."

"Nothing indecent I suspect."

Jim stepped away from UC, giving the man some room.

"Keep them closed, and when you open them up, picture everything you see outside as being the inside of your body— the ground, the trees, all of it."

"The inside of my body."

"Right. You're hiking up a hill that's inside your body."

"When can I open my eyes?"

"Whenever you wish."

UC blinked a couple times before looking to the east where the orange sun burned through cottony wisps of fog rising from the hollows of the slopes.

Jim felt the optical shift stronger than when he was with Christy back at that stream. This time the aliveness of the surrounding woods felt more energetic and visceral. The trees pulsated with a tactile vibrancy. The green of their needles and russet bark shown with new-born freshness. Even the moist air felt infused with nutrients, like food.

Jim breathed it in, unblinking. A film had peeled away from his everyday awareness revealing a world no longer detached from him, but more openly embedded. One where he could feel the forest as an organ of his anatomy— the lungs of a larger version of his body.

Looking skyward, he allowed this outer-inner perception to extend beyond the Earth. A saying came to mind, one he'd read by Teilhard de Chardin or an astrophysicist: *We are the universe experiencing itself.*

UC didn't say a word. And Jim didn't ask. He moved on, working to sustain his heightened point of view.

"This is true insight," he mumbled to himself.

Reaching the top of the hill, he saw an airy spaciousness beyond a line of redwoods ahead. He proceeded along the ridge and came to a sight that stopped him cold.

"Ohh god!" His body lurched as if stricken by a heart attack.

"You alright?" UC called up from the slope, struggling to ascend the last twenty yards to the top.

"They're gone! They're all gone!"

The landscape looked carpet-bombed. A hillside clear cut of all trees.

Being in such a wide open, impressionable state of mind made the shock of seeing such a rubble of stumps and slash all the more excruciating. Jim felt as ripped apart as the hillside before him. Christy's exercise exposed a grim reality: what's done outside happens inside. When you cut down a forest, a forest is cut down inside your body.

Jim's sensory field shriveled, his chest contracted as if trying to shield his heart from absorbing such a tortuous scene. The air felt suffocating. No blue jays or towhees could be heard, only the horn of a logging truck sounding off in the distance.

UC came clumping along. He found Jim standing next to an upturned root ball, its dark silhouette looked like a giant petrified octopus.

"Do you feel it?" Jim said, bowed over.

"Looks fairly recent," UC observed.

So shaken by the sight, the thought of shooting the devastation didn't cross Jim's mind. He asked, "Are they going to plant new trees here?"

"No doubt." UC lowered his body on the nearest stump. "But the pesky downside to reforestation is you no longer have the seeds from the older trees to germinate into a genetic combination that can withstand environmental threats and peculiarities that may emerge."

"What's that mean?"

"It means they'll be a weaker strain. Less resilient. Wouldn't you be with no daddy or mommy around?"

Jim gave a knowing nod.

UC lifted his free hand. "And these here along the crest of the cut are unprotected now, more vulnerable to wind-throw. Not to mention the soil…" he abruptly shut up.

There it was again, the blare of a horn. Jim had heard it moments before, but didn't connect it to the highway.

"That's a logging truck! We're close to 101!" UC jubilantly shouted.

22.
The John asked for you

For 16 years a corner of state forestry land served as a base camp for redwood activists, thanks due to the influence of a highly regarded ecologist and retired park ranger, known as The John.

The camp shared many of the amenities of a California state park, with tent sites, fire grates, running water and a cinderblock restroom with toilets and showers. As long as the camp was kept clean, and no one vandalized the property, built permanent shelters or platforms in the trees, or did anything improper, the campers were allowed to stay for a modest monthly fee.

This weekend the place served as a non-violence training ground for visitors coming to demonstrate at the Last Stand Protest.

Christy knew every curve in the dirt road that led into the camp so well she could drive it blind-folded. She slowed up to the guard shack. Recognizing her, the sweatshirt-hooded man standing in the four-by-four-foot structure perked a smile, leaned into the Jeep and gave her a warm hug.

"I'm staying at Mae Drummond's," Christy said. "But I came by to see if Ross Marley was here. You know Rosco?"

"Haven't seen him. But let me check the sheet, he might've come in last night." The man polled the names on a clipboard and shook his head.

"How about Jim Cassaway?"

"Cassaway..." the man slid his index finger down the list. "Nope, no one by that name."

Then where? Christy's anxiety made her skin shrink a size too small. She tried to logic it away. Maybe they came in so late they didn't get signed in?

She took a lazy spin around the campground. Waved to familiar faces who stood outside their tents, cups of coffee smoking in their hands. But no sign of Jim. Or Rosco's truck.

For all I know they could have gone back home.

Christy wondered if Jim would do that— leave her and his gear.

On her way out she told the guard, "I've got to run some errands for Mae, but if Rosco and Jim Cassaway show up, please, please, tell them I'll be back later."

"Will do. And hey, I forgot, a woman has been asking about you. Never seen her before. And yesterday the John came by looking for you."

"Right!" She remembered the note at Mae's she'd stuffed in her back pocket and, given her frantic state, neglected to open. She read the contents of the letter right there:

> Will pick you up at Mae's Saturday around noon
> and take you to the site.
>
> – John A.

Twelve o'clock didn't give Christy much time. She gave a goodbye wag of her hand and drove off, torn between finding Jim and meeting The John— which was the reason she'd come.

An hour later, a car rolled into the base camp and dropped off Jim Cassaway and UC Davis at the guard shack. They looked like damaged people—hobbling, filthy, and pissed.

23.
Be prepared for police brutality

A raging cramp rocketed Jim out of deep sleep. He jammed the heel of his hand into his calf, gritting his teeth as he worked the knot back and forth. Gradually the cramp loosened up and the pain subsided. He looked around, surprised to find himself inside a large teepee. Alone. A ruffle of voices outside.

Rising to his feet on swollen ankles he drew back the teepee's entry flap just as a red Frisbee floated into view and flopped at his feet. Jim picked it up and handed it to a gawky looking guy who'd come running up.

"Generosity," the man said, and slung the Frisbee out across a grassy clearing.

Jim stretched his neck in circles to relieve a kink as he took in the campground nestled among gigantic trees.

There were chirpings of birds.

The smell of coffee.

The unmistakable clang of pans.

Jim's memory returned in flashes— digging a shallow grave in the soft earth beside the fire road for Rosco's mangled body, coming upon a ravaged hillside denuded of trees, the logging truck's horn. He remembered using the tarp as a sled, pulling UC downhill until the man complained of the rugged ground gouging his back. When Jim decided to go off by himself and get help, UC opposed it, unwilling to be left alone. So, Jim carried the man on his back for fifty yards, then returned for the luggage, carried him another fifty yards, repeating and repeating the drill until they emerged from the forest at Highway 101, a short distance from a souvenir store. Its windows dark. Closed until 10 am.

The two sat on a bench, hunched over among an outdoor display of redwood carvings, everything from Dutch windmills and Indian heads, to eagles, bears and burl tabletops. He remembered UC murmuring on and on about the lab tubing, repeating, "They just better have the proper size." Lumber trucks droned past, quaking the ground, trailers stacked high with strapped logs.

Jim blanked on the kind people who stopped, picked them up, and dropped them off at the entrance to the base camp. They didn't give the guard a chance to grill them about their identities and their purpose there. UC, sprawled out on the ground, immediately erupted about Rosco's death.

"Listen to me! You need to call the police right now! We were attacked last night. They rammed our truck and killed our driver."

"Killed?"

"Do you speak English?"

"Who they?"

"Two masked men in a tow truck. Now will you call the police?"

"No way man, we're not calling no cops."

"They murdered the man for chissakes! Dragged him to his death!"

The stubble-bearded guard looked at the two in disbelief. Given their grungy and irritated state, packs and odd baggage in disarray, they appeared more suspicious than convincing.

"His name is Rosco," Jim said.

"Rosco?"

That got a reaction.

"Yeah, he was driving us here."

"Hang on." The guard stuck two fingers in his mouth, lifted his chin and whistled toward the campground.

While they waited for others to come, Jim asked if Christy Jones was there.

"Can't say. I just started my shift."

A big man approached, caveman wild with deep-set eyes, shoulder-length hair and a bristly brown beard.

"These guys claim they drove up with Rosco last night, and that he was killed by some dudes."

"We buried him out there."

"Where did this happen?"

"Along a fire road. God knows. It was dark."

"I marked the grave," Jim said.

"With Rosco's boot," UC added.

"Who else was coming from the south last night?" The wild man asked the guard.

"A yellow van," UC said. "The driver's name was Drum, or that's what they called him."

Hearing that, the wild man and the guard took a few steps away to speak privately with each other.

"Hey, I hate to interject." Jim pointed to UC's leg. "But his knee's busted up from the accident. Can someone take him to a hospital?"

Wild Man nodded and walked away.

The guard came back to them. "You here for the protest?"

"Me? No. I'm a plant biologist commissioned to conduct a forest study for The John." UC pulled a paper from his pocket and showed it to the man. "Here's the email."

The guard glanced at the paper, asking, "Do you know anything about the surprise announcement The John's going to make at the protest tomorrow?"

"No, I do not," UC said.

He looked at Jim. "And what are you here for?"

"Shooting a documentary about the protest for Christy Jones. All my gear is with her in that guy Drum's van."

That was the last thing Jim could remember. He wandered about the campground on rickety legs, hungry and parched.

"You look lost," a short woman observed.

"I'm looking for Christy Jones."

"Haven't seen her. I'm Rita."

Jim introduced himself. Rita gave a brief overview of the campground, pointing to where the restrooms were located, the kitchen canopy, the non-violence training area.

Jim headed to the restroom to clean up. Along the way, he passed people busy with campsite chores. One middle-aged man rolled a wheel barrow from site to site collecting laundry. "Wash day!" he called out.

Jim asked if he'd seen Christy. The man shook his head, jingling tiny bells attached to the ends of red, white and blue dyed dreadlocks.

Stapled to a large corkboard panel on the exterior wall of the restroom were aerial photos of clearcut forests, bald ridges and barren sweeps of ravaged land scarred with logging roads, much like the hillside he and UC had encountered. Names, handprinted on slips of paper were tacked to each photo: Vancouver Island, Mt. Baker, the Cascades, Pistol River. Next to the photos a sign was posted:

CODE OF CONDUCT

- We will be open, friendly and show respect for all people. This includes the lumber workers and loggers.
- We will not use violence of any kind— physical, verbal or dogs. This includes poking someone's buttons.

- We will not advocate destruction. We will not employ tree-spiking, machinery vandalism, or cutting power lines.
- We will not carry any firearms or weapons of any kind.
- We will not carry any illegal drugs or alcohol or hallucinogens. This is an activist camp. This is not a party.
- We will be aware of extreme fire danger and obey all fire regulations.

IF YOU DO NOT FOLLOW THIS CODE YOU SHALL BE REMOVED

After washing up, Jim stopped by the open-air kitchen. A line of folding tables was being cleared. Behind the tables people washed dishes in a sudsy horse trough. A large woman dressed in a peach-colored Hawaiian muumuu set a basket of red apples in front of Jim.

"Just got these in yesterday from Mt. Hood."

As Jim took a bite of an apple a sudden thought sent him rushing back to the teepee— *GOMES'S CAMERA!*

He threw back the door flap and was startled to see Wild Man standing inside. "Oh, sorry, I just…" Jim scanned the floor of throw rugs.

"Looking for this?" Wild Man lifted the strap of the hardshell case from behind a rolled-up futon.

Relieved, Jim checked on the camera, then thanked him.

"Name's Bruce, but around here they call me Bruiser."

Jim asked about UC Davis, the guy with the bad knee. Bruiser said he'd been taken to a clinic in Fortuna shortly after the two arrived. Jim had more questions, like: Where is the protest taking place? How big of a crowd? What do they expect in terms of conflict, police?

"Hold on," Bruiser stopped him. "Since you're filming the protest it would be good you joined in the training. You can ask your questions then. Starts in 30 minutes or so. We'll be gathering along the bank of the river."

Forty-eight people circled around Rita and Bruiser. As the story goes, Bruiser once served as a Sacramento police officer until he visited the redwoods on holiday and had an epiphany, or in his words, "a wake-up call from the All," and stayed on.

Rita stepped to the center of the circle, an empty cardboard box in her hand. She stood 5' 1" if that. All muscle. Dressed in denim shorts and a fatigue green t-shirt printed with the words: DON'T FOOL YOURSELF in neon yellow.

Bruiser marched around the circle like a drill sergeant, glaring into each person's eyes. "This is a gate action. You're going to get arrested. That's a given. And FYI, you are no longer hand slapped with a misdemeanor charge for trespassing, you'll probably be thrown in jail for up to twenty-one days under their twisted version of the Conspiracy Act. So get your head around that before you volunteer."

Rita dropped the cardboard box on the ground at her feet. "We'll need you to put your belongings in this box here. That means your cell phones and every kind of ID you carry— drivers' licenses, credit cards, the works. You don't have a name or an identity anymore, and you don't want one."

"You got a problem with that?" Bruiser stopped at a person who appeared tentative. "Do you want us to keep it safe, or have the police confiscate it and hold it for a couple weeks, checking your background, your text messages, emails and phone calls?"

The guy pulled his wallet and phone out of his pockets and set them in the box.

"Okay. Now, what is your job?" Rita asked.

No one answered.

"NorCal's job is to clear all demonstrators from the gate area by any means necessary. Your job is to what?"

"Stand our ground," one piped up.

"Dig in and delay them entry for as long as possible," said another.

Bruiser snapped his fingers at that statement. "And to exhibit non-violent behavior for others to imitate."

"Now…" Rita snatched a person's wrist, "…when they grab you, you'll have two options: go limp or go limp. They'll demand you get up. And what do say to that? You say: I'm protesting non-violently."

"Let's hear it!" Bruiser urged.

"I'm protesting non-violently!"

"That doesn't mean being passive or submissive," Bruiser went on. "You are a united front, delivering a clear message of resistance by putting your bodies on the line."

"Be prepared for police brutality," Rita said. "They'll do painful compliance holds."

To demonstrate, Bruiser enclosed his hand like a vice grip under a volunteer's jawbone. "Like this…"

"Gah!" the guy blanched, tried to jerk away, tear ducts squirting forth.

"Excruciating, ain't it." Bruiser let go. The man tripped over himself and collapsed, massaging his jaw.

"Don't fight them," Rita cautioned. "Don't swing at anyone. Don't even touch them. Keep your hands down at all times. They may shoot you with pepper spray or drop you with a stun gun before dragging you off to a police van or whatever."

Rita stepped up to a young woman, "What's your name?"

"Sasha."

"Wrong answer! Again, what's your name?" Rita covered the woman's mouth with her palm, and turned to others in the circle. Without your name or ID they won't know what to do with you."

Bruiser swept his forefinger around the circle. "They're going to tell you all kinds of things, lies, empty threats. Don't believe any of it. And don't argue with them. Their minds are cast in stone. If cutting down a two thousand-year old tree doesn't stop them, your words won't."

Rita plucked a thin stack of rubber-banded slips of paper out of her back pocket.

"You will not run." Bruiser advised. "It only shows you're scared of them. If they see you run they'll chase you and beat your brains in with batons. The police here spend hundreds of thousands of dollars on riot gear prepping for gate actions like tomorrow's."

"Local tax dollars at work," a voice interjected.

"After they dump you in a holding cell, you'll get a couple calls. Make this one your first." Rita distributed the slips of paper among the group. A phone number penciled on the paper. "Good counsel. Stick it in your shoe."

Bruiser took over. "Now we're going to do a role play exercise to help you learn how to deal with confrontation in a non-violent way."

The group split up into two lines facing each other, one on one.

"This is what we call a hassle line. It may not come to this, but if it does you will find yourself face to face with people whose very livelihoods are at stake. This is to prepare you in how to dialogue when you're being confronted with the emotional issues of the other side.

"You guys in this row will put yourselves in the shoes of a logger, or someone from the lumber industry. And this opposite line, you're you. We'll switch places later."

Jim happened to fall into the logger line, across from the man who'd just suffered through the compliance hold demo.

Once given the go ahead, the guy spoke first. "This land is not *your* land. This land is not *my* land. All the redwood trees that grow on it belong to the planet. We don't own them, so what gives you the right to cut them down?"

"You're not from here are you?" Jim countered. "What does a slacker like you know about what it takes to live here." Jim channeled the brute demeanor of the two thugs from the previous night. "These trees feed my family. Can you feed my family? No." Jim leaned forward, pressing his nose inches from the guy's face. "You couldn't feed poop to a fly."

"They'll make it personal," Rita coached the trainees. "Breathe people. And watch your body language. Don't tremble or paralyze. And don't argue. Just listen and let them vent."

The guy waited for Rita to finish, then stuttered a prepared response: "I know that I left my job to come here to protect these trees. Are your kids going to have jobs after the trees are all chopped down?"

"No," Jim seethed, "Their job will be chopping off your balls and sticking them in your whining little mouth."

Oops. Seeing the man cringe, Jim thought he'd gone too far.

Rita came over to him and his role play partner. She could see the guy buckling. "Keep your composure. You're losing it. Feel your feet on the ground. Your non-verbal communication and tone say a helluva lot more than your words."

The guy rubbed his hands together, stretched and relaxed his shoulders.

"Okay everybody, let's switch roles and change partners."

Jim found himself newly paired off with a strikingly attractive woman.

"I overheard you back there say you were looking for Christy Jones." she said.

"Yeah, you know where I can find her?"

"No, I've been looking for her, too."

"Christy hired me to shoot a documentary of the protest."

"Cool. Name's Dee."

24.
Where's the body?

Beldare sat at a lacquered redwood burl table on the deck of the lodge eating a flaky croissant and sipping Earl Grey. He leafed through his used, hardbound book on Pacific coastal forests, specifically the Post-it tabbed pages he'd notated earlier— sections describing the botanical makeup of the trees and regional vegetation.

He stopped reading when his hearing alerted him. Something did not feel right. He scanned the gauzy fog clinging lazily to the surrounding trees. The strange presence confounded him until he realized it was the spectacle of absolute silence. He didn't know it could be so loud. He set the book on the table, leaned back and listened to the monumental stillness.

It didn't last. Within seconds it was broken by the crunch of tires coming up the gravel driveway, followed by the idling drone of the Humvee. A door slammed. Beldare heard Chief Dixon talking on his cell phone, with Hardin no doubt. His gruff voice sounded so clear in these remote acoustics he could almost make out every word, and more distinctly, the man's agitated tone.

A safe-cracker in first impressions, Beldare saw Dixon and Hardin's relationship as a testy alliance, barely tolerable at best. As for their apparent disdain for him, Beldare figured it was two-fold: 1) having to relinquish power to an unknown entity, and 2) that he was making more money for his short stint than their salaries combined.

Chief Dixon's mind churned as he climbed the porch stairs. Dixon's father raised him with John Wayne movies: *Rio Bravo, She Wore a Yellow Ribbon*. Situations would arise where the boy would seek his father's advice. Most times his father would answer with the question, "What would the Duke do?" Although older now, in his fifties, problems and circumstances would still emerge where that question would jump forth, front and center.

One had just occurred.

Dixon strode around the deck and began talking as soon as he saw Beldare at the table. "Just got off the horn with Curt Hardin. Seems one of the patrols had an accident last night and some stranger's vehicle was totaled."

"Anyone hurt?" Beldare asked.

"One man. The driver."

"How serious?"

"Sounds *dead* serious." Dixon moved in close, bunting the man's chair with his knee.

Beldare half-turned with a shrug, then pinched a cloth napkin off the table and daubed the corners of his mouth. "Where'd this take place?"

"To the south. On a fire road."

"Were their faces masked?"

"Who knows!" Dixon fumed.

Beldare remained unruffled. "Let's get Hardin on speakerphone."

"Here…" Dixon plopped a newspaper on the table. It was folded to an article on page three with the headline: Rampant violence in redwood country.

As Dixon stepped through the sliding glass door into the lodge, Beldare took a sip of tea and speed-read the article in the San Francisco Chronicle describing random beatings, one with a golf club, another with a bullwhip.

"Got Hardin on the line," Dixon called out.

Beldare picked up the newspaper and went inside.

"They want more money," Hardin said through crackling static on the speaker.

"And where is the victim?"

"Hang on, I'm on another line. Been trying to sort out fact from fiction."

They could hear Hardin's muffled voice talking to someone.

Beldare handed the newspaper back to Dixon, pointing to a photo of a man's face with a white patch over his right eye. "We need more like that."

"Okay…" Hardin came back. "Just got confirmation from our source in the field. It's all true. The man whose vehicle rammed into a tree is dead."

Dixon recoiled with a grunt.

Beldare didn't flinch. "I thought I made it clear to merely give the appearance of death."

"You did, and that patrol told me it was a minor collision, and left it at that."

"Minor?" Dixon blurted.

"We'll work with it." Beldare could feel a wind at his back from Dixon pacing the floor. The man's anger filled the room like a heat wave. "Where's the body?"

"Buried along a back road. Apparently, they dragged the driver behind their truck."

"What? How could he be dragged? You just told me it was a minor collision."

"I called back and asked them that."

"And?"

"They're sticking to their story, where they accidently rear-ended another vehicle. They claim to know nothing about a death, or any dragged body. That said, now they want more money."

"So how did you find out about a dead body?"

"That came from the individual I was just talking to."

"And whose version do you believe?"

"Who do you think?"

Dixon lit a cigarette and sucked hard. He didn't sign up for no murder.

Beldare ignored the chief's alarm. "And this individual told you where the body was buried?"

"The general vicinity. He's familiar with all the back roads. So I sent him out to retrieve it and make it disappear."

"No!" Dixon blurted. "This was an innocent person for god's sake. Could be a local hunter or fisherman. We need to find his remains and contact his relatives."

The Duke would do no less.

Beldare waved a backhand at Dixon. "And that would be our undoing."

"The man deserves a proper burial."

"Bury him, yes, but well hidden. No body, no problem." Beldare said it so matter-of-fact, Dixon assumed he'd spoken the same words before.

"You got that right," Hardin agreed.

"That's not the point!" Dixon disputed. "This is…"

"In the meantime," Beldare raised his voice, cutting Dixon off. "We need more faked stories fast: 911 recordings, radio, TV, internet. I want to hear the cries of assaulted victims."

"Already happening," Hardin said. "We got chatrooms and twitter feeds buzzing about it. Got three more incidents on radio and TV news as we speak."

"Keep it up."

"And the officers manning the roadblocks report a reduction in outsider traffic."

"What about the crashed vehicle?" Dixon blew a flurry of smoke out his mouth.

"In process. It will be cleared up right away."

"And Hardin..." Beldare said. "You need that body to disappear."

"Consider it done."

Beldare leaned within an inch of the speakerphone. "The person you're sending to dig it up... is it your inside man?"

25.
Nature called

Rosco's boot vaulted end-over-end through the air before vanishing in a dark, cavernous grove of trees. Drum kicked dirt around the burial site, then tamped it down with a shovel, evening the ground. The heat of the sun felt unusually harsh. Or maybe it was the hellish nature of the task. Sweat slid down his spine, making his t-shirt stick to his skin.

The grunt work done, Drum scanned the area for any last signs of footprints and human activity. Then slapped his hands and patted his pants of loose dirt. He felt ugly, pathetic. He wanted to get to a shower and wash it off. In the distance, a low, purring motor sounded. He hurried up the embankment to the fire road to get a bearing on it. Sure enough, a vehicle was coming. He slid the shovel into the back of the van and slammed the double doors. Then, seeing his t-shirt smudged with dirt, he stripped it off, balled it up and tossed it through the driver-side window.

The vehicle came around a curve. He couldn't make out who it was, but they were honking the horn, irritating him all the more. He sauntered back and stood in front of the rear doors of the van, loosely folding his arms across his hairy chest.

It was Christy in his mother's Jeep. She pulled up behind the van, a grim look on her face.

"What are you doing?" she growled as she planted her feet on the road.

"Searching for Rosco. He never showed up at base camp. But you already know that."

She looked around the place. "Why stop here?"

"Nature called."

Christy's face remained rigid. She noticed a waxy sheen of sweat on Drum's skin. Something funny about this.

"Didn't know I needed your permission to take a piss," he said.

"Smart ass." She swept her eyes across the surrounding woods, then down the road, squinting in the sharp sun. "Got to be somewhere. They didn't just up and vanish."

"Who the hell knows."

"Well we would've known if we'd gone back last night. But you wouldn't listen."

"Forgive me for being responsible for the welfare of my passengers."

"They sounded in trouble. But no, no, not you." Christy shook her head at him. "Not Mr. Control Freak."

"Right there. That's it *right* there." Drum poked a finger at Christy's face. "That's what alienates everybody. That self-righteous, you-let-me-down look of yours."

Christy crinkled her nose. "Me? *I* alienate...?"

"All about what others should do *for you*. Who they should be *for you*." Drum heaved out his chest, posing as a statue of nobility. "Like you're their standard-bearer, their life coach. Well guess what?" Drum inhaled deep, as if to reload. "It just makes them feel inadequate. That's why they don't hang with you for long, 'cause you put out this you-let-me-down vibe. And the truth is, you really don't care about anybody."

"Bullshit! I care." Christy shot back. "I care a lot!" She slammed her flat hand against the rear doors of the van.

"Really?" Drum shuffled a couple steps away to distance her from the vehicle.

Christy moved with him, thrusting a finger at him. "Cared about you once, 'til you smothered it. Now I see someone I don't recognize. Not the Paul Drummond master survivalist and protector of the forest. The man who gave and gave. No. That person's gone, he gave up, replaced by this stranger who, because of a few setbacks, has left his soul to rot."

"Like you know what I've been through."

"Boo-hoo! Makes me sick just looking at you!"

"Then don't! Go! Get out of my face!"

"Gladly. Move your fucking van so I can get by."

Christy watched Drum strut away. Sure, things had been tough on him since the funding for his wilderness survival camp dried up. Okay, there's the broken engagement and financial debt, but how could he take the same downward spiral of drinking and apathy as every other defeated or unfortunate? As if tough times came with rigid plumbing everyone was forced to slide. And why did she think he was tougher than that?

She huffed, kicked the front tire of Mae's Jeep, got back in and veered it over onto the shoulder of the road for Drum to pass.

He turned the van around, slowed up to her side and cranked down the window. "You like him don't ya?'"

"What of it?"

"Maybe I should warn him about men you let get too close to you. How your heart all-a-sudden freezes up and you toss them out like empties to be recycled."

She flipped him off and bore down on the accelerator.

Drum glanced out the side-view mirror as he drove, seething at how Christy made him feel like a chump.

After she disappeared around a tree-lined bend in the road, he jammed on the brakes, hammered the seat with his fist, and yelled so loud a barn owl burst from a nearby branch. Behind him, Rosco's wrapped body rolled over and thumped against the wheel well.

Drum cut the engine, scrambled into the back and lashed the corpse against the side panel with bungee cords.

Maybe he was a chump. A bag man no less. It was eating away at him.

A quarter mile down the road Christy depressed the brake pedal. A tow truck blocked the road.

26.
You'll thank me later

C hief Dixon drove into the base camp and stopped at the guard shack. He hadn't set foot in the place in more than a year and given the recent murder, felt uncommonly nervous. But he had a message to deliver.

Beldare sat in the passenger seat, leafing through his notes, pondering the fact that NorCal Lumber Company did not have ownership rights to North Fork Forest. They'd obtained access to the Forestry Service land to do some salvage logging. Which didn't make sense to him. All this effort to haul out a few diseased and downed trees? How profitable could that be?

"Good day." The guard finger-twirled one end of his handlebar moustache. "Have you come for the non-violence training?"

"I'm not here to crash your party," Dixon replied. "Just want to inform people of some rather unpleasant developments over the past few days, and how they need to be super cautious. If you'll allow me, I'd like to speak to as many folks in the camp as can be rounded up."

While Dixon spoke with the guard, a large woman stepped alongside the Humvee glaring at Beldare through the side window. The woman was wide as a cow with milky brown skin. She had a black, shoulder-length mane striggled with curly white hairs, a meaty face and a spread nose. Indigenous, Beldare categorized. She carried a leather briefcase and wore a collegiate jacket over an oatmeal sweatshirt with layers of beadwork sewn into the fabric. Her owl-big brown eyes bore into Beldare, as if x-raying his soul.

He stared back, a bit unsettled by her unwavering attention.

Dixon was allowed entry.

"Here comes the Law!" the guard called out. "Keep it civil!"

Dixon parked where he was told, stepped from the vehicle, but didn't go far. Campers appeared from the shadows of the trees. A few shouted and waved their hands for others to gather. The non-violence training session was temporarily suspended. Jim followed the other trainees over to where a crowd circled around a tall man in a Stetson hat.

Beldare got out of the vehicle but walked only as far as its hood. He didn't notice the owl-eyed woman come up behind him.

"My name is Glenn Dixon. I oversee special law enforcement for Humboldt and Del Norte Counties. Some of you know of me. We've had our run-in's, but I'm not here to intimidate, interrogate or arrest anyone. I came to seek your help and give you fair warning about the severity of a current hostile situation. You may have heard about a band of ruffians wreaking havoc, beating up on people. We know none of you are them. But as far as we can tell, they're going after folks like you. So, what I'm asking…"

"They killed a man last night!" a young woman spouted.

"Yeah, Rosco."

"They tied his body to their bumper and dragged him to his death."

"Yes." Dixon stiffened. "We are looking into that." He noted the name 'Rosco' in his brain. "Did anyone here actually witness the crime?"

Jim started to raise his hand, but Rita elbowed him in the ribs and shook her head.

"This is the very thing I'm talking about," Dixon went on. "And this is why we set up highway barriers for people's safety. We're letting the locals through, and some tourists, but at their own risk. We don't want any out-of-town wannabees joining with these vigilantes to satisfy their bloodlust or whatever."

"Blah-blah-blah." someone jeered.

"Let the man talk," Bruiser hollered from the back.

"Thank you. Now we're doing what we can with the available resources, but we can only stretch so far. So, I'm asking for your help, to be our extra eyes and ears. We know their numbers are small…"

Beldare checked out the ragtag crowd of people surrounding Dixon, examining their body language to see if they believed him. He stopped scanning the stern and combative faces when he came upon the familiar features of a woman among them.

Dee Rotter.

The so-called Ingot Field Operative he'd met on the corporate jet, dressed down in tan shorts and white travel shirt, her long hair now black and shorn in a boyish, pixie cut.

She wore a wig on the flight.

"An outsider." came the voice of the owl woman in Beldare's ear, over-riding Dixon's speech. "An outsider, looking in."

Distracted, Beldare glanced over his shoulder, "Are you speaking to me, mam?"

"And yet you have a role in this."

Beldare rotated to fully face the woman.

Her eyes drifted to his chest, then back to his face. "A beehive inside you, buzzing with secrets. But you don't know what's really going on here, do you?"

"I'm not following," Beldare assumed the woman was mentally ill, drugged or drunk. He shrugged and turned back to the crowd, locking on Dee Rotter.

"No, you're not following," she went on. "You're conducting. But you can't hear all the notes."

Beldare couldn't shut the woman off, nor could he explain how her softly murmured words could drown out Dixon's forceful speech.

"Let me help you," she said.

He pivoted, and faced her again. "I don't need your help."

"You'll thank me later." She leveled a palm to her pursed lips and blew out a long stream of air toward Beldare's right ear.

He flinched at the tickle of her breath.

"There." She pointed to his ear. "Maybe now you'll hear what's *not* spoken."

He watched her ringed index finger descend and tap him mid-chest, like it was depressing a button. He winced, startled by the jab.

Abruptly, the strange woman walked away, joined by two other people.

Dixon didn't address the next day's protest and what law enforcement would do if any machinery was vandalized. He didn't have to. It was understood. Nor did he mention hunting down Rolf Zetzer, the accused murderer who'd snipped off his ankle monitor and fled.

"Anyway, that's all I have to say. If you have any information, please contact us. Thanks for your time."

"Yeah, yeah, stop NorCal felling trees and exterminating habitat, then we'll be happy to work with you," said the laundry man.

Dixon opened the door of the Humvee, burned in the back by the heat of a hundred defiant eyes.

"Do you know who that person is?" Beldare asked as Dixon wheeled the vehicle around.

"Who?"

"The large woman walking over there."

"That's Beverly. She talks to spirits."

Jim watched the Humvee pull away thinking at some point he'd like to interview the Stetson man for the documentary. Get the local law enforcement perspective for counterpoint.

As the crowd dispersed, Rita turned to Jim. "The police here are puppets of Lumber. Any information you volunteer to tell them will be twisted and manipulated whichever way it takes to reinforce their aims and amplify their power."

Jim felt choked off, neither believing nor disbelieving her. "But I know where he's buried. I buried him. I just don't know the exact road."

"Don't worry, somebody's on it."

Somebody. Jim strolled back to the training area wondering in hind sight if he should've captured Rosco's murder on video, even in the dark. Then go to the gravesite to shoot the digging up of his body. That's a real story, not some stunt.

27.
Shoulda picked a designated driver

"You're not saying you really believe in them," Kunkle said, as he and Driver fitted a metal yoke around the rear wheels of Rosco's pickup truck.

"Sure do."

"What, you mean like you've seen 'em?"

"No."

"Then how do you know?"

The two had returned to the site of the accident to haul the wreck away and clear the area. A country music song played from the tow truck's radio— Ray Boone singing, *Can't Keep Up with Your Face.*

"Way I see it, you got to believe in anything that can hurt you or freak you out." Driver said, walking back to the tow truck and grabbing hold of the hydraulic lever.

"You mean something like the boogie man?" Kunkle asked.

"Firm believer."

"Get outta here."

"No. Hey, believing in ghosts and vampires and all that, it don't cost you nothin.' And when you believe in them, you're not gonna shit your pants when they show up. You're already ready."

"Well I'm no way ready." Kunkle stared up the road.

"Relaaax, will ya. You got a little spooked, okay? We'll go back and search the road high and low after we're done here."

The hoisting arm whined. The chain flexed taut. The wreck made a crunching sound as it was jerkily urged away from the tree and hoisted out of the ditch, its dented hood creaking, bouncing, the front tires churning up loose dirt.

"They're not paying me nowhere near enough." Kunkle cleared his throat and spat.

"Hey, we clean it all up and no one's gonna know diddly-doo."

"Hold on," Kunkle snapped his fingers. "We got company."

Seeing the dust cloud headed their way, Driver climbed into the rig and shut off the radio. "Nothing to worry ourselves," he cautioned calmly. "Just doing our job."

His truck! Christy planted her foot on the brake pedal to slow the Jeep as she took in the image— Rosco's smashed pickup being lifted by the crane of a tow truck.

She stepped out of the Jeep, but kept the engine running. Two men stood like border guards, jaws fixed, steely eyes locked on her approach. The scene felt creepy, as if she was stepping into a malevolent force field.

"You lost?" one asked. A short, dumpish-looking man.

She didn't answer. Her eyes furtively scouring the site.

"Well you're just gonna have to wait for us to finish up if you need to get through," said the man handling the winch.

"What happened here?"

"She run into that tree there." The dumpy man twitched his head toward a redwood tree down the bank off the road. "Shoulda picked a designated driver."

"How did it happen?" Christy stepped close for a better look. A magnetic sign affixed to the side door of the tow truck read: WRECKING SOLUTIONS – 24/7, with a phone number under it.

"Not a clue, lady. We just got a call to haul her off to our body shop. Why, d'you know the driver?"

She nodded. Her breath accelerating.

"What'd she say?" The lanky winch man couldn't hear her as he locked the pickup into position.

"Says she knows the driver."

"That a fact."

A cold stare passed between the two men.

Christy peeked into the pickup's cab. Saw the shattered windshield, crumbs of glass on the seat. "Oh, god." Her hand muffled her mouth. She turned to the winch handler. "Did you see'em?"

Neither answered right away. Then the short one wheezed and said. "Nah. But he must be okay. He ain't here, is he?"

Christy registered a shift in the man's voice, a blunt tone of annoyance.

So where'd they go? Did someone pick them up? She walked to the edge of the road and scrutinized the area around the crash site. Camping gear splayed about the ground.

The pudgy man sauntered up behind her. "Yeah, left a mess."

"Who called you? The police?"

"No, we didn't take the call."

Christy drifted down the slope.

The man grabbed his crotch and exhibited an exaggerated over-bite to his cohort before trailing behind her.

She searched the forest floor, hunting for clues: what they left, what they took, any indication of what happened since.

She lifted a rolled-up ensolite pad and held it in a tight embrace as she recalled Rosco's voice on the walkie-talkie: "Mayday guys. We got some assholes on our tail and they're coming up fast."

"No-no… drop it," the pudgy guy demanded.

"I just need to know…" Christy didn't finish. Jim's video camera! He had that with him. She stepped among the scattered things, not seeing it anywhere.

He must have taken it. She swung around, staring up at the tow truck. Or they did.

"Stuff don't belong to you," the man said. "It all goes back with the tow. We got orders."

"Give me a second!"

She stopped at Rosco's cooler. Upright and open. It looked like someone rifled through it.

"I said, drop it!" The man reached toward the pad she held, seizing her hand.

"Don't touch me!" Christy backed away.

"Whoa… temper, temper."

She dumped the pad on the ground at the man's feet. Everything about the situation felt twisted and wrong. She wished she'd succumbed to buying a cell phone so she could photograph it all.

"I'm just really worried, okay? They were friends of mine."

"Did you say *they*?"

Christy nodded. "Uh-huh."

"And just how many they's of them were there?"

"Three…" Christy hiked back up the slope. "… three men."

Pudge followed, shouting at the winch man who stood watching them. "Says there were three men in the pickup!"

"Hunh," the man grunted, rubbed a rag across his palms as he stepped away from the truck, closing in on her. "And how'd you know to come along here looking for them?"

"I was…" Christy hesitated. Tension clamped her throat. Something about the question and how the man advanced, shrinking the space between them to a suffocating arm's length. His breath a stew of onions and greasy meat.

She side-stepped around him, distancing herself, and back-peddled up the road. "I-I'll check with the police. And the local clinics."

"Yeah, you best do that," he said.

"Okay, then. Didn't mean to interrupt your work." Christy turned her back to them, simulating a nonchalant every-thing's-fine stride to Mae's Jeep.

"Too late on that." Kunkle grumbled under his breath. Something had snapped inside, a neuron rupturing, tiny wires spitting sparks. He broke into a bumbling run, charging after the woman.

"Hey, whoa up." Driver reached out too late to stop him.

Christy hopped into the Jeep, relieved to be getting away, only to see the pudgy man's snorting red-veined face bloom in her eyes. He snatched the handle, yanked open the Jeep's door.

Shocked, she jammed the gear shift into reverse, punched it, ruddering backward, bolted with fear.

The door swung out, groaning on its hinges, levitating the guy's body into the air. Then, bucked by the rugged road, his stubby fingers lost their grip, slipped off, and he flopped to the ground, out of sight in a fit of dust.

"We're cool!" Driver shouted at him.

Christy didn't look back to see Kunkle stand up and stomp his feet.

"We are *not* cool," he hammered. "She's on to us. And those fuckers they got my name, no thanks to you!"

"Relaaax. We got immunity. That was the deal."

28.
A film?

"**N**o sign of her yet," Dee spoke into her cell phone as she stood near a knee-high stone wall that overlooked the Pacific Ocean just north of Trinidad. "I asked around and only got vague answers. But I met this guy she hired to shoot a film for her..."

"Wait, a film?"

"A feature-length documentary, so he claims."

"Is he with a crew?"

"Appears to be alone, far as I can tell."

"Doesn't matter, this has to be stopped." Hersh's voice took on a sudden strain.

"But..."

"But what?"

"I don't see a problem. I mean, everybody's got camera phones," she said.

"I know, I know, everything's recorded these days. A few photos and random video clips is one thing, but a fully produced piece, given what we..." Shit. Hersh held up mid-sentence. Thought better about what he was going to confide. "Well, you see where I'm going, I don't need to spell it out... just... something must happen to that man's camera and the footage."

Something? Dee didn't answer straightaway to the nebulous request. She watched a swell of seawater roll in a hundred feet below her, arc into a wave, and bash the cliff.

"Consider it special compensation," Hersh said.

Dee didn't respond, thinking through the how of it.

"In addition to your fee," he clarified.

A line of pelicans skimmed above the surf as another swell rose and curled, foaming white. Two sightseers strolled over next to Dee and took selfies. She stepped away from the panoramic view. Nature's beauty had zero appeal to her.

"Can you do that?" Hersh's voice now commanding.

"Yes." Dee saw a way. "I can."

"Excellent."

"I better get back to the camp. But I've got a question for you."

"All ears."

"By any chance have you heard this weird story about people who are, like, attaching their bodies to tree trunks?"

"I have, as a matter of fact," Hersh forced a laugh, unsure where she was going with it, and how to rid it from her mind. The less people know, the better.

"And?"

"What do *you* think?" he turned the question around.

"Rubbish from the looney bin."

"You may hear all kinds of strange, distracting rumors. Pay them no mind. Stay on point. Don't get side-tracked."

"Not possible."

29.
The Big No

"**I**t's not us-against-them as the media portrays. It's not oppositional. Loggers don't become loggers because they hate trees. They're not to be blamed so much as the ones in the high windows, punching the numbers."

A campfire flickered in Bruiser's deep-set eyes as he spoke. Jim had focused the video camera tight on the man's hair-furred face and tuberous nose, making him look like a giant from an Icelandic folktale.

"None of those businessmen live around here. Their profits don't go into the local economy. They go into yachts and penthouses. They go off shore. It does nothing to build prosperity for this place. And that speaks to their who-gives-a-shit mentality when it comes to the impact their tree-cutting has on the eco-system, and the habitats of so many lives."

This is good stuff. Jim thought, shuttling through the footage he'd shot earlier that evening. He was so impressed with the people at the camp he decided to use up some of the camera battery to interview them. Many came from other parts of the country, from Maine, Massachusetts, North Carolina, and after visiting, stayed on, some for years. Though all different, they shared a common alliance: they honored the redwoods. "We're living among a citadel of gods," one told him.

Jim stopped shooting with what he figured to be about ten minutes left of battery life, which he saved for the protest. He felt confident he'd get the rest of his gear back from Christy when he saw her there.

He pressed the playback button on the camera to watch some of Rita's interview. Her smooth face glowed like satin in the firelight, a sharp contrast from Bruiser's.

"Humans don't have exclusive rights to consciousness." Her words bit through clinched teeth. "Just because it doesn't walk on two legs, or speak English, doesn't mean it doesn't have a mind, or can't communicate, or feel. This forest is more evolved than us. It gives and gives. It doesn't take. It doesn't know *take*."

Jim heard footsteps approach. He hit pause as a woman sat next to him on the log bench. He recognized her face from the hassle line, but forgot her name.

"Get any good stuff?" she asked.

"I think so."

"I'm Dee," she said. "Remember?"

"Yeah," he nodded.

"Can I have a look?" She leaned into Jim to see the image on the viewfinder, her head nuzzling against his shoulder, picking up the audio on his headset.

"That's what's-her-name."

"Rita," Jim said as he pressed play. Rita's face came alive.

"People think this is just about saving trees, and it most definitely is. But that's not all. Tomorrow will be a last stand to say enough already. This is the 'The Big No.' *No* more profiteering of nature. *No* more slaughter of species. *No* more stripping, or drilling, or pumping, or fracking, or dumping. Our tolerance is *no* more."

"The big No," Jim had repeated to Rita.

"That's right. Inaction is our demise. Are we planetary stewards or a hopelessly failed experiment?"

"Heavy." Dee turned her face, nudging Jim's cheek. "And kind of preachy, don't you think?"

Jim shut off the camera. Something about the woman felt false, teasy.

"So, no sign of Christy Jones?"

"She'll be at the protest tomorrow. 'Like a moth to a flame,' I'm told." Jim didn't want to say he felt Christy abandoned him.

"Good. I've got a message to deliver to her." She put her hand on his forearm. "Can you show me more?"

30.
This is going down ugly

Jim got a ride to the protest site in the laundry man's rattling VW bus. Along the way the clownish activist expounded on the convoluted particulars of land ownership in redwood country, half the time steering with his knees so his hands could be free to accentuate his spiel.

"Even congress requires the Forest Service to sell a certain amount of timber."

"Wait, NorCal Lumber can get timber out of a federal forest?"

"Readily. The state and national parks are off limits, of course. But state and national forests, they're a different animal. NorCal lawyers have squeezed through all kinds of loopholes and knotholes in forestry legislation, re-drawing boundary lines, word-spinning terms, and reformulating what land is lumber-able."

The laundry man raced through a rapid-fire, head-scratching history of forestry ownership, land swapping, and loose logging regulations, and wrapped it up with, "If you're confused, then you know what's going on."

The gate action was about a quarter mile off a paved road, at the end of a gravel cul-de-sac with NO TRESSPASSING signs posted on trees. Jim could feel the rollicking vibe of the gathering under his feet a hundred yards away. He strode past cars and trucks parked bumper to bumper along the shoulders. No sign of the yellow van.

149

Gomes will kill me.

He searched for Christy among the faces only to realize that if he was ever going to find her and record a wide shot of the gate action, he needed to get up, high above the jostling crowd. He noticed people sitting cross-legged on the hood of a lumber company bulldozer.

That's it. He threaded his way through the protestors and clambered onto its roof.

From atop the bulldozer he saw cardboard signs bobbing in people's hands: SAVE THE REDWOODS, INDUSTRIAL FORESTRY IS A LUNG DISEASE, CHARLIE TANNER FAN CLUB.

A long green banner stretched across the iron gate shouted: STOP THE SLAUGHTER OF THE LAST STAND!

Many protestors sat beneath the banner, their arms chained to the gate. Others lay beside lumber equipment, some with their wrists lashed to the frames with padlocks and other constraints. Still others huddled, bunched tight with locked arms on beach blankets and sleeping bags. It appeared many had slept there and were planning a long, resistant stay.

On a small platform to the side of the gate, a threesome sang with guitar and fiddle. But their song was drowned out by someone beating a base drum, another blowing a vuvuzela, and the overall din of the throng. No hassle line here. The mood seemed festive, carefree.

She's got to be around somewhere. Jim unclipped the case, set Gomez's camera on his shoulder, and made slow sweeps of the bodies below, left to right, searching for Christy, checking every head for her hair, the color of redwood bark, and her signature crimson scarf.

Maybe she's going to speak. He zoomed the lens to a small clutch of people milling behind the gate. Seeing no sign of her, his energy sagged. She's probably with that guy, Drum.

If that's the case then I'm out of here. Shoot what I can and catch a ride back to the city with somebody. Need to return the gear anyway.

The trio stopped singing as a gaunt, gray-haired man with a Fu Manchu beard climbed up to the top cross bar of the gate and sat. He waved to a few people below as he was handed a megaphone from someone on the ground.

"It's a good day for a last stand!"

"The John!" Some shouted.

"Happy summer solstice everybody. My name's John Albers and I'm here to speak on behalf of the Save North Fork Forest Initiative. One whose aim is to stop all logging of the last large stand of old growth redwoods on the planet. As you know, they plan to start cutting a road in here tomorrow morning to do some salvage logging. This is an unauthorized entry, currently idling in legislation. So we asked them, "What's the urgency?"

People responded with a raucous slew of obscenities.

"Well, let me tell you," The John went on. "There's a reason they want to get in without delay. The same reason behind all the recent attacks that have kept our friends away. What do you think? Are these isolated incidents from a bunch of bad apples, or are they directed by NorCal?"

"NorCal!!!" the crowd clamored, followed by boos.

Jim went in for a close-up of the old man with the megaphone. Something familiar about his face. Right, he's the guy in the video I saw while waiting for Christy at the Safeway store— only a lot older.

"These are not loggers or millworkers. These are mercenary goons paid to silence us, limit our numbers, so NorCal can punch a road in here and fast track the clearcutting of North Fork. And what do we say to that?"

"No!!" the protestors howled.

Jim panned a number of fists punching the sky.

"Any old timers like me out there?" The John asked.

Several raised their hands.

"Glad you could make it."

"Older and bolder!" an elderly woman blurted.

"Then you can remember the mean and desperate measures they've inflicted in the past. But never such rampant bloodshed. Now ask yourself: why resort to such violent tactics?"

People shouted various answers.

The John lifted an open palm. "Let me tell you why! It's because something very magical is happening here. Something that will stop them from felling redwoods forever. Something that scares the living bejesus out of them."

He paused for the whistles and whoops to die down.

"I see some Charlie Tanner signs out there." The John pointed at a few. "Unbelievable as it sounds, the rumors are true. I am witness! This is not a prank or publicity stunt like people claim. Charlie Tanner is the real thing!"

"Tan-ner! Tan-ner!"

"Bless his heart, and the others who joined the woods before him." The John waited for the cheers to die down. "You know about Rolf Zetzer, the logger accused of killing his wife Kathy? Guess what, he did no such thing, 'cause Kathy joined the woods!"

A few cheers of "Free Rolf! peppered the crowd.

The John spread his arms high to the lofty forest surrounding them. "People have given their lives to save this last stand. Their bodies are fused within trunks of these giants! Praise to them!"

Although a lot of the crowd hooted ecstatically, through the camera lens Jim saw others shaking their heads, or shrugging in disbelief.

"Prove it!" one hollered.

"Yeah, show us!"

"Let me finish… let me… please…" The John waited for them to settle down. "Now, I ask you, are they going to cut down trees with people grafted inside them?"

'NOOO!"

"I think not," The John said. "Nobody's going to want the walls of their sauna seeping blood."

A news helicopter came into view.

"Wave to the chopper!" Somebody yelled. "We'll be on the six o'clock news!"

Although the big block letters on the side of the helicopter read KIEM. That was a ruse. Behind the pilot of the chopper sat Hardin and Beldare. The magnetic sign of station call letters was Beldare's idea.

The helicopter dipped down, circling above the protestors, passing its shadow across their heads.

"How many do you figure?" Hardin spoke into his headset above the cacophonous rap of rotor blades.

Beldare, who'd done density crowd counting in the past, calculated between nine and eleven hundred. Much less than the predicted six thousand, but still a lot to deal with.

"Where are they?" Beldare shouted into his mic at Hardin. "They're late!"

"On the way," Hardin belted back, lowering the binoculars from his eyes. "They needed to meet together first. Get into two trucks instead of four."

Beldare wished he could hear what the man with the megaphone was telling the crowd.

Jim watched the chopper and thought about contacting the TV station. Their news footage would add a bird's eye view of the event for the documentary.

The John pawed his hand up and down to silence the clamor. "They're dying to get an entry road plowed in here.

Start with some salvaging, remove a few snags to 'service the forest' as they say. You with me? Once that road is cut all their prayers are answered. The zipper's in place. They wait a few days, let us demonstrate and go back home, our moral duty done. Then like flash on lightning we'll turn around and North Fork will be gone. But if the public knew there were people inside just one of those trees, that would be the end. Nobody would allow *that* and they'd lose it all forever!"

"Where are they?"

"I want to do it!"

"Take me!"

"Please understand how careful we have to be in bringing this out, otherwise the saboteurs hidden among us will find ways to erase it like it never happened. So it's crucial we carefully document and safeguard it until the time is right."

Jeers and boos grumbled among the hubbub.

"Let me finish... please! We are now in communication with certain high-ranking people: scientists, state officials, religious and tribal leaders, who are being invited to see this incredible phenomenon for themselves. And when they do..." John hammered his hand in the air, "When! They! Do!"

A hail of hoots and yea's detonated. People hopped up and down, obliterating the John's introduction of a squat man in suspenders and flannel shirt who'd climbed up onto the gate by The John's side.

The John waved down the crowd as he handed the megaphone to the man.

"Hey there everybody. Name's Billy Metcalf. I worked as an edgerman at the Trinity Sawmill for twenty-four years. That was up until some months ago when I saw something red and sticky oozing out of a log on the saw deck that stopped me cold... that's not something you normally see..."

Billy Metcalf froze mid-sentence when he heard the screams. At the back of the crowd a skirmish erupted.

The attack was immediate and virulent.

"Holy mother of..." Metcalf dropped the megaphone to his hip. He turned to The John, "You seeing what I'm seeing?"

The John grabbed the megaphone. "People in the back, what's the problem?"

An area cleared as protestors scattered, revealing figures in flesh-colored masks wielding baseball bats and chainsaws.

"This is a non-violent protest! Hey! This is a..."

Nobody was listening anymore. Too busy scrambling every which way to escape.

"This is going down ugly." Billy Metcalf hopped off the gate and hustled away.

The John sounded off: "Whoever you are, you need to stop now. If you have a grievance, we're all ears, come up here and share it."

Watching from the chopper, Beldare was aghast at the melee. "I said harass. I said disrupt and disperse, I never said to go after them with chainsaws!"

"Yeah well, one of the units dropped out," Hardin said with a sly grin. "So they decided to make up for it with power tools."

All was chaos and dust on the ground. Some people sprinted flat out down the road, driven off. Others crawled around, battered and bloodied by whirling bats and golf clubs.

"This is all wrong!" Beldare hollered. "Where are Dixon and the police?"

"They're on their way." Hardin reported. "Okay, take us lower," he ordered the pilot, wishing he was down there beating on heads.

"No more delay, bring them in now!" Beldare ranted, his face red as a welt.

In the past, with previous jobs, Beldare might resort to strong-arm persuasion as a last means to solving the problem. But he'd never seen it done first hand. They'd always been enacted by others, 'handled' somewhere else. Yet now, facing these vicious beatings, he fidgeted in his seat, his insides knotted, as if his own body was being bludgeoned with each successive blow. Stop it! He wanted to scream. But was helplessly not in control.

Jim was also shaken by the punishing sight, but stayed dutifully detached, in documentary mode, capturing the clash from the roof of the bulldozer, first with sweeping pans of the action, then pushing in on isolated assaults.

Those chained to the gate and other machinery chanted, "Non-violence! Non-violence!" Some used picket signs as shields. Most ran blind to get free of the onslaught.

As far as Jim could tell, Christy was nowhere to be seen. Which was a good thing. He didn't know what he'd do if he saw her being thrashed. Among the flurry of screams and whelps of pain, he heard the whacks of baseball bats cracking people's skulls. The chainsaws weren't cutting or maiming anybody that Jim could tell. More for show, apparently. The thugs waved them around to threaten and incite mortal fear in the protestors. Which they succeeded doing with grins behind their masks, savoring the orgy of adrenaline and terror.

Jim caught sight of a kid drawing back a slingshot and flinging a stone at one of the masked men who was lashing the back of a protestor with a bullwhip.

Jim then turned the lens on two women kicking out the knees of a chainsaw-slasher. When he dropped to the ground they ripped the nylon mask off his face, just enough for Jim to capture his identity on video. The man swung the saw madly in the air, driving the women away. He clawed his mask back on. Then looking up, he spotted Jim on top of a bulldozer with a video camera aimed directly at him.

The brute lurched to his feet and came hurtling around people toward the bulldozer.

Uh-oh! Jim slung the camera case strap over his shoulders. No time to fit the camera in it. He lowered his body off the roof, merging into a blur of legs and crooked faces. He dodged around the panic-stricken people and tore off across the road into the woods. When he stopped for a quick look back, he saw the chainsaw man chasing after him.

"Ain't gonna hurt you!" the large man panted in pursuit. "Just need that camera!"

Jim zigzagged around enormous trees. I can outrun him, he thought. The man kept coming, busting through head-high ferns.

Tripping on a root, Jim nearly lost his footing. As he regained balance he didn't see the snag of a partially fallen tree until he rammed his forehead into it. The collision knocked him flat.

"Just drop it!" The man gained on him.

Jim couldn't hear him or anything except a metallic ringing in his ears. A momentary oblivion. Then a geyser of fear ignited his awareness. Get up and run! He forced his body upright and trundled off dazed, hairline sparks strafing his vision. He left the camera case where it lay, slapping back branches and fern fronds until he spotted a hollowed-out log.

Large enough.

He crawled inside, brushing back cobwebs and scooting as far back as he could, winded, a seam of blood drooling down the bridge of his nose.

"Where'd you go?" the man advanced.

Jim's hearing returned as the low, DUM-DUM idle of chainsaw grew louder. And with it, another sound, the

CHINK-CHINK of the man's belt buckle clinking against the chainsaw housing with each hulking stride.

"Ahhh, there you are." The man peeked in the log. "Hey champ, all I want is your damn camera. Just hand it out."

"I can't. It's not mine." Jim hit the record button, pointed the camera at the man's masked face in the opening. A red light blinked in the viewfinder. He thought the battery had a minute or two left. Not so. In the ensuing chase, he'd forgotten to turn it off.

"You got nowhere to go, champ." Drips of the man's sweat hissed on the hot blade. "Okay then, say goodbye to your balls."

The man revved the throttle trigger and BRRTHMM! the machine flared to life, its steel tongue whirring, deafening.

Jim curled tight against the back wall of pithy wood, holding his ears, caressing the camera in his arms. The chainsaw's raging teeth swept back and forth inches from his tucked knees, chewing into the sides of the log, spattering chips of wood in his face.

Jim blinked back the flying debris. He was about to try negotiating with the guy. He'd keep Gomez's camera and give him the digital memory card with all the footage. But the man pulled the saw out and moved away from the opening.

Jim didn't budge. He could still hear the DUM-DUM of the idling machine. Then a high, menacing whine rang out. The man was dropping the teeth down through the top of the log right above his head.

Get out and run! As Jim started inching his way toward the opening, the noise suddenly abated, followed by the thump of something hitting the ground.

A boyish face peered into the hollow. "You Cassaway?"

Through his crackled vision Jim saw a kid gripping a slingshot in his hand— the one from the protest.

"Christy Jones sent me to find you. Come on, it's okay now."

Jim crawled out of the log, apprehensive, reeling, the ache in his skull starting to rage.

The masked man lay prone, grimacing, rubbing his temple. The kid stood over the man, slingshot stretched back, a golf ball clenched in its webbed pocket.

The man squinted up at the hard, white ball and tried to protect his head with outstretched hands. "No-no, for Christ's sake…"

"Lucky I don't take that saw to your legs, mister. Then you'd know what a tree feels."

"What's all that shit about non-violence?"

The kid relaxed the sling. "That wasn't violent. You just got kissed by a rock." He stuck the slingshot in his back pocket, gestured to Jim. "Let's go. I'll take that."

The kid took hold of the camera and headed back, picking up the case where it lay at the snag. Jim stumbled along behind, his head smarting with every step. They crossed the road and pushed on into the forest on the other side. The uproar of the riot grew fainter the deeper they rambled.

"Okay stop. Sit down. You're good here." The kid kneeled, lifted the lid of the case and set the camera inside.

Jim collapsed. Somewhere during the chase, he'd lost a shoe. But that didn't matter now.

"I'm Kip," the kid announced as he unscrewed the top of a leather bota bag. Bright eyes. His hair a tussle of curly blonde locks. "Here, drink."

Jim wiped off the blood that drained down his face, and took the bota bag to his mouth.

"I need to check something," Kip said. "Don't move. Stay hidden. You're no good if you get arrested or found. They'll destroy your video and you."

Jim's head teetered, still woozy. "And Christy?"

"I'll take you to her. Later." Kip pulled a lemon drop from his fanny pack. "Here, suck on this."

Then he vanished.

Jim tipped his head back against the trunk and let out a stuttered sigh. He didn't feel like ever standing up again. He blinked at the god-rays of sunlight fanning through a copse of trees. He'd already forgotten about the lemon drop. He tipped his body over onto the damp earth and closed his eyes as sirens wailed in the distance.

He'd only blanked out for a couple minutes when a strange kid shook him awake.

"What's your name?" the kid asked.

"Huh?"

"What's your name?"

"It's Jim. Why?"

"Look at me. Do you know where you are?"

Jim looked around. Nothing made sense.

"Drink this."

Jim swallowed some water from a bota bag.

"What's my name?"

It didn't register. "How would I know?" Jim said.

The scrawny kid had bronze, laser-intense eyes. Dirty fingers, strong as talons, one gripped a slingshot, the other flicked the strap of the camera case. He wore a caramel-colored bomber jacket over a t-shirt with a red orb emblazoned in the center, ringed with the words: LET'S NOT DO WHAT WE DID TO MARS.

"Time to move," the kid said, slinging the strap of the camera case over a shoulder. "Stay close. Step softly."

When Jim dawdled, the kid urged him on, moving through the forest barefoot, feral, with an elastic stride.

31.
This is a crime scene

Chief Dixon led the convoy of police cruisers, vans and SWAT trucks to the gate action. Whirling lights and sirens snaked around clusters of terrified protestors fleeing the scene.

Designated police came hustling into the riot, focused only on the masked marauders, tasers drawn. The men dropped their bats and chainsaws, threw their arms up. In a flash they were cuffed, frisked, told their rights and herded off.

It was all well choreographed.

The chaos calmed. The dust settled. The bruised and bloodied squirmed and moaned on the ground.

Another police unit advanced, tasked to clear the gate area. Dixon gave a speech to the remaining hundred or so diehards.

"You're safe now. We've arrested the hostiles. However, this is still an unlawful assembly and you are trespassing on government property. I ask you to leave so that we can tend to the injured."

Ambulances pulled up. Surprisingly early.

"This is a crime scene people. We need you to clear the area. You can leave now without harm or arrest. If you're unwilling, then you are making it more difficult for the medics. I suggest you think about your friends, step away and let the medical people attend to their wounds."

"Since when do you care?" someone barked.

A line of sixteen police advanced in full tactical riot gear, their faces tense behind hard acrylic shields, armed with batons, pepper spray canisters, and automatic weapons.

The John linked arms with Bruiser and other activists who were chained to the iron gate, chanting, "This is a non-violent protest. This is a non-violent protest."

No compliance, no surrender.

Dixon gave the GO sign. The police swarmed the gate with bolt cutters. The protestors were clubbed, zip-tied, dragged off and muscled into awaiting vans.

Hovering the site in the helicopter, Hardin and Beldare watched it all unfold with minimal police action applied. Hardin had the pilot lift up higher to take in more of the landscape. He peered through binoculars, his eyesight keyed to any movement, any speck of color or shift of shadow.

"Ah-ha." He spotted a figure fleeing the protest into the woods to the northeast. "Come on…" he coaxed, "show me… show me the lair." But the person vanished in the trees.

He told the pilot to orbit the area in wider and wider sweeps.

He's looking for squatters, Beldare presumed.

About a mile from the gate action Hardin spotted motion in the forest canopy.

"There!" He tapped the pilot on the shoulder and pointed to a meadow. "You see that clearing? Take it down there."

"Roger that."

The chopper descended to within ten feet of the ground, flattening the grasses into a rippling vortex.

"Gotcha!" Hardin pumped a fist in the air. "He was right. He thought their action camp would be nearby."

Beldare didn't know who Hardin was referring to. He gawked out Hardin's side window, unable to grasp what the man was so excited about.

"Over there. Don't you see'em?" Hardin tapped the curved glass. "Three o'clock!"

Beldare saw nothing but a stand of trees.

"Look again. See the platforms and bridge planking running from tree to tree? It's like an Ewok village tucked in there."

Beldare keened in on specific trees where he caught glimpses of silhouettes moving among the limbs. He wondered how these people managed to haul all those boards way in there and build such high platforms with no one the wiser.

"Okay," Hardin said. "Take her up." Then he tapped Beldare on the shoulder with a soft fist. "We got'em. Now, here's how it's going to go. We call in our team of monkey men— the arborists. They'll wrap cables around the trees, shinny up and tear all the suspended decks and shit down. Hoo-ha! Done and gone."

Beldare shook his head.

Hardin's eyebrows pinched, "What, you got a better idea?"

32.
She's in Sweetwater

From the trees at the fringe of the clearing, Kip and Jim watched the helicopter sky away. Kip didn't move. Long after the swirling wind and racket of rotor blades receded, he remained motionless, ears perked. Jim watched him, waiting for a signal, which eventually came with a lifted finger.

"Someone's been following us, trying not to be seen."

Kip had grown up in the forest. A nature boy through and through. Born Christopher Kipple, he'd been parented by a number of communal activists over his 14 years. The redwood forest was his playground, his school. Everybody knew the wild, unwilling mascot of the cause who never missed a rally or gate action. Though he preferred the outdoors, Kip could find a welcome bed in any one of their homes.

"Okay, we're going over there." Kip led Jim across the grassy meadow to the action camp on the other side.

Strange sounds echoed in Jim's ears as they entered the camp. Footfalls drumming on top of his head. Looking up he saw people tramping along suspended bridges from tree to tree. A woman met them, saying, "That was no news chopper. We've been found."

Kip introduced Jim. He didn't get her name. Maybe it wasn't given. His brain in a fog. All he heard was, "Christy Jones's film maker man."

"Is she here?" he asked.

"No," Kip said. "She's in Sweetwater."

"Sweetwater?"

"Farther in. But you're in no condition." Kip told the woman that Jim needed to be checked out for a concussion.

They walked him over to a makeshift table made of 2x8 boards and sawhorses. The woman looked at the gash on Jim's forehead. Then checked his vision, asked a series of questions. He showed all the symptoms of a concussion: wobbly memory, slurred speech, reality displacement.

After the nameless woman sauntered off, Jim asked Kip, "Why wasn't Christy at the protest?"

"The John persuaded her not to go. She'd be in serious trouble if she got jailed. So he pressured her to stay and work on the maps."

"The maps?"

The Nameless Woman reappeared. She popped the fasteners on a fishing tackle box that served as the action camp's first aid kit. She twisted the cap off a tube of antiseptic ointment, applied it to the wound and wrapped Jim's head with a cloth bandage. Then she removed his one shoe and bloody sock, and daubed the blisters and lacerations with the cream.

It stung as much as it soothed.

"What's Sweetwater?" Jim asked her, pointedly.

"Sweetwater Woods," she said. "A remote section of North Fork, deeper in."

"Told you we were being followed." Kip bent his head toward a figure jogging toward them.

Dee Rotter, breathing hard.

"Hey, hi. I needed to get out of there and I got lost. But then I saw you two guys."

Kip gave a subtle shake of his head. The Nameless Woman caught it and asked, "Who are you?"

She turned to Jim. "It's me, Dee, remember?"

"No, talk to me." The Nameless Woman shot Dee a stink-eye stare.

"I was at the gate. Barely escaped with my life." She let out a breath. "Please, is it okay if I just hang here. I'm still shook up from it all."

Kip wondered why the woman's eyes ricocheted between Jim and his camera case on the ground.

The Nameless Woman tapped Kip on the arm and whispered, "I'll handle this. Take him to the blue tent."

Kip shouldered the strap of Jim's camera case. "Follow me."

Jim didn't move. He stared at Dee's face, not recognizing who he was talking to. "Where did you say Christy was? Sweetwater?"

"Me? I didn't say." Dee said.

"He's got a concussion," the Nameless Woman said.

"That explains it."

"No, I'm fine. Just need to see Christy. She's got my gear."

"I need to see her, too," Dee explained. "I've got a special message to give her."

"And what message is that?" the Nameless Woman asked.

"I'm to drive her back for her court appearance."

That struck home. But Kip didn't buy it. "I'll go get you-know-who," he said as he guided Jim away. Dee started to follow them.

"Not you, honey," the Nameless Woman stiff-armed Dee in her shoulder, firmer than intended, driving her back against the table, jarring the boards. "You're going to stay right here and shut the fuck up."

Woo... Dee silently resisted the temptation to retaliate. It didn't last. In an instant, she crumpled the woman to the ground with a swift punt behind the knees.

"Teach you a lesson, 'honey,' about knowing who to push around."

'Hey!" A tall, long-necked man rushed in, hunting knife in one hand, abrasive sharpening stone in the other. "Stop right there!"

"It's okay. I asked for it." The Nameless Woman struggled to her feet. "Just escort her out of here."

The man pointed the knife toward the southwest, the way out of the action camp. "Okay, you. Let's vamoose."

"Sweetwater... Sweetwater...," Dee repeated quietly to herself as they crossed the meadow. "Hey, I know you have to check everybody out, but just listen to me." She cozied close to the man. "I need to reach Christy Jones. You know her, right?"

"I know a lot of people," he said, stropping the knife blade across the whetstone as he walked.

"Well, I'm supposed to get her back to the city for her court appearance. Do you know where I can find her?"

"She didn't tell you?"

"We were to meet at the protest, but she didn't show."

"Can't say."

"Then can you at least tell me where Sweetwater, or Sweetwater Woods is, and how I get there?"

"How do you feel about getting lost?"

Reaching the tree line on the other side of the meadow, Dee waved him off. "I can find my way back to the gate from here. Thanks."

He stood for a long minute, thumbing the sharpness of the knife blade until Dee disappeared in the far trees, then he headed back to the camp.

After dozing for a few hours Jim woke up and stood outside the blue tent in the half-light, his head tolling a dull ache.

The camp was quiet. A couple people shuffled along a deck high overhead. Another descended to the ground by rope.

Was it a dream, his delirium, or real? Jim wasn't sure. But the image of UC Davis remained fixed in his mind. The man had looked into the tent, one hand leaning on an aluminum crutch, holding something in his other hand. Jim recounted him saying, "I never thanked you for all you did for me. So I brought a souvenir from the test I conducted. Something for your film." UC held up a glass vial of rosy-colored fluid and set it on the floor of the tent by Jim's side. "I'll take you to the source in the morning. Prepare yourself for the shock of your life."

Kip appeared with a couple cheese and pickle sandwiches. They sat outside the tent as tree shadows lengthened and the air dilated into night.

"Is UC Davis here?" Jim asked, between bites.

"Who?" Kip didn't recognize the name.

"UC Davis."

"Never heard of him. So how you doing? You remembering anything?"

"Yes and no. I remember you," Jim said.

"That's a start."

"I remember a helicopter."

"How about a masked man chasing you with a chainsaw?"

A chill jolted Jim's nerves. He started for the tent.

"Your camera's safe. I'll get it." Kip departed and soon returned carrying a black guitar case. "Remember that woman who followed us here?" Kip opened the case revealing the Sony video camera, packed snug with a towel.

"What woman?"

"Said her name was Dee. She came into the camp asking about Christy and eyeballing your camera. They took her away, but I knew she'd be back. So I left it out beside the tent just to see."

"The camera?"

"No, the case. I stuffed it with a heavy branch and like I thought, she took it. She's gone now."

"Oh no." Jim could hear Gomez scorching his ears.

"Sorry about losing it," Kip said. "But these things, they're worth knowing."

33.
They're going to smoke us out

Someone shook Jim's body, jarring him awake. He heard thunder, people scuttling, urgent shouts from high in the trees.

"Incoming!"

"Wake up people, we got trouble!"

At dawn, five men had hiked into North Fork from the gate. They stopped in the clearing, opened up duffel bags and pulled out hazmat body suits.

A police chopper descended. From its sled rails hung a large bulbous netting. The hazmat men released cords, and the bundle spilled its contents onto the ground— bales and bales of mysterious foliage.

The chopper lifted and hung in the air two hundred feet above the meadow. The hazmat men gathered up the vegetation and spread it into a hip-high hedge along the tree line in front of the action camp.

People on the platforms watched incredulously through the branches at the developing scene before them.

"What's with all the plants?"

"Got me."

The bushes were damp, their leaves limp, making them difficult to identify.

But Kip knew.

"Poison oak. It's poison oak! They're going to smoke us out!"

"You have five minutes to evacuate," said a Hazmat-suited man. "Otherwise you will suffer the consequences."

The tree-sitters got the message. Commotion and alarm kicked in, mixed with nuclear rage.

"You evil, evil assholes!" someone hollered.

"Be smart, people! Come out now and you'll be safe. If you don't, you will become very, very sick."

"Sick? Are you shitting me! It will rape the lining of our lungs!"

Eighteen people walked out. One working an aluminum crutch. They knew that breathing poison oak smoke can kill you. It swells your trachea, cuts off oxygen and makes death arguably the best option. The smoke would also adhere to clothes. Its soot particles would carry the oil onto the skin. A living hell.

Still, a few stayed, disbelieving the lumber company would sink to such a heinous act. But one thing remained clear— it was over. The action camp caput. No denying that. In time men would invade the site, scale the trees, root them out, and tear it all down. The task would take hours and hours, but burning poison oak revved the evacuation to hyper-speed.

Those who gave in were corded together and escorted away, spitting their outrage.

Then the hazmat men splashed gasoline on the bushes, lit matches and flung them in. A grim, spreading fire unfurled gobs of thick black smoke.

Kip rustled Jim out of his tent. "I got your camera. Let's go, right now!"

The hazmat men drew back from the burn. One of them lifted his chin to the sky and twirled his right arm in clockwise circles.

The helicopter lowered.

"Wait. What are they doing?" Jim looked to see what was causing all the ruckus. "Who are they?" he asked. But Kip wouldn't have it.

"No time!" He yanked at Jim's arm.

Perplexed, Jim followed Kip into the woods to the north, away from the camp.

The chopper fanned the smoldering bushes. Acting like a bellows, it sent the smoke high into the canopy where it filled the platforms, chasing people down by ropes, leaping off branches.

After a few seconds, the chopper plunged to within a foot from the grasses, pushing the smoke into the camp at ground level as everyone grabbed things in a panic and raced to vacate the area.

"Shit!" Kip stopped, wedged his fanny pack into the guitar case and set off, shouting. "Got to run now!" He coaxed Jim into a sprint. "Hey! Hurry up! And toss your clothes. The smoke will stick to them."

Jim glanced back. A dense cloud came billowing toward them, whipped by the rotors.

Kip started stripping as he ran, first his jacket, then t-shirt. With his free hand, he unzipped and kicked off his jeans and undershorts.

"Your clothes!" Kip called back. "Get 'em off! Now!"

Jim stumbled through the woods, tossing off his vest, shirt and pants, layer after layer, down to bare flesh.

Kip looked back at Jim tapping the top of his head.

Jim understood. He removed the bandage that wrapped his wound.

They ran naked, legs and arms whacked by ferns and punctured by blackberry thorns. The forest right behind filling with a dark haze.

After running flat out for five minutes, they reached a clear, smooth-running stream that meandered between mossy banks.

Kip reached down and dug up fistfuls of mud from the bank and slapped it to his skin, to his face and limbs.

Jim watched, then mimicked Kip.

"Everywhere." Kip said, and slathered the mud on Jim's back and neck. Jim did the same. Little by little no skin was exposed, their bodies were coated a glumpy brown head to toe, dotted with little pebbles.

Kip gestured for Jim to keep moving, to follow him along the slick-squishy bank beside the sparkling water.

At one point, Kip held up a hand to halt. They'd outdistanced the smoke. Jim thought he heard voices, a rustling nearby. He looked across the stream where Kip's eyes were fixed. On the other bank, three figures emerged from behind ferns. A red scarf crowned the head of one.

Jim's eyes lit up.

"Ahh," Christy blew out an elated sigh as she waded into the stream. They met in the middle.

"I thought I lost you," she said, near tears. She pressed her cheek against his cheek. "Thanks for finding him, Kip."

Kip nodded, covering his privates with the guitar case. "They set fire to poison oak. Smoked us out."

"Sadistic bastards!" one of the men with Christy said. "We could hear the chopper and thought the worst. But not that."

"Come," said the other man. "We'll get you some clothes and food."

"I have all your video gear." Christy said as they crossed the mirror-bright water to the other bank. "And something else." She took his muddy hand in hers. "Something for the experientialist."

34.
There's this interval

T he drying mud cracked and crumbled off Jim and Kip's bare bodies as they threaded single-file along a narrow deer trail through salmon berry bushes that skirted the stream. Along the way, Jim recounted Rosco's gruesome murder and burial.

"Tow truck men?" Christy's body twitched and she shared her frightening encounter with them.

After about a mile, the group turned away from the stream and climbed up around a thickly wooded hillside to a level area dappled pink with flowering rhododendrons.

Ten minutes later, they came upon the remnants of a wooden cabin nestled among the trees. The once Weaver homestead formed the center of the small Sweetwater camp. A century-old ramshackle structure with slab-cut siding and a roof recently covered with a brown tarp stapled to its hand-sawn rafters.

This wasn't an encampment like North Fork. No platforms or bridge-work hung in the upper branches. There was only one small deck, erected forty feet up a tree which served as a crow's nest overlooking the valley below, and some tents tucked in the trees away from the cabin.

The ground rules were ironclad: no fires, no flashlights or lamps. No portable stoves or loud speech. Nothing to give away their location. When going out to fetch supplies, people had to take different routes each time, keep to deer trails, and leave no sign of human activity.

After washing the mud off their bodies from five-gallon buckets of cold water, Jim put on the sweatshirt and pants he had hurriedly stuffed in his gym bag back in the city. Kip was given some over-sized clothes to wear, borrowed from The John's tent.

Jim sat outside the cabin going through the video gear while inside people spoke in hushed tones about the North Fork smoke out, and how it impacted their plans. They listened to Kip and Christy talk on Jim's behalf. Bringing a stranger into camp who'd not been fully vetted was prohibited.

The meeting broke up. Jim was loaned a pair of sandals and a backpack to carry his video gear. He took these offerings to mean he passed inspection. Christy told him otherwise.

"Kip and I vouched for your integrity, but your presence here is provisional. Don't take this personally, but your every word and move will be scrutinized for a while. Understand, everybody's on edge and extremely protective. The good news is they gave me permission."

"For what?"

"Are you ready?" Christy smiled.

Jim recounted the string of events since he agreed to come along: breathing exhaust fumes, getting pissed on, burying Rosco's mutilated body, suffering a concussion, and running naked from poison oak smoke.

"Why not," he gave a throaty chuckle. "Made it this far."

Christy and Kip led Jim down a slope and up another, switching back and forth through the silent woods. Seeing Jim lagging back, Kip stopped to warn him, "Stay close. Don't stray. It's easy to get lost in here under the canopy."

Reaching a plateau, they entered a grove where a woman sat cross-legged in front of a goosepen at the base of a redwood tree. As they approached, Christy turned to Jim, tapping an index finger to her lips.

The three quietly sat behind the woman on the mattress of forest litter. Jim noticed a pair of boots on the ground next to the opening.

"This is Holly," Christy whispered to Jim.

Holly dipped her head, acknowledging the three of them. She had a round Asian face with dark moats of sleeplessness under her eyes. Beside her was a rolled-up sleeping bag, a small lunch box and a clear container half-full of water.

Jim could hear subtle, intermittent stirrings coming from inside the tree. Christy motioned for Jim to lean in closer for a better view. He craned his neck around Holly and saw a bent figure enveloped in what looked like a delicate netting of milky-white hairs.

Holly glanced at Jim. Then, gentle as a lullaby, she spoke to the person inside the tree. "You're doing really well. The tree is connecting with your spine. Let it in. Reach for its touch... relax and receive. Reach... relax... and... receive."

Jim scooted in closer. The cavity of the tree gave off a musky smell and felt warmer than outside the trunk. The fibrous threads cross-stitching the figure had a slick moist sheen. As Jim's eyes adjusted to the darkness, he saw the man's head contorted to the side, the skin taut, as if the skull was trying to push free of the stretched, blue-veined flesh of cheeks and chin.

Jim's throat heaved. He scooted backward, swiveled his body so he could lean against the outer bark. He inhaled a deep breath of the damp, fermented air, his stomach flipping somersaults.

There was no getting around it. This was no apparition his concussion concocted. This was undeniably real. Corporeal.

"He's going to make it," Holly muttered in Christy's ear. "He's around the corner, almost home."

"Any…?" Christy mimicked talking with her hand.

Holly shook her head.

Christy checked on Jim, mouthing, "You okay?"

Jim lifted a thumb, and exhaled a truncated exhalation.

"Would it be alright if Jim records it?" Christy asked Holly.

"Yes," she consented. "But no names."

Jim took his time setting up the camera, fidgeting with its settings, and positioning it in front of the hollow trunk of the tree.

"This is day two and then some," Holly shared, speaking into the camera mic. "The critical period has elapsed. By morning his breath will pass to the tree's."

Jim hunched over the camera, adjusted the focus and opened the iris wide to gain as much light on the subject as possible. Looking through the viewfinder helped distance him from the sight. He punched the record button and asked Holly to describe the metamorphosis taking place in detail. She offered bits of information. But her attention needed to be undistracted while coaching the volunteer through the transmutation.

After shooting for a couple minutes, Christy tapped Jim on the shoulder. "Stop filming." She thanked Holly, and stood up, motioning Jim and Kip to do the same.

Before leaving, Jim recorded establishing shots with Holly's back to camera, a close up of the volunteer's boots at the base of the tree, and wide pans that took in the entire grove.

"So, Mr. Experientialist," Christy beamed, having served up visual proof of the metamorphosis to Jim. "Was that real enough for you?"

Jim shook his head. "I don't have words. I saw it, no question, yet part of me still doesn't believe my eyes."

"Admit it, I just delivered you your ticket to the world," Christy slipped her arm through his and they headed back to the encampment.

"Truly. Thanks. Now, I just need to get Holly to clarify a couple things I was too dumbfounded to ask."

"Like what?"

"She said that at some point during the third day, they go into a sleep-like state. The tree takes over and her assistance is no longer needed. But did she also say that some are rejected?"

"It's like anything," Christy said. "Just because volunteers believe they can endure the strain of it, the process brings out subconscious resistances. Could be a lack of trust, the body's fear of death or change, the unknown, or simply the need to control. And whatever it is that is blocking their transition will amplify the pain."

"You mean some don't make it?"

"Evidently there've been a few who tried to do it alone and were rejected. There was also an instance where two people got together in a goosepen and it turned into a disaster. A lot of people need help letting go. That's where Holly comes in. She's like the midwife."

"I get that."

"And it takes a toll on her."

"I bet."

"We need more Holly's," Kip noted.

Jim stopped mid-stride, looked back to where they'd been. "And the person's boots left at the tree. What's that about?"

"To help us find them. The John put me in charge of the maps to flag their locations, the groves they're in, so we can keep track. The shoes and boots mark the exact tree."

"Maps…" Jim mumbled.

"You okay?"

"Just a lot to take in.

They continued on.

"I'd like to interview The John," Jim said, out of the blue.

"Well, you may have to wait on that, he's bound to be in jail a while. It's like his second home. But you can interview Rolf."

"Rolf? The logger guy?"

"Yeah, he's here at Sweetwater."

As they neared the cabin, Kip urged Christy to tell Jim about 'the interval.'

"Oh right, there's this interval. According to Holly there's a short length of time when the tree speaks through the volunteer's mouth. It's while they're in a semi-conscious state. And for about a minute the person's voice changes and what they say comes from the redwood tree's consciousness. Sometimes Holly hears a humming or murmuring. But a couple times the communications have been clear. She said one tree told her how grateful the forest was for the sacrifice people were making to help them live on."

"What?" Jim gave a confounded face.

"Makes me cry just thinking about it."

"Hold on. The trees... talk?"

"Uh-huh."

"In English?"

"If the volunteer was from Paris, the tree would probably speak French." Christy laughed. "What, too many shock-waves for you in one day?"

"I-I'm speechless."

"Well evidently the trees are not. At least not while the volunteer's vocal chords are still workable. Come on, Rolf should be waking up from his nap, and it's my watch time on the lookout."

"The interval," Jim said aloud.

"That'd be cool to record that," Kip said.

"Yes, Kip," Jim agreed. "Yes, it would."

35.
The toughest, most dangerous work

Rolf Zetzer was still napping when they returned. So, Jim recorded a man named Oscar making up a batch of 'alchemy paste' inside the cabin. Oscar explained how the potion was the simplest of recipes. All it required was a dozen handfuls of fungus carefully dug up from deep under a nearby grove of old growth trees. "The special ones," he called them. And using a mortar and pestle, beat it into a thick, chalky batter with a few drops of stream water.

Oscar swabbed a dab of the paste in Jim's hand. It felt like gritty pancake dough.

"The paste is a catalyst for the transformation," Oscar said, stirring the mix. "First the palms of your hands and the soles of your feet are perforated with the dry fungal nettles. This opens up the pores. Then the paste is applied, slathered on both the hands and feet, where it's absorbed into the blood. That's it. It's that simple. Except for one thing. Not all trees are equipped to convert a humanoid, and the mixture is only viable for so many hours."

Jim was handed a bag of the dry fungus and a bag of the paste as props to shoot for the documentary. He thanked Oscar and stuffed the bags in the front pocket of the backpack he'd been given.

Outside, Jim set up the camera while Kip fetched Rolf. The thickset man looked careworn, his shoulders slumped as he approached. He had puffy, bloodshot eyes, a crooked little scar over one eyebrow, and hands big as oven mitts. Jim noticed the tips of Rolf's fingers were marbled white as if they'd been dipped in candle wax.

After introductions, Jim positioned Rolf in the frame, seated on a log. He fitted a wireless mic to the collar of the man's wool shirt.

"Ask away," Rolf said.

Jim clenched the headset to his ears. "How long have you been a logger?"

"Been felling trees since I was thirteen. Started out helping my dad. I'm 44, so that makes it thirty years and change."

"Can you share some of your experiences as a logger?"

"I'll say this. it's the toughest, most dangerous work there is, bar none. You have to love it to do it. And I did, 'til things changed."

"What changed?"

"Letcha in on something. It's an art to fell a single redwood. To drop it in a precise spot. Ya gotta be dead on. That's twenty thousand tons topplin' outta the sky. You don't want it busting other trees down on top of your head. You got to be fixed in the moment, your tips on fire, listening to the stitch and crack of the wood fiber, the whine and tug of the saw. Don't want it kickin' and rippin' your arm off. Back before I lost my hands to white finger I was DaVinci. God was I good." Rolf lifted his head, snored out a breath. "Hell, there's no art in a clear cut. Big chomping machines, and a lot more money for the man. Factory work, it robs the art."

"What made you stop?"

"Kathy. She went and grafted her body to a tree."

"Your wife. The one you're accused of killing?"

He bit his lower lip before speaking, "Right, my wife."

"What was it like to be suspected of murder?"

"Oh, I *am* a murderer." Rolf floated his right hand up toward the surrounding forest. "I've killed ancient trees. Two-hundred and fifty footers."

Jim nodded, but kept on subject. "I mean, for killing your wife."

"Pfft, I knew they'd make me out to be some maniac."

Jim zoomed in for a tighter shot of Rolf's face. "Can you tell me how it started? With the tree people."

"Can't tell you when or where exactly." Rolf scratched at beard stubble. "All I can say is it goes back some. You hear all kinds of things about missing folks around here. Seems like every month somebody's lost in the woods. Easy to do. No horizon. Thick canopy. And the fog takes away the sun's path. People tell stories how the forest took'em, or a furry ape man, or some demon spirit.

"But then there came that day a year ago last spring. It'd been dry for a week or so, unseasonably dry. We were thinning out a section, had to fell a couple of big boys in the way. Buddy o'mine, Ed Ruggles, he's workin' a tree when blood spatters out of the trunk, spitting on his chain saw. Thought he was hallucinating. Dipped his finger in the red sauce dripping out of the wood, tasted it, and that was that."

"What was that?"

"He left the saw stuck there. Never went back."

"Ed Ruggles."

"Like me, third generation logger. As I said, you hear all kinds of things living here. There's a native legend sayin' how the First People would bury their dead inside the trees. But this blood was fresh, and there was some cartilage-like gristle in it."

"You saw it?"

"Uh-huh. Wasn't like Ed to split like that. We're talkin' one tough cowboy. The man took pride being a feller. And he was one of the best. But that… that incident changed him."

"How so?"

"Should've kept his mouth shut." Rolf shook his head. "That was all she wrote."

"You mean, what? They murdered him?"

"Didn't stop the rumors. Like the lady poet, Carla Sayers, a friend of Kathy's, she'd disappeared in the woods leaving a note."

"What kind of a note?"

"Left it in her shoes, about making a plaster from the fungus. Said she was going into a tree. 'Blending' I think was the word she used. Bunch o'horseshit I thought and told Kathy as much. I mean seriously. But Kathy worshipped Carla. Went to school with her. So that stuck a wedge in our marriage, stewing up battles on the home front. And Kathy, she'd always had a sense about other stuff."

"Like… what stuff?"

"She was rock solid certain terrible things would come to us because of what I did for a living. 'Karma.' she said. 'Can't avoid it.' Urged me to stop. Said folks were tampering too much with living things and tippin' the balance. Forest spirits were in her ears, elves and whatnot, telling her to leave me and seek redemption. I thought the wheels had come off the wagon."

"What happened then?"

"I encouraged her to get help, talk to somebody, therapy, whatever. Next thing I know she's high-tailin' it, driving way out into the woods like she was in a trance. She knew where she was going. And I followed her. Lost her a few times. Then found her inside a charred-out hollow, her hands all fuzzy-like. 'Come on out of there!' I pleaded. Then, after a while…"

Rolf hesitated, sniffed and shut his eyes. Jim sensed the man quaking inside as he relived the incident. So, he laid off, didn't push the interview, and waited for the man to settle.

"I stayed with her there talkin' a long time, real long time. Tried to pull her out. She wouldn't have it. Told me to leave. When I came back the tree had taken her."

Rolf scooped his beefy hands into the wells of his eyes.

Jim checked the battery level on the camera, almost gone. He thought about replacing it, but Rolf looked back at the lens, cleared his throat.

"That was biblical," he said, tears draining down the sides of his ruddy cheeks. "You don't come away from that the same man, sonny. No, you do not."

"Just came from seeing it myself. I know I'll never be the same again," Jim said.

"A loved one?"

"No."

"Still, you get my meaning."

Jim nodded. "What did they have on you in terms of evidence that you'd killed your wife?"

"Right, so after that I quit my job. Told another logger about it. Even brought him to Kathy's tree. It didn't sit right. He was sure it was the devil's work. A few days later some folks broke in while I was out and bloodied up my trailer. Fed me to the sharks."

Kip came over. He pulled some rolled up papers from a cardboard tube. "Sorry to cut in but you wanted to see the maps right away."

"Oh, yeah, thanks buddy." Rolf looked at Jim. "Excuse me a second."

"That's fine." Jim paused the video.

Kip slipped a rubber band off a satellite image of North Fork and Sweetwater Woods and set it in Rolf's hands. There were eight red dots marked on it.

"There's Marianne, Emily and Tanner in North Fork." Kip pointed. "Plus, the five people here in Sweetwater that Christy marked. That little red square is the cabin."

"I've been meaning to ask how many." Jim stepped over to take a look at the maps.

"Seventeen so far," Kip explained to Jim. "Based on counting shoes."

Kip opened up a second, larger topo map. "Here's a larger look of the region."

Over Rolf's shoulder Kip finger-tapped nine more dots on the regional map. "That's Stevens… over here is Bodkey… we know Carla's somewhere near about here… there's a few no names down in this area…. and your Kathy would make seventeen."

"Not counting the early ones." Rolf snorted a series of breaths, squinting at the map. He slid his index finger across the wobbly topographic rings. Kip handed Rolf a red felt-tipped pen. Rolf removed the cap and pressed the tip on the map.

"That's Kathy's place." Rolf tapped the map. "Right near Carla." He handed the pen and map back. "You need to keep spreading them around. At least one in every grove." Rolf said.

"One in every grove," Kip repeated.

"And don't let those maps fall into the wrong hands."

"No way." Kip rolled up the maps, stuffed them in the tube and hustled back to the cabin.

"Okay," Rolf groaned. "We done here?"

"Last question." Jim punched the record button. "What's next for you?"

"Tomorrow morning, first light, I'm off to give my good-byes to a few old friends, then find a tree near Kathy. It's several miles from here."

"You're going to do it."

"Uh-huh." Rolf nodded. "Just hope there's a tree willing to have me."

Jim shut off the camera. "Thanks for sharing your story. I know you're on the run, so I hope you don't get caught."

"Slim chance of that. I'll be going by water." Rolf stood up and walked away, only to spin about-face. "If this comes out, they're done for, sonny. And they know it. They'll bloody every trailer from hell to breakfast to keep this news from coming out. So you get it out there. You tell 'em."

"I will," Jim said.

As Rolf lumbered away, he whacked his temple with the heel of his hand. "We went too far. Too frickin' far."

36.
Leave the toad

It was late afternoon. Hardin, Beldare and four arborists marched into the North Fork action camp to assess the burn site and tear down the suspended platforms. Hardin needed to confirm the place was completely empty of tree squatters before he and Beldare reported to Hersh.

Their protest plan and crowd removal had gone extremely well. Only forty-five arrests. The vigilante patrols were freed, paid and went home satisfied.

The poison oak bush fire had burned down to smokeless, ghostly cinders. The men stamped through them into the eerily silent camp.

As the arborists scaled the trees and dismantled decks and bridging, Hardin combed the site.

"If you come across any weirdness, holler," he called back to Beldare as he rambled off, clearly on the hunt for something.

Beldare didn't ask what 'weirdness' Hardin so eagerly sought. He wandered about the encampment and soon found himself strolling along a moss-lined footpath, the ground soft and spongy under his slip-on's. With each venturing step the voices and battering sounds of the men dismantling planks diminished.

Beldare was familiar with New England's hardwood trees, a spectacle of color every autumn, but this was different. Being among these giants felt other worldly. The stillness and serenity beckoned him to continue ambling on, his head lifting and bowing as he took in the sheer height and girth of these rust-colored columns. The trees made him feel like a tiny, transient visitor. And that felt grand.

The waning sun tickled through the branches, casting lacey patterns on his gray sweater vest. As the path curved around the green fan of a large fern, he caught sight of someone in the corner of his eye and staggered to a stop. There, for an instant, the specter of Beverly, the owl-eyed woman who confronted him at that camp appeared, then snapped into a human-shaped shadow on the bark of a tree.

Beldare walked on, unable to shake her presence watching him, stalking him. He'd never encountered anyone like her before. Unnerved, he was about to go back when something glinted in the sunlight off the footpath ahead.

At the base of a redwood he came upon glass vials and a roll of clear plastic tubing. The ground was cleared away, the tree's roots exposed. A tube the diameter of a straw had been inserted into the largest root. He circled the trunk, pondering its purpose. It looked to be some kind of delivery apparatus, like the chemical treatment injections he'd seen used to fight Dutch elm disease on the east coast. He kneeled for a closer look at a plastic container that held a reddish-colored fluid. A length of tubing extended from the container into the forest beyond. Perplexed and intrigued, he decided to investigate where it led.

Traipsing off path through the woods, Beldare tracked the tubing as it curved around trees and bushes to no apparent end. Not one to give up without an answer, he continued on. The tubing ultimately led to a tree with a camp stool, and oddly, a pair of worn cross-trainers. Here again, the soil had been cleared away, the tubing inserted into an exposed root. In the trunk, a dark cave.

Beldare sat on the camp stool and peered inside.

Hardin called out for Beldare, but there was no response. "You happen to see that short old guy?" he asked an arborist. "Must've gone back to the gate," the man said.

Hardin gave up hailing Beldare. He crossed the meadow in the thickening twilight, disappointed that he didn't find one of Them.

Beldare was not at the gate.

"Where the hell…?" Hardin rubbed his upper jaw, an annoying toothache had begun to flower. He strutted around as two NorCal workers spray painted blue diagonal slashes across the bark of trees, marking the ones to be cut for the new road.

"Rain's coming," one said.

Hardin gazed at the western sky. "Guess we just leave the toad," he said, and headed to his company truck. "Never gonna find him at night." He fished a satellite phone from his rucksack. Richard Hersh answered right away.

"Happy to report the North Fork camp has been emptied," Hardin proclaimed. "We cleared it out completely. Trees are being tagged as we speak. So they can start felling tomorrow and cutting the entry road on schedule. Want to know how we did it so fast? You gotta hear this. What? No, no sign of one yet, but we'll keep looking. What's that?" Hardin shifted in his tracks, trying to understand what Hersh was saying. "Sweetwater? Who told you that? Yeah, I know where it is, but I never…"

37.
I have a confession

Made of weathered boards pulled from the old home-stead's outhouse walls, the lookout deck was only wide enough for one person to sit. Kip's perch, on a branch ninety-feet higher in the redwood tree, gave a full 360-degree view. Given his concussion, Jim was satisfied to have reached the lower one.

Between the long, graceful limbs he could see for miles through binoculars to the west and southwest— range after range of hills, softening in paler and paler tints of blue. He bit into a stick of turkey jerky as he tried to make room in his world for what he'd witnessed only hours before at Holly's tree.

Besides his world being rocked, the subject of the documentary had shifted. The Last Stand protest would still play a part, but a lesser one. The focus now was this mind-boggling transmutation, and the people willing to give their lives to save a forest.

Jim's adrenaline fired up as he realized the project had grown bigger than first surmised, expanding beyond regional interest to an international audience. His ticket to the world indeed. And he must finish it fast. Be the first, before some other producer or TV network nabbed the story.

Is that what that flirty woman was all about? Trying to steal the camera? The thought rattled his body— the fact that he had something extremely valuable to protect.

Adding to his tension was the lie festering inside. It was time to fess up to Christy about the false self he'd been portraying, and face the fallout.

Jim gazed to the west where the late sun sat on the rim of the coastal range. He panned the binoculars to a tree that stood above the rest. As he watched its feathery branches wag in the breeze, he wondered what it would feel like to be that tree. Outside in the elements day and night. Questions followed— one's he never thought to ask: Does a tree have senses? Can it see, or hear the birds on its limbs? Smell smoke from a fire? Is it aware of distant trees being chopped down?

The sky suddenly darkened. To the west, a wall cloud had blotted out the sun. This was no fogbank scrolling in off the Pacific. This was a storm front, roiling midnight black, swollen with rain.

The scurrying of chipmunks, cries of birds and other woodland creatures spread the weather news. In the distance, voices from the cabin. The meeting breaking up. Soon he heard a scratchy sound and saw Christy's red scarf appear as she worked her way up the trunk by ropes.

"Hey, you," she called up.

Jim leaned over the deck. "I could hear you guys from up here."

"It got a little heated. The upshot is they're not going to wait. With North Fork down, it's only a matter of time before this camp is discovered. So they're leaving in the morning to try to bring people like the governor and whatever big talkers they can persuade to come right away."

Jim helped Christy pull herself up to the branch across from him.

"I mentioned the video you shot. They considered taking it but thought it better to keep it safe with you for now. Oscar and Emma are going to check with hospitals, see who got caught in the poison oak smoke, and get word to The John about speeding up the plan. So it's just going to be you, me and Kip to watch the place."

"What about Holly?"

"She's wasted and getting sick. Needs to take a break for a few days. How's your head?"

"It's been split open more ways than one."

Christy chuckled. "We better move. Rain's coming. We need to gather sleeping bags and take down hammocks."

Jim descended behind Christy. He grabbed hold of the knotted rope and eased his body down branch to branch, before taking the last sixteen feet by rope ladder to the forest floor.

"I'd sure like to record the governor and whoever else they bring here. In fact, I know some notable people they could contact in the city."

"Like who?"

"There's a renowned rabbi, a couple physicists, a zen master... people I interviewed for a documentary I did."

"You have their names?"

"Yeah, I even have some of their numbers in my... oh..." Jim patted his back pockets.

"Those aren't your pants. You stripped them off, remember."

"Yeah, but I didn't have my wallet in those either. It's at the base camp, in a box somewhere. Rita knows."

Jim followed Christy along a narrow trail. En route, Jim spotted Oscar, and then another man, strolling soundlessly among the trees.

"They're shopping," Christy whispered back to Jim. "Looking for a tree to enter someday."

A few minutes later they came to a grove where a couple hammocks hung.

"First the sleeping bag." Christy untied a stuff sack dangling from one hammock, and handed it to Jim. "Hold it open."

"I have a confession to make," Jim said, as Christy crammed the sleeping bag into the sack. "Something I've been holding back."

"You mean how you thought I was a nut job?"

"No. Well, yeah, that's, I mean we all have our blind spots. And there are those who cling to false hopes only to realize it's a lost star. I figured I was getting to know yours up front in a big way."

"I bet." Christy tied the draw strings together and set the bag on the ground.

"And it troubled me. Having to see your humiliation when the fantasy blew up in your face. So I'm sorry if I came off distant or cynical whenever the word 'morphing' came up."

"Fair enough. And now?" Christy unhooked the hammock strap girdling a tree trunk.

"Now…" Jim mimicked her action, unstrapping the other end of the hammock. "Now you could say anything and I'd believe it."

The cloud bank submerged the forest in shadow.

Christy glanced up, then back at Jim. "That's your confession?"

"No-no." His lips pressed white.

Christy walked toward Jim, rolling the hammock into a cylinder, secretly hoping he was about to share his affection for her.

"I'm not really a staff producer at News Bang."

"Oh." Christy nodded, suppressing a slump of disappointment.

"In fact, I'm basically a freelance grunt." Jim let go of his end.

"That's it?" She cradled the rolled-up hammock under an arm.

"Yeah, why?"

Christy strode over to the other hammock. "I knew that. I knew it back when you interviewed me for Earth Day. What, you think I'm drawn to people for their titles?"

She sounded irritated, nervous. But it wasn't about him. It was Mae's pestering voice in her head: *Tell him how you feel!*

Drops of rain patted the ground. They rolled up the other hammock in silence.

"Let's get these into The John's tent."

Jim picked up the sleeping bag and trailed Christy through the woods, unsure what had dampened her mood.

"Okay, my turn." she said, keeping a half-step ahead. "I came here with one single intention, or so I thought. And yes, my decision was motivated by recent events. I told you what happened and how I retaliated." Christy slowed her stride. "But I didn't tell you how it pushed me over the brink, I mean, I was hysterical. Off the charts."

She stopped between two enormous trees and faced him. "That's why I didn't get back to you. I didn't want you to see me like that."

Hearing why she didn't return his calls gave Jim a lift. He'd often wondered if it was because of the story he'd shared that day on the beach.

Christy moved on. "Then, when The John told me the Tanner metamorphosis was real and would I come, I jumped. The timing. It was like I'd been summoned by destiny. But it's not as impulsive as it sounds. I looked at it twelve ways to Sunday. I mean, I'd just been betrayed and arrested, so I needed his swear-to-god assurance. And even with that, until I saw it with my own eyes I was treading air, clinging to a lost star, like you said."

They came to a small clearing where a large canopy tent had been erected.

"I get it." Jim said, "You decided to join the…"

"Partly as an escape, I admit, but also as a way to give my all. These trees certainly give theirs'." Christy unzipped the tent door.

"It's okay, Christy."

She flung the two hammocks onto the floor of the tent. "I'm telling you this because…"

"I know. I mean, I pieced it together. You said on the phone how you needed to say your last goodbyes. You sold your car. You weren't at the protest. And then today happened, and…"

"Jim…" She took the sleeping bag from him.

"Much as I want to stop you…"

"Don't… please." Christy raised her hand for him to stop talking, appealing for his full attention. "If I don't get this out…"

Jim took a step back, giving Christy room for whatever she was struggling to express. Her breathing had noticeably quickened. Her upper body gyrated, as if wrestling to escape invisible bonds.

"You see, all that's… you changed it." A sparkle of rain blinked from her lashes. "When I couldn't find you the other night, I knew it. Hell, I began feeling it on the beach, the day of the sand dollars. But it all became obvious when I saw you on that bank this morning, naked, caked in mud, like you'd risen right out of the earth. My god, right then, right *then*…"

Christy stopped moving, pressed the sleeping bag to her chest. "How do I explain it? It was like, like the moment you reach the flower center, you know, the heart of the labyrinth. I can't help myself. I want to be with you."

Jim hung on her every word as fat raindrops tapped their heads and popped on the tent roof.

"So there. That's my confession. I said it. Now I feel as naked and exposed as you were, mud and all."

Jim saw an opening, but she persisted.

"I'm a fiery woman. Over-zealous at times. I've made a lot of enemies. I'm due in court tomorrow. Not going to happen, so I'll be in contempt, most likely go to jail and…"

Jim could no longer keep his body away from her. He snatched the sleeping bag out of her hands, tossed it down and opened his arms.

"Say no more, Christy Jones."

Rapt in his embrace, she said, "I never knew I had feelings like this."

Jim's heels touched down, feeling the pulse of her heart pound against his chest. "I…" He was about to speak but held back.

She eased away. "What?"

"Nothing." He'd also planned to confess how he was homeless, but that seemed irrelevant now. "I'm right where I want to be."

Christy loosened the knot of her red scarf. Jim watched her hair unfurl, bounding on her shoulders, framing her face like a wreath. She tugged him toward the tent.

"Wait," he said, realizing this was one of those rare, once-in-a-lifetime moments. He set his right hand on her waist, clasped her left hand that held the scarf, and began to hum a waltz. Christy fidgeted at first, then slid into his trusting steps as rainclouds let loose, sizzling the air around their ears.

38.
Mother nature my ass

Argus Beldare awoke in the pre-light of dawn shivering uncontrollably. He huddled in the cupped recess of a fallen redwood's upturned root ball. It had been his shelter throughout the rainy night. He rubbed his stiff, clammy hands together and stamped his feet.

It had been a rough time. The roughest he could remember. Sounds of the forest kept waking him, spooking him. Nocturnal calls and rustlings between downpours. Screech owls, black bears, emaciated wolves prowling the woods. Who knows? He'd shake awake to the grunts and clumps of something moving nearby, the sharp crack of a twig, a snort or a snuffling, something breathing out there, a predator smelling him, flared eyes peering from the leaves like candle flames, piercing the blackness.

Cowering in the retreat of the root ball, he gripped a branch and jabbed its tip into the drizzly air like a spear, trembling, fearful for his life. "No," he murmured to himself. "Not that way. I won't be eaten alive."

When rainclouds thinned to reveal the crescent moon, its momentary sliver of light played tricks with his vision, turning the shaggy redwood bark into distorted faces, leering from limbs above his head, some skull-like, some bloated, wrapped in a snarl of scarlet veins. When he closed his eyes, others shuttled across his vision, ghoulish faces in the windows of a death train smearing past with frenzied glances, seeking him and him alone.

Common sense told him to wait out the night rather than become permanently lost. But after such a terrifying experience, he wished he'd taken the risk.

She brought him in there. That woman, Beverly. She'd lured him. He knew it. He'd seen her silhouette emerge from the trees. Unmistakable. That was no illusion. That was her shadow pointing to the plastic tubing that led him to that hideous tree.

At first, he couldn't register what he was seeing inside the hole of that trunk. A swatch of color. Fabric of some kind. As his eyesight became accustomed to the dark, he recognized the tucked legs of a person enveloped in a fibrous, cocoon-like mesh.

"That's a man…" Beldare stiffened, gave a fitful shake of his head, unwilling to grant such an occurrence. "But w-what?" he stuttered, to no one in particular. "What would cause such a thing?"

He kicked the stool over, knelt down closer, staring into the charred cavity, mesmerized by the unshakable image, as uncanny as it was repulsive.

And then, before his eyes, the tip of a wick-thin tendril lifted from the ground near the person's feet and twitched.

"Ah! Did you see that!" Beldare pivoted on his knees, shouting to no one.

A cloud took the light and a wave of dampness cooled the air. He jolted to his feet, only to realize that in his curious pursuit, he'd lost all sense of time. He needed to return to the others.

He followed the tubing back to the first tree. But the footpath he'd taken somehow disappeared. Without a trail to follow and night creeping in, the woods became a grim stranger. "Can't see the forest for the trees," he'd muttered to himself.

Rain fell. He went about hurriedly at first, feeling desperate, only to give up and look for a dry place to wait out the night. All the while he couldn't shake the sight of that bent-over man inside the tree. That wasn't some strange affliction. No, that was voluntary.

The transmutation was one thing, morbidly nightmarish. But equally startling was the tube running a red fluid from the tree's root, as if distributing the person's blood to another tree. Why? Was it some kind of experiment? Or an act of resistance being scientifically documented?

Hardin's last words came back to him: 'If you come across any weirdness, holler.'

That's when Beldare realized what was happening behind his back. The reason for all the secrecy. Hersh's 'extenuating circumstances.' It was more than a raid to flush out a bunch of tree sitters so a road could be cut. It was to stop the world from seeing such an unthinkable act of defiance.

But why would people sacrifice their lives?

It reminded him of the Buddhist monks who set themselves on fire in protest of the Vietnam war.

"Because it's their only way. Their last stand," he answered aloud.

Argus Beldare's parents wanted him to become a civil engineer. He defied them and studied to be a lawyer. His aspirations changed when he helped a fellow Harvard student avert expulsion after an exam-cheating incident. The student's father heard about it and hired the twenty-year old to handle 'some mischief.' Beldare walked away from Harvard law and never looked back. He became a crisis management consultant, trailing Dante into the purgatory of everyday corruption and corporate crime, and deeper still into the icy, inner circles of greed-made human hells.

Throughout his career, Beldare came to know a spectrum of personalities, mostly power-mongers with delusions of grandeur. Many of them intelligent, obscenely wealthy white men. Would they perform a selfless act like the man inside that tree? Give beyond themselves? Never. They'd resort to dark deeds, do whatever it took, even murder, rather than sink an inch from their thrones. That's how they'd make their last stand.

Just before daybreak, a primal outpouring of rage overtook Beldare and he unleashed a raw, convulsive roar.

Relief came with the first faint light of a new day. The storm passed. He strode out from under the root ball and stumbled through the forest, turning his trusty redwood spear into a walking stick, mulling it all over in his mind.

That's the urgency. It's not to salvage a few downed trees, it's to wipe out the people inside them.

Coming upon the narrow track of an animal, he followed it, winding among the redwoods and rain-glazed ferns to an opening— the meadow by the action camp. He knew his way back to the gate from there, which had now become a well-worn path. Footprints filled with rainwater made by the hazmat men and the fettered activists they'd smoked out by his big burn. A tactic that now painted him in shame.

The area around the gate showed the remnants of a siege. The ground a mess of muddy debris, wadded and soggy blankets, bags, pieces of broken picket signs and puddles reddened by blood.

Beldare stood at the gate basking in the warmth of the morning sun as he pondered his next course of action. Across the way, he noticed one of the monster tires on a logging vehicle was punctured, its hard, knobby tread bell-bottomed in a pool of water. This was to be the day the lumbermen would start cutting their road.

A rumbling joggled the ground. Must be them now, he presumed. Sure enough, a NorCal company truck pulled up. Curt Hardin at the wheel with that perma-smirk on his face.

"Where've you been?" Hardin strode from the truck, outfitted for hunting elk. An untucked woodland camouflage shirt, matching pants, and black combat boots laced to the shin. "Thought we lost you."

"Spent the night in the woods," Beldare said.

"I told you not to go wandering off."

"No, you did not."

"Yeah, well Hersh is pissed. He expected a full reporting from you. But it's cool, I filled him in." Hardin caught sight of the flat tire on the buncher. "Motherfuhhh." He pulled out his cell phone and took a couple pictures. "Got any idea how much those tires cost?"

Another vehicle approached. Dixon, driving the Humvee.

Hardin waved at him, and pointed at Beldare.

"Look who spent the night out."

Stepping from the cab, Dixon checked out the short man. "That was some gully washer. Looks like you managed to stay dry."

"Okay, okay, so much for small talk." Hardin unfolded a topographical map and propped it on the front fender. "More to do. Let's see what crazy ideas you got for this next ..."

"My work is done here," Beldare interjected.

"Not so fast. Nobody's done. Not yet. We got one more deal. This here is the Sweetwater sector. It's a beast of an area. I lined up a tracker guy to help us."

Beldare didn't look at Hardin's map. He glared at Dixon. "Why was I kept in the dark?"

Hardin and Dixon exchanged snap-glances.

"Have you seen it?" Beldare's question resounded like an order. "Have you watched a person being slowly absorbed into the trunk of a tree?"

They feigned ignorance. Then Hardin asked, "Who told you about that?"

"I saw it with my own eyes." Beldare pointed at Hardin. "And you knew this."

"We'd seen a video, heard some rumors like everybody else. That doesn't mean it's real," Dixon said.

"Whoa! You say you saw one? In a tree? Where? Back in there?" Hardin shot a finger at the ex-action camp. "I knew it! Oh my god, you gotta show me. You gotta take me there right now!"

Beldare glared at Hardin. "I don't have to show you anything. You've been holding this back from me all along."

"Like the chief here said, we weren't sure of nothing. We needed to have it verified."

"Verified? By whom? Who would you hire, a forensic mutation specialist? All you need are your own two eyes."

"Yeah, well maybe we thought it was a crock o'shit, you dig? Some dopehead's idea of amusement," Hardin reasoned. "A stunt, ya'know, I mean who'd believe any of this shit, right? Riiight."

"Hersh knew. Which explains his secrecy."

"You got to admit it's a freak of nature," Hardin said.

"So you *have* seen it."

"Bits and pieces at the mill..." Hardin confessed. "And some witnessed accounts."

"And once you had actual proof of this freak of nature as you call it, when was that exactly?"

The two were silent.

Beldare answered his own question. "Well I can tell you, it was long before I was brought in, that's when."

"Listen mister, we really didn't need you," said Hardin. "Hersh demanded your 'superior tactical supervision.' But we didn't. You were dialed in to the depth that he decreed." Hardin refolded the map and pointed a corner of it at Beldare. "Only a handful of people know. And once they're gone, which we shall dispense with in short shrift, this will all be a camp-fire story."

Beldare looked up at the enormous trees that dwarfed them, working to contain his anger, sniffling air out his stuffed nostrils.

"You're upset. You were kept out of the loop. We get it." Hardin turned to Dixon. "Better that he knows now."

Dixon didn't offer a reply. He lifted a pack of Camels from his shirt pocket, tapped one out and lit up.

"So… are you with us?" Hardin rubbed his jaw and spat. "Cause we're going to clear Sweetwater out completely and put an end to all this shit once and for all."

"You don't get it." Beldare threw his arms up into the air. "You people."

"Oh, we get it, we got it, and now we stop it."

"No, you don't. You're sinking in the quicksand of your own crap." Beldare turned his attention to Dixon. "This supersedes spreadsheets and job security and grubbing stock-holders. This is Mother Nature speaking to *us*. As for me, I manipulate the filth and greed of *human* nature. I alter the course of corporate debacles, I make cesspools disappear, but I never, ever meddle with *Mother!*"

"Mother nature my ass, this is sorcery," Hardin squared off with Beldare. "Hell, they're probably cutting heads off chickens in there, and if we don't stop it, we'll be sucked in by their satanastic powers."

Beldare glared at Hardin. "Are you that dense?"

Dixon stood squint-eyed and mute, sucking smoke.

"Listen little man, you were hired to do a job." Hardin tapped the map on Beldare's chest.

"Don't you touch me." Beldare axed the map out of Hardin's hand with his stick onto the wet gravel.

"Yeah, then you can walk, you stunted ugly fuck."

"That's the first good idea I've heard come out of your mouth. Yes. I *will* walk." Beldare stroked the knobby top of his walking stick. "Please thank Mr. Hersh for hiring me. The experience has been... well, words fail." He turned to Dixon. "Oh, and if you see Beverly, give her my thanks as well." He planted the redwood branch on the ground and set off.

Hardin sprung to his truck, unclipped the hand gun from the door's side panel and took aim between Beldare's shoulder blades.

Dixon knew it was for show, but still played along. "No-no. Hey! Pump the brakes. That's not going to solve anything."

"He knows."

"So do I. You going to shoot me?"

Hardin exhaled a snort, lowered the weapon, and tossed it on the driver's seat.

Dixon took a last tug on his cigarette, flicked it on the ground and extinguished it with the steel tip of his cowboy boot, only to pull another from the pack.

"Nobody'd believe him anyway." Hardin plucked the map off the road and slapped it against his thigh to shake off the water.

Dixon didn't say anything. He took drag after drag watching Beldare stride away, tapping his walking stick to the metronome of his steps.

"We don't need his pissant tactics," Hardin spouted. "Planting stories, burning bushes. Enough of that shit. Time to make some noise the old-fashioned way."

Smoke cannoned out Dixon's nostrils, followed by a bull-grunt from the back of his throat. His eyes locked on the squat man's body shrinking in the distance.

"So what are we waiting for?" Hardin snapped. "Hel-*lo*? Sweetwater?" He started to unfold the map. "Now here's how this is going to…"

"What would the Duke do?" Dixon interrupted.

"The who?"

"The Duke. John Wayne."

"He'd finish the job, that's what he'd do."

Dixon opened the door of the Humvee, reached in and grabbed the satellite phone.

"You calling John Wayne?"

"It's me," Dixon spoke into the unit. "Cancel that operation. Repeat, cancel it… that's affirmative. We are *not* going to proceed."

"What are you doing?"

"Calling off the dogs." Dixon crushed his cigarette out as Beldare disappeared around a bend in the road. "Far too much damage has been done in the name of a lie." He stepped up on the running board and slid behind the wheel.

"What? You've got a most wanted man on the run. Remember Rolf Zetzer? What you wanna bet he's holed up in Sweetwater? Now, if I'm not mistaken it's your sworn duty to apprehend that man. So do what you're getting paid to do— your fucking job!"

"Duke wouldn't do it." Dixon lit up the engine. "You're on your own."

Hardin looked stupefied. "You shittin' me? I don't believe this! Okay, fine. Go! I don't need you. I've got all the help I…"

The Humvee motored away.

Hardin burned. "What would the Duke do?" he mimicked Dixon sarcastically. "He just got you fired, that's what he did!"

Hardin climbed back into his truck. He was about to call Hersh and share the latest development, but thought better of it. He'd only come across as a whiner. Instead he punched ten numbers into the truck's phone— numbers Hersh had given him of an unnamed shooter.

Beldare walked up the dusty road with a spring in his step, absorbing the warmth of an ever-lightening sky as he passed under the stately arms of the giant trees. A smile shone on his face. He felt young, carefree, like a kid again. And with it came a sudden, irresistible urge to listen to Franz Liszt on a stereo, and eat orange marmalade, straight out of the jar, with a spoon.

39.
Looks like I'm rollin' with Zorro

The back road was overgrown with vegetation. Once grooved by the wheels of a horse drawn cart a century past, and decades later bulldozed and spread with crushed rock, left untended, the forest reached out to reclaim its land.

Branches screeched across the fenders and roof of Hardin's four-door company truck as it lurched and splashed through potholes following the tread of freshly engraved tire tracks. He slowed to a stop when he saw an SUV parked at a fallen tree that blocked the road.

And there she stood, the look-at-me-don't temptress from the airport, only she'd become someone else— a ninja assassin with spiky, toothpick-short black hair.

"Well, lookie here." Hardin pulled up to her, window down. "Name's Curt Hardin, and you are?" He didn't wait for a response. He killed the engine and stepped out. "Hersh said I'd be meeting up with a trigger. Never expected it'd be you."

"Life's just a cabaret of shitty surprises." Dee Rotter had been waiting for an hour, since noon, arms crossed, antsy.

"No, I sure didn't have you pegged for no bounty hunter. Bad read. And just look at you."

Which he did.

Her slender, acrobat's body was clothed in a black, skin-tight unitard that ended in thin leather slippers, like ballet flats. She had a gun belt tightened around her right thigh and hip pouches on her waist belt, obviously for ammo.

"Looks like I'm rollin' with Zorro." Hardin turned his attention from her to the road ahead.

"Where's your army?" Dee asked.

Hardin didn't answer that. He didn't want to explain what went down with Dixon. How he felt deserted and naked without police support. He kicked the log with his battle boot. "So this is the end of the line."

The location was Hardin's call— the closest to Sweetwater Woods by road. He didn't foresee a log jam. He looked back in the direction they'd come.

"Okay now, where the hell's my tracker?"

"Your who?"

"The guy who's gonna lead us to their nest, that's who."

"Looks like you've been stood up."

"Better not be."

"Can't take a step without him, huh?"

"In case you don't know it, and you don't, this is one rugged area, thick woods, steep terrain, easy to get yourself lost in the blink of one of those lashes of yours."

Hardin tossed his cell phone on the driver's seat. Zero chance of picking up a signal in this remote forest. He grabbed his map and unfolded it on the hood.

"Sweetwater... Sweetwater... okay, here's about where we are... and here's... yeah, right *there*." Hardin tapped a thin, wiggly line on the map. "This is the same year-round stream that runs through the North Fork Forest back behind their action camp."

"I was at that camp," Dee said. "That's how I heard about this place."

"You're the one who tipped off Hersh?"

"Correct."

"Better than my spy. Well in that case, can you tell me where they're holed up?"

"Don't know that."

"How about the number of people in there?"

"No, and I don't care. I'm only here for one," Dee plucked a photograph out of her hip pouch.

Hardin instantly recognized the person. "Huh." He gave a stone face, unmoved. He wouldn't give Dee the pleasure of seeing how impressed he was with her being a professional contract killer. Or show any trace of alarm that her target was Christy Jones.

"If you see her, give me a shout." Dee slipped the photo back into the pouch on her belt. "She's my prize. Mine and mine only."

This was not the same woman Hardin met at the airport. The one he wanted to bed, slack-jawed at first sight. Her face had become hawk-like, the sea green eyes hardened to nail heads. The once sultry voice clipped sharp.

"And what do you intend to do with her body?" Hardin asked.

"Feed the wildlife."

Hardin folded and pocketed the map. He looked back up the road. Still no sign of his tracker.

Sound carries upward in these canyons. From a treed slope, thirty yards above them, Paul Drummond could hear their every word. He'd expected to see Hardin and at least half a dozen armed men mustering, with dogs even. But if it was just Hardin and the cat woman, all the better. Still, the strange woman's ominous vibe gave him a chill of foreboding, and he didn't scare easily. He stood motionless in the shadow of a redwood watching Hardin lift two belts of 12-gauge shotgun shells from the truck, which he shouldered, crisscrossing his chest Zapata-style.

"Alright, time to gun up."

Dee rolled her eyes.

"So, you got your agenda." Hardin strapped a wide belt around his waist and slid two pistol-grip Roadwarrior shotguns into side holsters. "Mine is to eliminate all of the tree mutations. Destroy the monsters, and with your help expire any undesirable witnesses."

Dee wasn't sucked in by the rumors. Only the whereabouts of the Jones girl aroused her interest. Whatever demonic human sacrifices going on in the woods were not her concern.

"Sorry, can't help you there. Your business is your business. And I'm fine with going our separate ways at any time."

"Whatever," Hardin said. Shooting another human being didn't faze him. A few years back, he'd joined a search party of Sheriff deputies on a manhunt to capture an escaped convict who'd broken into a fishing shack. Seeing the twenty-two-year old peeking out the door, Hardin drilled two bullets into his chest before the guy could lift his arms in surrender. The thrill of that kill faded much too fast. But now it was coming back, revving his blood. And in this case, these people were the real thing— bona fide NorCal enemies.

He stared at the road behind them, listening.

"Looks like your tracker guide got lost. So what are we waiting for, your courage to kick in?"

"Ever been in a real wilderness before, Dee? If that's really your name."

"Yeah."

"I mean all alone?"

"I did backwoods training."

"Nothing like this I bet. Orienteering out here is a whole 'nother mother."

Even Hardin was apprehensive about finding his way back without Drum.

"Then stay. I'm going in." Dee stepped away.

Hardin watched her bend at the waist and set the SUV's keys in the shadow of the front tire.

"My hunch is their nest is somewhere near the stream, or not a far hike from it. I say we stay on the road until it dead-ends at the water, then follow it in. There used to be an old homestead back in there, so I'm told. Probably come across an old track that leads in to it, long overgrown." He blanched and rubbed his upper jaw. The toothache firing up.

"What's with your mouth?"

"Nothing."

The two straddled the fallen log and headed down the narrow forest road. Hardin crept along its shoulder. "Look for foot paths, a trailhead, any clues, a busted twig, shoe impressions, and listen with wide open ears."

After they were out of sight, Drum descended the hill and took to the road. He stopped at the woman's SUV, palmed the car keys she'd hidden behind the tire and trailed after them.

Hardin and Dee took to the winding road in watchful silence. After twenty-five minutes Dee said, "At some point we're going to need to split up, 'cause you're going to scare my prey away with those bone-busters of yours."

"Shh!" Hardin stopped abruptly. "Hear that?"

"What?"

"The water sound."

Dee stopped. "No."

"Maybe it's time to brush up on your backwoods training, darling. That's the stream up ahead."

Dee shut her eyes to listen. "Oh, that."

"Yeah, that."

They took to the fringe of the clear running waterway, swatting at mosquitoes. Adrenaline surged through Dee's blood. No longer did she need to put on a cheery, sisterly act for those scruffy, hyper-pious tree huggers at base camp with their dirty fingernails and yellow teeth. Now she could be her total potent self, kill mode, where rage and pleasure fused to a fixed point between the cross-hairs. This was her fourth contract. It was out in the open. No waiting in shadows, clocking routines, slinking around underground parking garages. And she was going in light— a single, 9mm Machauser Sterben, operator-fitted with exo-suppressor and micro-baffling for added sound absorption. The silencer made the firearm weighty, but she could handle it. Simply locate the target, end the chick's life, and bolt. Seventy-five thousand bouquets. Not a bad payday for four days in the field. More than enough to move her twin sister back into that private mental healthcare facility in Vegas. And, if the documentary dude happens by, that'll make a sweet gratuity.

But first things first. She needed to put some distance between her and this swaggering prick.

40.
Your inside man's gone rogue

Dixon's face burned brick red as he paced the driveway at the base of the porch stairs that led up to the lodge. He had picked up Beldare jauntily walking along that North Fork road and taken him back to the lodge to fetch the man's luggage and drive him to the Eureka-Arcata airport. On the way to the lodge, Beldare schooled Dixon on how to salvage his reputation: "You write a letter stating your vehement rejection of the tactics employed by Ingot and NorCal over the past week, such as hiring vigilantes and the forced evacuation by burning poison oak, which caused grave injury and hospitalization. How you refuse to participate in any further activity and are taking a leave of absence, or mental health time to recover, so on and so forth. Send the letters or emails to NorCal administrators, to Richard Hersh himself, and to your local government officials."

While at the lodge Dixon planned to "shred, delete, and incinerate all materials with thorough immediacy" that connected him to the death and havoc that transpired. Minimize all trace of his involvement, trash admissible emails that spelled out their game plan, along with the false news reports he and Hardin drummed up.

Dixon told Beldare he was willing to accept responsibility for his actions. "In due course," Beldare cautioned. "But that doesn't mean you have to make a preemptive confession, or pushpin every scrap of evidence on the walls of City Hall."

Just thinking about breaking from Hardin and NorCal's grip felt liberating to Dixon. Everybody's in service to another, but he could now choose who that would not be. Unfortunately, it meant letting go of his budding ambition to be mayor, which, although tough to give up, relieved one more stressor from his life. Now he could go clamming, surf fishing, hitch the Airstream to his truck and tool up the Oregon coast with his new friend, Naomi. And if nothing surfaced, all the better.

Except something had surfaced, and that something was lying on the porch of the lodge.

Nostrils flared, Dixon punched Hardin's numbers on his cell phone a second time and pressed the unit to his ear.

"Come on… come on…"

Up on the porch, blocking the front door, lay a large bundle mummy-wrapped in a dirty tarp.

"Pick up godammit!"

Rosco's exhumed body had been dumped there, very recently judging by how no critters had feasted on it. The dead man's rigid right forearm poked through a fold in the tarp, its flesh in tatters, exposing the elbow and knuckle bones, stippled black with dried blood. The hand's middle finger stood stiff at attention, its nail hanging by a hinge of skin, pointing to the overcast sky where a buzzard spun in slow, delirious wheels.

Hardin didn't answer the call.

"This is Dixon. Your inside man's gone rogue. He left notice at the lodge. Copy me on this. And you better watch your ass!"

41.
Clear the boots

Sunlight played on the crest of a small waterfall, flecking it with dazzling gems. Jim and Christy sat side by side on the bank of the stream pumping water with handheld filters, then pouring the potable water into two dromedary bags.

While they worked the pumps, they made plans to leave Sweetwater Woods. They'd wait until the others returned to the camp, stay at Mae's for a night, then pick up Jim's wallet at the base camp and bus back to the city. Christy would deal with her contempt of court offense. Jim would take the sneakily borrowed gear and video he'd shot to *News Bang*, and return the camera to Gomez. They'd face the music of their digressions. Many apologies. No excuses.

Jim thought of Miko, his life-saving nurse who now lived in Portland. How he wanted Christy to meet her. And Christy was eager for Jim to meet her father. All they could promise each other, given the financial and legal unknowns, was that they would find a way to combine their lives.

Paul Drummond kept a cautious distance behind Hardin and the cat woman, soundlessly padding the loamy earth among ferns and grasses that edged the stream. Hardin was no dummy in the wild. He stayed close to the water like a life line. Drum had taught him well, back in the day. Maybe too well.

In his teens, Drum ventured deep into Sweetwater woods. He remembered this rivulet, which at that time ran swift with winter rains. He also recalled a derelict cabin, farther in, hidden among the trees.

Hardin stopped walking. Something gripped his attention. "See that cleft mark." He kneeled, pointing to a depression in the mud. "Rain's disintegrated most of the track, but that looks to me like the imprint of a boot heel."

Dee slapped at mosquitoes as Hardin surveyed the area, looking for more indicators. All he found was a deer trail, leading south into the woods. He waded across the ankle-deep stream, crouched beside a massive, moss-covered stone on the opposite shore, and finding another suspicious indentation, rose to his feet.

"Okay, we cross here."

Dee glared with dread at the stream. If there was one thing she hated most, next to having her period, it was sticking her feet in cold water.

As Jim and Christy worked their water filters, Jim's producer's mind made plans.

"After we're done here, I'll go shoot establishing shots of the forest, get panoramas from up in the lookout. Then I'll start organizing the footage, make selects, start making a chunk cut with the editing program on the laptop."

Christy stopped pumping and smiled at him, feeling for the first time that everything's going to be good from now on.

"I'd still like to interview some lumber company people for their perspective," Jim said.

"I know just the one who can set you up."

"Great, and hey, what if we weave in your story? About your dog and what they did?"

"No-no, don't make it about me."

"The doc will need some personal stories for viewers to relate."

"Fine, just not mine."

"Whee-woh! Whee-woh!"

Christy cranked her neck. "Hear that?"

"Whee-woh! Whee-woh!"

"The bird?"

"That's Kip's call." Christy's face fell slack. "Something's up. We better get back to camp."

They jammed the filters and dromedary bags in their packs and headed up the slope.

"It can only mean one thing— an intruder," Christy said.

"Could be hikers, or a hunter, right?"

"Doesn't matter, we can't let them see the tree people."

They waited at the lookout tree as Kip descended to a low branch, binoculars dangling around his neck. He pointed to the southwest and held up two fingers.

Christy gestured for Kip to stay in the tree, be their eyes, and took Jim by the arm. "Let's clear the boots."

"Who is it?"

"Don't know, but we need to ditch the boots and cover the openings with branches. Whatever will camouflage them."

"There's five, right?"

"Yes, and they're spread way out in different groves."

"I kind of remember the one where Holly was at yesterday." Jim gestured. "Up and around over there."

"Good, you take that tree. Hide it well. If you hear one sharp bird whistle from Kip, that means all clear. If you hear two, it's trouble."

"Hold on. What about the camera and all the video footage in the tent."

"Oh, right, okay then, go get that first and, and… we'll meet up at Holly's tree."

"See you there." Jim started off.

"Wait." She pulled Jim to her by his sweatshirt and buried a kiss on his lips. "Be safe."

After fifteen minutes of hiking along the north side of the stream, Hardin and Dee came across a mishmash of depressions in the bank.

"Here we go… look at this. We got two, maybe three people. Fresh, too." Hardin tip-toed the periphery, visibly excited, tracing two sets of prints, one shallow, the other treaded, definitely made by boots. "And they went…" He pointed up the rise. "… thataway."

Dee held back. "You go ahead." She'd let Hardin stir up the chicken coop, while she lingered there and nailed her target when she fled the roost.

"Suit yourself."

Drum stayed back. He couldn't follow Hardin without the cat woman detecting him.

Dee arched her lithe body, stretching her spine. She worked her shoulders up and down, loosening the muscles. When she started doing knee bends a mosquito intervened, circling her head. She spent the next minute slapping the air, until finally, extending her bare wrist, she waited for the pest to land on the vein and slap-smashed it to atoms.

Christy didn't bother to look inside the tree. She picked up the pair of hiking boots at its base and lobbed them into the brush. Then she scavenged the area for branches and flat slabs of decomposing bark to lean against the opening. The others at Sweetwater talked about practicing a drill to conceal the tree people, pull tents and hammocks, clear out the cabin and disappear. But that was just a lot of talk now.

Christy had half-covered the opening when it hit her: The maps! The intruders can't get the maps! Kip, she remembered. He stashed them in the cabin.

The thought spurred her into a frenzy to finish hiding the goosepen.

Kip sensed the presence of the man hiking up from the south before he actually saw him through binoculars. He was armed and advanced sneakily, his head on a swivel. He'd stop behind one tree, look this way and that, then move on to the next.

Kip tight-roped out on a high branch to better identify what looked to be a hunter dressed in camou colors and combat boots.

Reaching the grove where the land leveled off, Hardin spotted a tent, pitched between two trees. He eased the stubby shotgun from its holster and quietly approached, cocking his head, alert for someone inside. He tapped the nylon fabric with the nose of the weapon. Nothing stirred. Peering into the tent he saw an empty sleeping bag and some clothing. He straightened up and slowly rotated his body, panning the site. No one around. He kicked at two of the corner stakes, flattened them under his boot, releasing the guide wires. The tent tipped, shimmied and collapsed. He lifted his chin and rubbed his upper jaw.

That's when Kip recognized a face he'd seen before.

NorCal. Bad sign.

He whistled twice, took a breath, then repeated the distinct, high-pitched warning call.

Christy had just finished concealing the cavity in the tree when Kip's sharp whistles sounded. She didn't hesitate. She raced to the cabin for the maps.

Jim didn't register Kip's alarm as he headed up the slope to find Holly's tree after retrieving the can muttered. He

"Somebody's gotta be somewhere," studied the ground backed away from the fallen tent posite directions. He where two tramped paths led o right shoulder, lightly leaned the shotgun barrel a ger. "My-nee-mo," he said, tapping his index finger o

and took the path that hooked to the northeast. He hadn't gone far when he heard a dull stamping, followed by a rustling, whisk-whisk sound.

Christy Jones was not the sly type. She didn't know how to creep around sneakily. Even if she could, there was no time to waste. She sprinted in a blind rush, slapping back ferns and branches to get to the cabin and collect the maps before anyone found them.

A lone figure came into Hardin's view, swiftly striding through the woods from the north. Long legs. Some kind of red headband. He gave chase, lifted the barrel of the shotgun to the sky, yanked the trigger and blew a hole in the stillness.

Christy shrieked and held up. Shockwaves reverberated through the forest. Wings of unseen birds fluttered high overhead.

"That got your attention, redtop." Hardin said, marching toward the woman whose back was to him. He cracked open the shotgun, flicked out the empty shell, re-loaded, and snapped it shut.

Jim had just reached the grove with Holly's tree when he heard the discharge. He spun toward the sound, rocked with fear.

Kip was crossing to another redwood, limb to limb. When the shotgun fired, he slid the slingshot out from his hip pocket. With his other hand, he unzipped the fanny pack and fingered a clear glass marble.

Christy whirled around, winded and shaken from the report.

"Well look rookie..." Hardin's voice rose an octave seeing the woman. He lowered the shotgun in line with her chest.

Christy's teeth clenched. She recognized him too— the slits for eyes and cock. demeanor. 'Hyena' others called him. She never knew his real name, but she'd seen that fixed grin at the back of rallies and public meetings. Always at the back, scoping out the people, tattooing their faces to memory.

"Yeah, you know me alright," Hardin said.

"You have no authority here," she spat.

"And neether-neither do you. So that puts us in a zone where anything goes." Hardin tipped his head back and called out, "Hey-hey, I found your prize!"

To Christy's left, a few feet beyond a couple clumps of sword ferns, the land dropped off— a deep, seepage ravine shingled with maiden-hair ferns, its bottom thick with rhododendron bushes. She inched her way in that direction.

"Whoa!" Hardin barked. "Don't you move a tit. Got someone who wants to meet you. And while we wait, you're going to tell me where your friends are."

Christy didn't answer.

"Like Rolf? Rolf Zetzer?"

"Gone."

"Ah, so he *was* here. I knew it."

She nodded, thinking the man had come to capture the fugitive.

"And where'd he go?"

"Didn't say."

"Who else is here?"

Christy didn't answer. She dug the toes of her boots into the spongy earth to gain traction.

"Let me put it to you this way, I'm looking for the ones *in* the trees."

Christy shook her head. "Don't know what you're talking about."

"Oh, you know perfectly well what I'm talking about." Her body flinched

Christy decided to make

in anticipation of bolting

"Nah-nah! Don't move now. I'm not going to shoot you, not unless you try to run."

"No, but I'm shooting you!" Someone shouted from the trees.

Hardin swung his eyes toward the man's voice.

"Smile for the camera!"

It was Jim, twenty yards away, leaning half-hidden against the bark of a tree recording the scene.

Hardin caught a glimmer of the camera lens, offered a wide smile, then stretched his neck and hollered, "Hey Zorro! Where the hell?"

Neither Jim or Christy could see who he was calling. But Kip could. Below him on the ground a slender figure, dressed all in black, stepped panther-like across a puzzle of entwined redwood roots.

"*Whee-woh! Whee-woh!*" He whistled 'trouble' again, as the strange cat woman veered toward Hardin's voice.

Kip recognized her face in profile. The one he'd pranked with the camera case.

Dee emerged from behind a tree, a dark visage, as if a shadow just detached from the ground, grown legs and began walking.

"There you are," Hardin said.

His body stymied Dee's line of sight. She side-stepped to her left and seeing the red headband and then the features of the woman's face, her heart leaped: Yes, that's her, alright. She smacked her lips as if savoring a delicacy.

Hardin said. "You're welcome. And I'll take a finder's fee, thank you."

"Out of my much."

"Gladly," Hard death, heh-heh." He looked at Christy. "Have a nice

The cat woman closed in, arms extended straight from the shoulders, two hands molded around a handgun with a long barrel, its aim fixed center mass.

"Who the devil...?" Christy muttered. But this was no time for introductions.

Hardin rambled off. "I'm going for the camera dude."

Dee wanted him too, and for a distracted second her eyes darted in Hardin's direction.

Christy tucked her knees and kicked off. She plowed through the high ferns and leapt for the ravine.

Dee whirled, trigger-poised, tracking the runner, when something punched her between the shoulder blades, knocking her off kilter.

Pfit! The gun went off.

Christy tumbled down the slippery slope and into a dense cluster of rhododendrons.

Stunned, Dee spotted the marble as it rolled on the ground at her heels. She spun back and charged after Christy *pfft! pfft!* firing round after round into the flowering thicket, leaves and pink petals bursting to bits in the air.

Christy disentangled her arms from the branches and crawled on her stomach along the bottom of the rain-drenched ravine. Finally stopping to catch her breath behind a lichen-encrusted log.

Kip took to the air, leaping from branch to branch, tree to tree.

Dee unsnapped her ammo pouch, an[d] *grily slammed* in a fresh clip. Whoever hurled that *le will die today.* She crept along the ledge of the ra*ther had* lunged, eyes and weapon hing*ther in outstretched* hands, bar taut, primed for *vement below, the first* titter of a leaf.

Kip lemur-swung his body to a lower branch, frustrated with himself. He'd meant to strike her head, clock her senseless. He worked to calm his thumping heart as he placed a golf ball into his slingshot.

There she stood, below him, fifteen yards away. Kip wanted to get closer, but there wasn't time. He drew back the webbing to his chin and let fly.

The golf ball struck Dee in the elbow, knocking the gun out of her hands. "Gaah!" She grimaced, stooped to retrieve her weapon before scuttling behind the shield of the nearest tree, pissed and hissing, her elbow a screaming fire. She tugged it tight against her torso. "You are dead. You hear me! *Dead*." She scanned the area for the culprit, first at ground level, then elevating her sight higher and higher, up the ladder of branches. Something there. Someone's head. *Pfft! Pfft! Pfft!* She emptied the magazine.

Hardin reached the tree where the camera dude had stood. He hunkered down, studying the impressions in the forest floor as Drum once taught him, letting the tracks guide like arrows pointing the way. These showed little tread, but a crushed puffball mushroom was definitely fresh. More impressions led him to an open glade. And there, looking oddly forlorn at the foot of a redwood, he spotted a scuffed pair of boots. The once thick carpet of dry needles around them had been trodden down in front of a charred opening in the tree.

Peering in the darkness, Hardin recoiled. "Oh my fuggin' god!" The sight of the dead person stiffly encased in a spider-like web keel him back. "It's one of *THEM*." He waited for his hands to stop shaking. Then, without a second look, he pressed his left side aming shotgun into the open the trunk, stuck the muzzle of the He dropped the weapon, fired. A pulpy, glop resounded.
e other shotgun, extended it

deeper into the tree and fired again. The blast spattered fleshy nubs out of the hole, some sticking to his pants.

"Ahh yuck!" he shuddered.

Dee clamped her teeth as she tried to rub away the throbbing pain in her elbow where the golf ball chipped the bone. She braced her back against the thick, cushiony bark of the redwood. Things had changed. Now her focus was split between her target and being a target. She hoped that distant barrage was Hardin hitting its mark. She listened for any sounds, only to hear the bustle and screech of alarmed birds high in the canopy. Nothing from the ravine.

Dee stilled her breath, coaching herself: Give her time. She'll come out. Just wait right here for as long as it takes and then nail the bitch… if I haven't already.

She had.

Christy lay bleeding beside the decaying log. A bullet had entered her back, kidney high, and exited just above her pelvic bone. The scalding wound convulsed her body. And with Hardin's gun blasts, she concluded the worst. Choking back heartache, she mashed her lips to muffle her cries.

For an endless minute, the forest turned eerily quiet. Then came the dull, yet unmistakable tamp of footfalls. Someone near. Christy tried to hide in the log's shadow as best she could. Soon she spied legs descending the bank of the ravine, followed by a guitar case and gear bag, and finally Jim's face.

"Christy, it's alright, it's me." he whispered as he skidded down the slope and crawled on all fours to her side.

"Ahh," she sighed, relieved to see Jim alive. She waved for him to come close. Her face muddied, hair down, sopping.

Breathing hard, he knelt and pressed his cheek against hers. "You okay?"

She bowed her head. "To see you, yes, but…" she moaned, "…no, I'm…" She lifted her right hand, revealed the wound in her side, blood wicking through her dirtied travel shirt.

His eyes blinked hard, unwilling to deliver the grim image to his brain. "Oh nooo," he gulped. He could see it was critical. He unstrapped the backpack, which still held the dromedary bag.

"Where's your scarf?"

She shook her head.

He pulled off his sweatshirt, wrapped it around Christy's torso, and set his hands against the wound to stanch the bleeding.

Christy cringed, then whimpered.

Jim wanted to ask what all this was about. Were they after her? Were they after the tree people? But there was no time. She needed immediate medical help. But how to do that with these killers stalking them.

Rising on his haunches, Jim peeked over the big log and through the thicket of rhododendron branches. He had an idea: create a decoy and make a run for it. He opened the backpack, pulled out the water-laden bag, reared back and hurled it up the ravine as far from them his arm could heave.

Kip landed on the earth. He was out of marbles, rocks, and golf balls. All he carried was a pair of binoculars and an all-purpose, fixed blade knife in a sheath on his belt. No match for guns. He needed to get to the place where he'd smacked the cat woman and retrieve his golf ball. But he'd lost sight of her. Looking around he spotted a swatch of red snagged among the ferns across the way.

A crash jolted the forest, like branches cracking, followed by the soft report of shots fired in rapid succession.

There she was, the panther, sidling down the slope of the ravine, gun poised.

Kip side-stepped behind bushes and trees, padding his way to Christy's red scarf which he patiently disentangled. He stashed it inside his shirt and backed away, only to bump into a solid form. It wasn't a tree but someone with large, moccasin-shod feet.

Reacting by reflex, Kip's hand lunged for his knife as he spun around.

Drum seized Kip's wrist and lifted a finger to his lips. He knew Kip had lost faith in him. Most everybody had. He looked squarely into Kip's fierce eyes, set his right palm on the young man's heart and said, "I'm with *you*."

Kip eased his grip on the knife. He believed the big man. He tugged Christy's scarf from his shirt and shared his plan, twirling a finger toward the forested canyons to the east.

Drum got the message and nodded.

Kip poked Drum in the chest, then pointed to the west, to the cabin. "Get the maps," he mouthed silently.

Drum shook his head and whispered, "Maps?"

Hardin approached the cabin. "It's over, people. Come out now. You don't want the other option."

After blowing apart the morbid human entity inside that tree, he lost the camera dude's tracks and decided to find his way back to the tent he'd flattened earlier and take the footpath that snaked off in the other direction.

It led to the old Weaver cabin. Not a word or sound came from inside. He circled the rundown building and peeked into the one and only window, its gray, weathered muntins crooked, glassless.

The place was vacant, but recently active.

The wooden door groaned on rusty hinges as Harden urged it open with his shotgun and stepped inside.

He found an ice chest full of food. Plates and cups on shelves. Buckets of silverware and water. In the center of the room stood a wide redwood plank table with foldable camp stools. In the corners, four canvas sleeping cots.

Hardin slid out a cardboard box from under the table. It was full of curious items: a ceramic mortar and pestle, a brown grocery bag full of some sponge-like substance, and a jumbo-sized Ziploc bag of white pasty stuff. Drugs, he figured, pulling the seams apart.

"What is this shit?" He set the weapon on the table, stuck a finger in the sticky batter and daubed his tongue with it. "Blech!" He spat it out on the floorboards and dropped the baggie back in the sack.

His eyes wandered the space and stopped at a high shelf. Something up there. A long cylinder. He reached up and nudged the cardboard tube down.

"What do we got here?" Hardin popped the end cap, and shook out the rolled-paper contents. He slid the rubber bands off and unfurled it across the table, revealing a topographical regional map. Curled within it, an aerial photograph, both freckled with red dots.

Dee heard shuffling, followed by a voice, hushed and urgent, floating in the air beyond the ravine: "Christy, come on, I've got you."

She heard the crunch of twigs, the swish of leaves brushed aside, and saw a flash of red flicker between columns of trees.

There! Her headband!

"Hurry up." Came the muted voice. "Let's get out of here."

Must be that camera guy with her. Alright then, two birds…

Dee unwound the silencer from the Machauser to lighten the load on her bruised elbow. Sound was not an issue out here in the boonies as she first thought. She pouched the suppressor and took off in a brisk stride where she'd last seen her target's red scarf.

Crouched behind the log, Christy and Jim heard her name being called. She thought she recognized the voice, but her mind fluttered as her torso spasmed from the scalding bullet wound.

Climbing the side of the ravine, Jim scanned the forest to see who'd called Christy's name. He saw the cat woman's silhouette lope off through the woods, seemingly beckoned by the voice. No sign of the man with the shotguns. Or Kip.

"She's gone." Jim slid back. "Christy, let's go. We need to get you to a doctor."

Christy shook her head. "Too far.

"Come on." He extended his hand. "I'll help."

"I won't make it, Jim. Too much blood."

"We have to try."

"That man…" she gulped. "He'll see us. He'll kill us both. And you need to…"

Her eyes misted as blood dribbled out the sweatshirt onto her fingers.

This can't be happening! Who would want to murder Christy? And why? Jim sagged, overcome with helplessness. But she was right. There wasn't going to be an ambulance. The nearest medic was miles and miles away.

Without speaking, Jim and Christy came to the same conclusion together: only one thing to do.

She clutched his arm. "Yes… yes!"

Kip's scarf diversion was working. He hustled along, bobbing the bait from the end of a branch, coaxing the cat woman farther and farther away from the ravine, like a matador taunting a bull with fleeting glimpses of red.

42.
Look, it's all here

Hardin had just figured out the meaning of the red spots on the aerial photo when a shadow devoured his body, making him lunge for the shotgun on the table.

Drum's large frame filled the doorway.

"Kee-ryst!" Hardin stamped his foot. "Gimme a heart attack!"

Drum stepped across the threshold, his eyes prowling the cabin, taking inventory before fixing them on Hardin.

"Hooph!" Hardin exhaled his fright. "So where you been?"

"Who's the woman?"

"Never mind that. Look, it's all here." Hardin swatted the enlarged satellite photo. "Where every frickin' one of those freaks are at. Got a bigger topo here that shows even more."

"Who?"

"Who do you think? I just blew one to smithereens. Shoulda seen it. What a horror show! Now you can help me find the rest. They're spread out all around here."

Drum stepped over to the table.

"Tell me you're packing pain killers," Hardin said.

Drum shook his head.

"Shit. I got this mean muthafuggin' toothache. Here, take a look." He hooked a finger in his mouth, titled his head back and opened wide. "Whaddya see?"

"A dental bill," Drum said, peering over Hardin's shoulder to the dots on the aerial image.

"Yeah, well, the sooner we take care of this, the sooner I get to a dentist." Hardin tapped the stock of the shotgun on the table. "Now here's how this is going to go."

43.
Please, let me down

Christy flinched with every step, sputtering breaths. She had one arm wrapped around Jim's shoulder, while her right hand pressed against the wound. Jim hefted her along a winding deer trail, anxious, his eyes flitting about, inspecting every tree trunk they passed.

The fact there were no killers in the area gave Jim scant relief. The woman he vowed to spend the rest of life was wilting away in his arms. All he could do was help her to a tree where she could join the woods before it was too late.

But where?

"Stop. Jim, I need to stop." Christy moaned, dragged both boots along the ground.

"Not yet, we've got to get you to…"

"No-no. No further. I have to rest. Please, let me down… just for… a minute."

She loosened her grasp from around his neck, and slid limply to the earth.

"Christy…" Jim bent over her crumpled body.

"I'm sorry… ow!" Christy's eyelids pinched from stinging pain. Her limbs quivered. "Let me just catch… my…"

"You will hang on," Jim demanded. No way was it going to end like this. He looked up at the trees. "Little help here. Hey? Any way you can help me help her?"

When her eyes re-opened, something had dramatically changed.

She was alone.

44.
Didn't see that coming

Paul Drummond stood cross-checking the red-dotted aerial photograph in his hands with the landscape before him.

"We there yet?" Hardin flanked him, becoming more and more impatient with the search.

They'd given up locating one of the dots on the map, and went off seeking another.

"We should be close… if this map is right…" Drum said.

Ten yards away, he caught sight of an arched shadow at the base of a redwood. Closing in, he came upon a pair of leather ankle boots, half-filled with fallen needles. Inside the hollow, a strange, alien shape.

This volunteer's transmutation was further along than the one Holly midwifed. The one Hardin had blasted to bloody chunks.

Drum squatted.

Cream-colored netting crisscrossed the body like a cocoon. Though veiled, the face was still recognizable as a woman— kneeling, her hands together, palm to palm, knitted in prayer like a marble statue in a cathedral niche.

Drum's breath recoiled an audible gasp.

"Hey? You got one over there?"

Drum didn't answer. He stared, captivated.

"Bingo! We got a winner!" Hardin hustled up. "Gross, huh. Almost heaved my guts back at that other one."

Drum leaned back on his ankles, glanced at Hardin, then back in the goosepen. "It's real. It's really, really real."

"Damn straight it's real. You think I'd come all this way if it wasn't? Now move your ass. You don't want to get any on ya." Hardin drew the shotgun from its holster and nudged Drum with the barrel. "Come on, get out of my way, man."

But Paul Drummond didn't budge. "It's... a godsend," he stammered, the aerial photo sliding loose from his fingers.

"I said move it!" Hardin roared.

Drum ripped the weapon from Hardin's hand and rammed its walnut stock into the man's crotch. Hardin bent over like a folding chair with a guttural "Oof!" only to be clipped in the chin with a second strike, knocking him off his feet. Drum pounced, wrestled the other shotgun from Hardin's other holster and scrambled to his feet.

It was all over in five seconds.

Disarmed, groveling in near fetal position, Hardin groaned in shock and humiliation. His face reddening with insult and rage. One hand glommed onto his testicles. The other was balled into a fist hammering invisible nails into the forest floor. He tried to talk, "Yish... spftt!" But he couldn't make words with his mouth, only bubbles of spit.

"The element of surprise," Drum spoke. "Didn't see that coming, did you?"

45.
A magnificent tree

"Ohhh..." Christy moaned as hands tugged at her armpits.

Jim lifted her limp body off the amber matt of needles and woodland debris.

"I found one."

"It's you." Christy exhaled a withered breath. Her face drained of color, having aged years in minutes.

As Jim muscled her body along, a memory flashed—Miko his nurse, walking his weak, bony body across the sand toward the crashing surf at Ocean Beach.

"Don't ever leave me like that," Christy said.

"It's not far." He urged her up a gradual slope.

Rounding a tree fern, they entered a flat, open glade, the ground a green bed of wood sorrel encircled by mammoth trees.

"There, Christy... that one..." Jim tipped his head.

Although delirium smeared her vision, one of the trees in the grove stood out. It had a collar burl and a small cave in its trunk.

"Yes..." She gritted her teeth. "Slow down, please."

But there was no time to spare.

A scrub jay squawked from a branch as Jim lowered Christy's body at the foot of the redwood.

"Is it a good tree?" Christy asked.

"A magnificent tree." Jim went straight to her boots, yanking loose the laces.

"I hope... I hope it will accept me."

The tree's base was broad as a garage. "It will." He set the boots beside the opening.

"Oh no, the stuff." Christy's heart sank.

"I got it." From a pocket in his backpack he plucked out the baggies of fungus and paste Oscar had given him.

"There is a god." She strained a sigh. Wanting to help, she took the bag of fungus from him and tried to pull the seal apart. "You will see me through this?"

"All the way." He peeled off her socks.

Christy's hands trembled. She didn't have the strength to open the baggie.

"Here, let me." He pinched some stiff fungus from the bag and scored her palms and the soles of her feet, stippling the skin.

"I'm scared."

Jim didn't answer. He scooped the paste with his fingers and slathered it on her hands and feet. A single question crowded his mind: How do I keep her alive long enough for the tree to admit her?

She shook her head. "I don't want to leave now."

"You came here to do this, remember?"

"No... yes I did, I did, but then you..."

"Yeah, my fault, I guess."

"Yes." She swallowed and belched, "Damn you."

Jim cracked a giggle and offered her some of the white paste. "Here, put some of this on there."

She took a handful and swabbed it sloppily on her wound, cringing as it triggered burning jolts.

"Okay..." He motioned to the hollow in the tree trunk. "You ready?"

Christy gazed at him groggily. Then scooted backward.

"Wait." Jim kissed her tenderly. Her heartbeat throbbed his lips. "Now, in you go... into the birthplace of your new life."

"Oh god..." she panted, "Promise you'll visit."

Jim helped her into the darkness one flinching inch at a time until her eyes became two seeds of blue light.

The exertion sapped her. "Feel... faint." She wheezed and lowered her chin to her chest.

"Stay with me," he pleaded. "Christy?"

Nothing.

"Come on... you're a fighter, you can't give in yet."

No answer.

"Talk to me." He ducked his body into the opening. A thick odor of humus filled his nostrils. "Shit! Say something god dammit!" He nudged her shoulder.

"Huh?" she gasped. "Did you just swear?"

46.
Give you a head start

Curt Hardin sat, stripping off his socks. His smirk now a black and blue swelling. Ammo belts lay beside him next to tipped-over combat boots.

"You came to me!" he spouted. "I didn't go to you! You came to *me*!"

"I did," Drum agreed, digging the muzzle of a shotgun into Hardin's brainstem.

"Begging!"

"Yeah."

"I'll pay you back, you pleaded. I'll pay you back." Hardin flicked off the sock.

"Now, your shirt."

"I'll work off the loan. Whatever you need, just name it, I'll do it."

"Yeah, I said something like that. But that was before I became an accessory to murder."

"I never killed that guy."

"Everybody loved Rosco."

"Never touched him."

"The shirt!"

"What! I got no weapons on me."

"Off!" Drum stepped back, giving him room.

"Aw, fuck!" Hardin worked the buttons. "You can't be serious about saving these evil mutants? Open your eyes, it ain't natural!"

Drum didn't respond.

"Then what? You want more money? Is that it?"

"Nah."

"Come on, let's talk."

"Never been good with money."

"No shit. You should have invested in lumber, duh."

"I said, lose the shirt."

"What are you doing?" Hardin pulled the camou shirt off his back. "Let's say we call it even. Okay? You did the job. You disposed of the body. So you don't owe me nothing." Hardin flung the shirt. "Loan paid, alright?"

Drum orbited Hardin and faced him. "The pants."

"No-no. Drawing the line there, pervo. This is far as I go. You're not going to shoot me, anyway."

Drum hunched down, eye level, curling his trigger finger in Hardin's face. "See this finger? Hey!! Do… you… see… this… finger?!"

"Yeah-yeah."

"It's itching to blow your head off your neck."

Hardin averted his eyes from Drum's forefinger. "You won't do that. You don't have a killer in you."

"I do now. Know why? Because at my lowest of lows you used me like a broom. Look at me!" Drum tapped Hardin's chest with the nose of the weapon. Hardin squinted at him with a sneer. "What do you see? Huh?"

'A loser."

"Close. You see a nobody with nothing *to* lose. So blowing your head off is no different than killing a tick. A *tick!*" Drum forced a maniacal, high-pitched laugh.

Hardin flinched. The guy's wacked.

"Buuut…" Drum stood. "Just maybe I'm willing to give you a chance." He stepped back, bobbing the barrel of the shotgun up and down. "On your feet."

"Easy… easy…" Hardin stood, apprehensive, lifting his hands chest-high.

"Your pants… off!"

"Alright-alright." Hardin loosened his leather belt. "But I'm not the one who stuck you in a hole, you did that all by yourself."

"Yeah, and what was I thinking— coming to you of all people."

"That's what I'm saying. And this is the thanks I get for pulling you out, when no one else would even look at you." Hardin stepped out of his pants and kicked them aside. "This is how you pay me back?"

"That's far enough. Keep your skivvies on."

Hardin's body stood exposed. A muscular upper torso on wimpy legs, as if he devoted all his weight time on curls and bench work, while his lower body got zip attention. Spindly legs white as ointment.

"Now, here's how this is going to go." Drum felt a tickle quoting Hardin's habitual line. "The hunter becomes the hunted."

"So that's it? Your little survival school tracking game?"

"No game. You ready? I'll give you a head start. Thirty seconds. How's that for gratitude? Pretty charitable wouldn't you say?" Drum grabbed the other shotgun off the ground.

"I say fucka-you-you."

"Or should I make it ten seconds? Or, how about I tie you up and stick you in the tree with that woman there."

Sparks of hate shot from Hardin's eyes. He couldn't look at the woman crouched inside the tree.

"Yeah," Drum said. "That's a better idea. Why didn't I think of it? Oh, I just did."

Hardin smoldered, rigid as stone.

"Which is it going to be… Curt? The tree?" Drum aimed one of the shotguns at the goosepen. Then pointed the other to the northwest. "Or back to the stream, on the run from me?"

Hardin envisioned his route to the stream— take to the water all the way to the road… then nab the keys Dee hid under the SUV tire and drive away. Yeah. That's a can do. Besides, Drum's gotten slow, he's overweight, too much liquor and dope. Too much woe-is-me.

"Thirty seconds." Hardin said.

"Start your engines. One thousand one… one thousand two…"

Hardin kicked off, racing as fast as his bare legs could take him, whisking past fan-leafed ferns, hurtling logs, arms flailing, frightening black-tailed deer that launched from brush and pranced away.

Drum raised his voice. "One thousand six! One thousand seven!" He watched Hardin take the bait. He'd tricked him when he said: 'back to the stream,' and pointed the weapon to the northwest. A sleight of hand. The stream was to the south.

"One thousand ten!"

The white blotch of jockey shorts bounded in and out of tree shadows, shrinking smaller and smaller until they disappeared where the land slanted away.

A funny sight. But Drum didn't break a smile. Too much time and distance had passed since he left Kip. He patted down Hardin's discarded pants, pocketed the wallet and truck keys. Then he strapped on the man's gun belt, holstered the firearms, and shouldered the two bands of ammo. He picked up the aerial map, and, before trotting off, bowed his head to the woman inside the tree.

"Bless your heart. Sorry about all this."

47.
End it

Kip could feel the woman closing in. He had an extra-sensory ability for picking up a foreign or predatory presence in the forest. Some said he was born with psychic antennas, a fox's hearing, a hound dog's nose. He denied it. "You just make your ears the air. Listen to the creatures. The chatter of birds. They'll tell you."

At one point, he dropped the binoculars as bait. A little farther on, he knife-sliced the ball of his thumb and squeezed dollops of blood on the fronds of conspicuous ferns he passed. Anything to keep the lure alive. "The road's not far. Top of the hill. We're almost there," he'd say in a forced whisper, and flash the red scarf like a dangling carrot for the woman to trail.

He knew she was no fool. He had to be careful not to get shot as he steered her deeper and deeper into back country. Maybe she was trained in land navigation, but darkness comes early among these giants, and she'd have to be very skilled to find her way back tonight, if ever.

So would he, for that matter.

Dee came upon a fern leaf spotted with blood, then another, a few steps later.

I knew it. I knew I'd winged her.

She listened as she light-footed between the trees, following the voice and rustlings. The hunt was on. She'd take out the man too, whoever he was. Could be that documentary dude who froze up when she flirted with him at the camp. Or the one who'd whacked her with that fucking golf ball.

Just need to get close enough. One clear shot. Finish the job. Bam! Way out here, who's going to know?

She tracked them into steeper, mountainous terrain. Over one canyon and up the next. Where the hell are they going? Was there a road anywhere around here?

She'd lose them momentarily, then catch a flitting shape moving fifty yards away. Always just out of range. Beckoning her. Taunting.

Time to get ahead of this. Blitz them, she concluded, growing more irritated with the pursuit. Kick it up and run with everything you got. So what if they hear me!

Judging by the path of the blood, she headed up a rise, sprinting when she could, pushing her body to the max. Better to go all out. End it. Yes. 'End it' became the mantra, a kettle drum pounding in her head.

48.
Ask the planet

At one time, Paul Drummond could find his way out of the thickest of redwood forests, however remote. He'd been lost before, voluntarily. As a teen, he and a Hoopa Indian friend would venture deep into the woods to challenge their orienteering skills. Once they picked a fog-laden day. No sun. No path. No food. Nothing to guide them. Only a canteen of water and a pocket knife. By the flip of a coin, Drum was blindfolded, walked farther in, spun around and left there without a compass. He had to count to a hundred before removing the kerchief from his eyes. The wilderness survivalist version of hide and seek took him two horrendous days and nights to get out.

Experts say when you're lost in the wild, the body tends to walk in circles. Best to stay where you are, seek or make shelter, and wait for help to come. Sage advice. But Drum decided to experiment with what his friend's father once told him: "If there's no sun, and no one's coming to find you, then ask the planet under your feet. It knows where the north pole is."

Drum wasn't sure how Kip would fare in the dense woods where he'd diverted the cat woman, especially now, with distances deepening in shadow and nightfall near.

I should go look for him, he thought, but his heart was drawn to find Christy first. He hurried back, his mind reeling from seeing that woman's cocoon-like mutation inside the tree. He couldn't wait to tell his mother about it. Mae will volunteer her body to a redwood tree in a blink. Hell, I'll carry her in my arms all the way into Sweetwater if I have to.

Drum made it to the cabin, sucking breath, a stitch in his side. He was out of shape and dying for a stiff drink. He couldn't remember the last time he ran, or even jogged. He glugged water from a gallon container. Hid the maps and one of Hardin's shotguns under a loose plank in the floor. Armed with the other weapon, he headed off to where he'd last seen Kip, figuring Christy would be nearby.

But there was no sign of her. He was about to holler her name when a gunshot cracked like distant thunder. Followed by another. And another.

Drum's head jerked to the east.

No! Not Kip!

49.
It's taking already

At Christy's urging, Jim slipped on the sweatshirt that had wrapped her wound. He dashed back to the ravine to retrieve the camera and gear. She promised she'd still be alive when he returned. But finding her tree took longer than he figured. He thought he knew the way back, but the changing light and lengthening shadows shifted the surroundings in a short time and the prominent landmarks vanished.

Panic set in. He wanted to call out, but it wasn't like she could holler back. Besides, if he shouted the likely response would come in bullets or buckshot. So he back-tracked to the ravine one more time and picked up their trail.

"Oh god, good," he sighed, seeing her eyes blink in the darkness as he kneeled at her tree. "Sorry I took so long."

"Look," she said, showing Jim her hands and toes, "It's taking already." Tiny filaments rose through the pores of her skin, and were spreading into a downy matt. She stroked it with a finger. "Soft as moth wings."

The other good news: the paste clotted the wound and stopped the bleeding.

Jim looked from her hands to her eyes. Although faint and depleted, she appeared to be accepting her fate, content to be in the cradle of the tree's hollow, and wanting her metamorphosis to be recorded.

Jim fastened the monopod to the camera and planted it in the cushy organic material in front of the tree.

"There's money… in my fanny pack," she said.

"Oh-kay?" Where is she going with this?

"Give some to Kip… and use the rest for our film."

"*Our* film, yes." He opened the iris on the lens, adjusted focus. The late sun cast a tunnel of light into the grove, giving Christy's face dramatic definition.

"I so wanted to be there with you when it came out."

Jim looked away, struggling to maintain the clarity of attention needed to record her against waves of anguish.

Christy groaned and shut her eyes. He could see her chest heave and collapse erratically. Her eyes drift. Her lips slacken.

Don't go yet, please, please! Jim begged as he attached the lavalier to a sheaf of bark on the inner wall of the hollow.

"It tingles," she mumbled. Her feet beginning to bristle with fuzz.

"Okay, let's check the audio. Christy? Could you say something…"

Her eyes lifted with a gasp. "I could have made a life with you."

Jim's heart detonated.

"I needed you to hear that," she added.

He turned his head, covering his mouth with a hand, fighting not to cry out. She will *not* see me break. Not now. Not when she needs me stable and strong.

He pretended to adjust something on the camera housing as he struggled to sustain a mask of composure.

"My father… he'll need to know. Will you tell him? He's staying at my place."

"You can tell him yourself." Jim zoomed in for a close up, filling most of the frame with her face. Then punched the record button. "You're on."

"Hey-hey, Dad… I won't be appearing at the trial after all. I'm sure that will make some people very, very happy. But given this, these circumstances... as you'll see, I'm staying here... with my friends the redwoods... and, and I feel honored..." A tear bled down Christy's cheek. "Love ya." Her breathing became chopped. She gulped, "Everything hurts."

"Yes it does." Jim remembered Holly, her caring assurances. And being at that house in Sausalito watching the male nurse coach the woman giving birth. "Christy, look at me... you can do this. You need to hold on till the tree welcomes you."

Jim spoke as if he knew it would. Like he'd midwifed these transformations before. When he really didn't have a clue. But he didn't want to lose her, not yet.

"You've made it this far. Look at me, look at me and say, "I will do this."

Christy sucked in an urgent breath. "I will..."

"For the trees."

"Yes... for the trees," she shuddered.

"Good. Just hold on."

"Heh... look at us?"

They stared at each other without a word for a whole minute. The whites of her eyes dimming with the sun's descent.

Three bursts resounded, distant, one after the other.

Gun shots.

"What?" Christy asked, seeing Jim jerk his head to the east.

50.
Aw, shut up!

Dee's all-out sprint worked. She'd managed to reach the place where the two had stopped. Maybe they tired, or got lost trying to reach wherever the hell they were going. But there it was— her target's headband, stationary, a red flag half-hidden among the green foliage.

Bull's eye.

She narrowed the gap between them, sidling up stealthily, the muzzle of her firearm nosing between the leaves. But something was wrong. She could feel a surface tension on her skin as she drew near— an absence awaiting her.

Sure enough, when she pounced, there was no one, only the red scarf tied head-high between two branches planted in the dirt. A rag, laughing at her. You sucker.

She pounded her foot. Looked about crazily.

No! They were just here. I *heard* them. They can't be far.

She cupped an ear, holding her breath, alert for the slightest sound.

Nothing.

Her anger boiled over. She let out a mongrel's growl, ripped down the scarf, and flung it.

A Stellar's jay squawked its alarm from a branch above her head.

"Aw shut up!" She fired at it, first one round. "Shut the fuck up!" Then two more.

The resounding blasts quickly passed, swallowed by the vertical enormity of the forest.

Hearing the shots, Kip cringed as he crept down the shoulder of the hill. He felt relieved the chase was over. She almost outsmarted him.

Would she find her way back? He couldn't say. He wished he'd taken her deeper in, but darkness had seeped into the trees, spreading its blanket. He didn't want to risk getting lost. Who knows what he would find back at the camp. And he'd promised Rolf the maps would be safe.

51.
Picture yourself

Jim couldn't see Christy's face anymore, only hear her fitful, anxious breathing. She sat frail, leaning against the back wall of the hollow, her energy ebbing away, slow as the twilight that shaded the grove.

"You know..." he confided. "... back when I was lying in that hospital bed not knowing how much longer I'd live, I'd close my eyes and do a surrendering exercise to shed my fears. It was something from an old mystic by the name of Hermes Trismegistus. Anyway, if you follow along with your imagination, it may help, okay?"

"Uh-huh."

"First... visualize yourself before this lifetime... before you had a name. Be in that space... feel it as best you can... and breathe it in." He gave her a moment. "Then... as you exhale... release that picture, that feeling... and come back."

Silence. Jim waited a few seconds. "Alright?"

Christy whispered, "Yeah."

"Good, now picture yourself in the womb... mother's womb... and breathe in that sensation."

"Warm," Christy shared.

"Yes, warm..."

"Hmm..."

"And exhale... let it go." Jim waited a moment. "Okay, now picture yourself as a young person... feel the energy of youth… breathe it in… and then… release it. He didn't wait for her response. "Now experience being an old, old person…"

"That's easy."

"I bet. So… you're an elder… having lived a long life."

Jim could hear her breath settling into a rhythm. "You're doing good. Now, imagine yourself having passed away… you've let go of your body and you are in the world beyond this physical world."

Jim gave her five seconds. "And let that go with your out breath."

Christy released a long exhalation.

"Okay… lastly now… picture in your mind all these times and experiences, all of them at once: before you were born… in the womb… being young… growing old… passing on, and being in the life between lives. All these states, all these places, all the feelings… all together."

Jim waited another five seconds, listening intently. Christy's breath had evened out. "And when you're ready… let go of it all."

"Mmm," she hummed.

"According to Hermes, this is how one begins to see with the eyes of the divine."

"Ah, I like that."

"Good."

"And that worked for you? In the hospital?"

"It helped me see how life is transitory. We're all passing through. And, yet we can get fixated on this short-term reality, hoarding it even, like it's the one and only, when there is no end but a long, indefinite string of changes, physical and non-physical."

"Oh!"

"What happened… Christy?"

"I think it's touching me... oh..." She made whelping sobs. "Oh god... I think I can feel the tree... the trees... yes, I can feel them!"

"Can you describe it?"

"Like a wind. A tugging current coming up from the ground. Mmm, like the roots are reaching into me, pulling me to them. And something else... oh, I can hear it."

Jim looked into the camera's viewfinder, a knee-jerk reaction. There was really nothing he could see in the darkness. "Hear what?"

"Reminds me... when I was a girl, tree-sitting. Some nights I'd wake to sounds that were not in my ears. Like I'd tuned into the trees' wavelength. Their speech. This... this is that sound. I can hear them."

"What does it sound like?"

"Ocean waves."

52.
You're going to need
some shoes

"It's blood," Drum said, rubbing the sticky substance between his fingers. He was squatting beside a log in the area where Kip told him he'd last seen Christy Jones.

"Nooo." Kip sagged. "That cat woman must have shot her."

For Drum, finding Kip during the night took a stroke of luck, a wrenched vertebra, and a great-horned owl. After hearing the shots, he hustled into the steep forest to the east. He didn't know where the kid had gone, if he'd been murdered or wounded and left for dead. Although armed with a shotgun, Drum was not a savvy gun person. Never liked guns. Even handling one felt alien. His confrontation with Hardin was a bluff. Murder was not his nature. Just the same, if he encountered that cat woman, he wouldn't hesitate to blow her away.

Night lowered its curtain. He could barely see his hand in front of his face. After cracking his shins and tripping over one too many stumps and snags, his lower back buckled. He keeled over, racked, flat on the ground. He lay there aching for a long time until, inspired by the greeting hoot of an owl, he let out a three-count whistle to see if Kip would pick it up.

Kip whistled back.

An hour and a half later, after slogging down a canyon and following the stream, they reached the cabin, banged up, famished, and determined to search for Christy at first light. As they chomped trail mix in the dark, Drum asked Kip to walk him through the transmutation process. Kip knew it was for Mae.

Drum rose gingerly from a crouched position, bracing his lower back as he scanned the stirred-up ground near the log, hunting for clues among the minutiae. Kip stood by, holding one of Hardin's shotguns guard-ready. They chose not to call out Christy's name. No telling if more shooters were coming into Sweetwater.

"Here we go," Drum followed a trail of blood drips dotting the ground litter up the slope to the north.

The farther they tracked, the more Drum's emotions battled. He'd been hoping to atone, seek Christy's forgiveness for his gruff, biting remarks. Even declare his regret their relationship never panned out. He also wanted to express his awe at having witnessed the person in the tree, and admit how he'd doubted her. But with every drop of blood, he felt more and more immersed in grief.

Coming upon an open grove, Kip held up fast. Hearing something, he gestured to his ear. Drum raised his shotgun. They continued on, ears perked.

There, some thirty yards away, they saw a person sitting at the foot of a huge redwood.

"It's Jim, shh…" Kip lifted an index finger to his lips.

They couldn't see Christy, but they could hear Jim speak with tender, hopeful words.

"You're not really dying, Christy, you're re-becoming."

"He's helping her join the tree," Kip whispered to Drum as they padded through the green sea of sorrel.

It seemed quite intimate. And for Drum, every caring word out of Jim's mouth blistered his ears.

"He's good." Kip remarked, waving Drum to stoop down with him and not disturb Jim's gentle counsel.

But it was too heart-crushing for Drum to watch, knowing he'd missed his chance to tell Christy all she meant to him.

Sensing a shift in the air, Jim looked around. Not seeing anything, he continued his affirming words. "It's working, Christy. Keep releasing any last resistances... so you can live on... with this beautiful forest."

Jim had set his emotions aside and concentrated on seeing Christy through the difficult, at times excruciating, metamorphosis.

"You know this is why she came here," Kip said. "That was before she and Jim…"

But Drum had snuck off, soundless as a ghost.

Kip stayed on, watching for a while before giving a whistle.

"Over here." Jim offered a sleepy smile and waved.

Kip stood back from Christy's tree, curious yet respectful. He saw that Jim had erected a low-lying lean-to out of scavenged branches, roofed with sheaves of bark to protect the camera from the elements.

"It's okay," Jim scuttled over to make room for Kip. "The tree is with her. You can see it."

Kip squatted and peered in. White fungal threads twined around Christy's folded legs. A lacework of strands thin as dental floss covered her hands which lay palm-down on the earth.

"She fought hard to stay alive for it. The fungus coagulated her wound and stopped the bleeding. She's still breathing, but it's very faint. It won't last. Her heart is barely pumping. I believe the tree was able to sustain her life until she'd made the change…"

"That cat woman," Kip spoke through gritted teeth.

Jim nodded. "We heard you beckon her away.

"Don't think she'll be coming back."

"You're my hero. How about that other guy?"

Kip shared how Drum showed up, disarmed the other man, and sent him running off in only his jockey shorts.

"Where's Drum now?"

Kip snapped a glance back in the direction he'd come and shrugged. "Can't say. He was here. Maybe went back to get his mother."

They sat quietly. Kip tilted his head to take in the towering height of Christy's tree. Jim could sense the kid's unspoken sadness.

"I think she can still hear us. If there's something you want to tell her. I need to stretch a bit."

Jim labored to his feet. He stepped away from the tree to give Kip privacy but his legs were weak as twine, and having not slept or eaten, he managed to go only a few feet before tottering and collapsing in the sorrel.

Kip raced to his side, opened a water bottle and tilted it to Jim's lips.

Jim slurped it down in ravenous gulps.

'You need food." Kip set the bottle down and offered Jim some trail mix.

Jim dug his hand into the bag.

"What if I spell you for a while. Let you rest."

"Thanks, no," Jim said between bites. "Can't leave her now. But... there is something... I wonder if you'd be willing to run an errand for me? It's big."

Kip's eyes blinked wide. He helped Jim to his feet and supported him as they ambled back to Christy's tree.

"No telling when people will be returning to the camp, but I can't wait." Jim lowered himself to the ground. "We need to get this video into the world fast." He unclipped the lid of the guitar case and handed Kip two memory cards. "That's all the footage I've shot. It's got the Holly piece, Rolf's interview, the protest, Christy… and some sound bites from base camp."

Kip palmed the cards as Jim ripped a piece of paper from a notebook and jotted down words and numbers.

"Take them to this address in San Francisco. Have you ever been there?"

"No."

"But you know of the city?" Jim handed Kip the note.

"Course. I'll go."

"There's a bus station around here, right?"

"Eureka."

"Good. The sooner the better." Jim lifted an envelope out of the fanny pack and handed Kip a stack of twenties. "Here's money to buy a ticket and food, hotel and stuff."

Kip looked at Andrew Jackson's face. Fluttered the bills with his thumb. He'd never held so much. Then he read the note. "News Bang?"

"It's an internet news company. That's their main production office. Call the number. Tell Bryce Wiley who you are, and that I sent you with footage that will shake the world."

"Wiley…"

"Yes. Have someone from News Bang pick you up at the bus depot when you arrive. Okay?"

Kip nodded eagerly.

"And this is important. You need to show the footage to Wiley and Gomez." Jim clicked shut the guitar case.

Kip stuffed the money, the note and memory cards into his rucksack. Then pulled out a cardboard tube. "Can you keep these safe while I'm gone? It's the maps to all the tree people."

Jim knew the value of what Kip was handing him. "Do you know all their names?"

Kip tapped his head. "Most."

"These are missing people. Give Wiley the names you know. Have him check them out."

Kip rose to his feet and strapped on the rucksack.

Jim thought he heard something move inside Christy's tree. He checked on her, then turned back to Kip, who stood immobile, glaring at him.

"I never rode on a bus before."

Jim rocked with muted laughter. He looked at this back-woods teenager with scratches across his cheek and nose, twigs sticking out his curly hair, dressed in The John's oversized canvas pants with cuffs folded above dirt-stained feet, the soles hard as hooves.

"You're going to need some shoes."

Kip looked at his bare feet.

"To get on the bus." Jim scuttled on his knees and grabbed Christy's boots. "See if these fit."

Kip sat and laced them up. They fit, but when he walked around they looked clunky as boxes.

"Okay," he said. "Guess I should get going."

"Yeah, we're miles from Eureka."

"No problem." Kip plucked keys from his pocket, jingled them in the air. "That cat woman's rental car. Drum gave 'em to me to get back."

"Wow. You can drive?"

"Kinda. I'll take back roads."

"Well, alright." Jim extended his hand. "This is a big thing you're doing. Hope you know that."

Kip gripped Jim's hand tight and hammered it down in one swift motion. Then he picked up the shotgun.

"No-no, you can't take that." Jim pointed at the weapon. "Sorry."

Reluctantly, Kip laid it down and clumped off. After only a few yards he stopped, removed the boots, laced them together and sprang away.

53.
Not much farther now

Swollen by rain-fed mountain streams, the river flaunted its wealth, sliding its shiny mirror between sandbars and cobbled banks on its long passage to the Pacific.

The river carried Rolf Zetzer throat-deep in the drift of it, curving past clusters of redwood trees standing true as pillars bearing up the sky. Staves of filtered sunlight spangled off the gray-green water and flickered on his watchful eyes. His work boots, tied together around his neck, bobbed as he buoyed along.

He'd been carried for miles, until finally he spotted the landmark— an old tumble-down sawmill where a million logs had once been debarked and cleaved.

Rolf kicked and hand-paddled to the shoals across from the mill.

Water drained down his arms and legs as he hulked from the river, splash-spotting the egg-shaped pebbles. He sat dripping on the shore, watching the river move along, sniffing a familiar fragrance— a plant that grew along the riverside. He drew its herbal scent into his nostrils. Wormwood? Artemisia? Kathy knew. She'd bring sprigs of it into their trailer home.

Rolf lifted the work boots from around his neck, unknotted the laces, plucked out the wet baggies he'd stuffed inside, one with fungus, the other with the chalky white paste.

He pushed his bare, water-wrinkled feet into the leather, tied the boots tight, grabbed a baggie in each hand and stood.

"Not much farther now," he said, turning from the bank and lumbering into the forest.

54.
Har-din!

Dee Rotter sat on a rotting log, scratching her ankles that itched and kept angrily itching no matter how much she bloodied the skin with her nails. Some kind of bad rash erupted after a restless night spent sleeping on the damp ground.

She'd been looking for a way out of the forest all day. Even climbed to the top of a hill to get a higher vantage point, only to find her view blocked by trees. Her tactical field training and hard target marksmanship were useless. And feeling like an utter fool for being led astray intensified her rage at having failed the assignment.

Her stomach grumbled as she got up and headed down a canyon, furiously lost.

"It's not over. I'll find them. I'll finish them."

Distracted by the bright yellow of a banana slug, Dee didn't watch where she planted her heels. She slipped on a slick fleece of moss and skied off a steep eroding bluff. Clawing the ledge in a death panic, she kicked a foothold in the dirt and clung there. Her Machauser Sterben slipped from its holster and plummeted thirty feet of air before discharging a round when it hit. Looking to see where it landed tipped Dee's balance.

"Nooo!"

She struck the rocky streambed and blacked out.

The pain of a shattered pelvis soon woke her. Pain so paralyzing Dee could barely suck a breath. She tried to crawl out of the chilly water, but the act of moving sent spikes of lightning through every nerve. She crumpled in spasms, her mouth half-submerged in the shallow stream, gasping bubbles.

Get up. Come on now, defy it.

She lifted her neck. Noticed her gun propped in a notch between stones, out of reach. Spitting blood, she rolled over slowly, but finding a position free of pain was fruitless. She ended up moaning on her back.

With another night seeping in, 'You're only as good as your last hit' no longer looped around her mind like a revolving door. The bite of failure had lost its teeth.

Dee wavered between tantrum and tears.

Both won over.

"Har-din!" she wailed, rasping her throat raw. "Har-din! Help me godammit!"

Minutes passed.

The stream babbled on and on.

She crooked her neck toward the gun. Its black tunnel stared back at her.

55.
Well done, Dee!

R ichard Hersh was feeling good. The previous afternoon the CEO texted him:

> Court trial delayed.

> Defendant a no show.

He knew it, of course. But the message felt redeeming. He re-read the text three more times. Each time he pumped his fist. "And she's a no-show forever! Well done, Dee!"

Just one pesky concern— no word from her yet.

Maybe she's hiking out of the woods. Or taking care of that film maker.

The next day, Hersh flew to Eureka to meet with her. Hand off her final payment personally. He'd check with Hardin that night for a progress report on eliminating the tree freaks.

While awaiting Dee's call in the hotel's seaward lounge, one of Ingot's lawyers texted him:

> Got notice of new
>
> witness for defense.
>
> Woman claims she
>
> was hired by Ingot

266

to entrap Jones.

Had change of heart.

We must talk asap.

"Sir... sir... your wine?" the waitress asked.

The label was a blur. Hersh's lips parted, but no words came out.

56.
Easy there, momma

Hardin stumbled into a clearing of tall grass, out of breath, his legs and forearms bleeding from lacerations. The redwood slivers in his feet had already reddened with infection. He never found the stream, or the fire road where he parked his truck. He spent the night shivering under a piled heap of fern fronds. Nested there, he thought of ways to make Paul Drummond suffer before killing him. Things done in prisoner of war camps he read about.

In the morning, mortal doubts began their attack. He had to make it out by end of day or else he'd die.

Finding the open field was a welcome sign. Now he could get his bearings. In the distance, a slender vine of smoke rose above the woods. He exhaled a sigh. But as he headed toward it, he sensed movement in his periphery.

Two elk under the tree line. One sitting, chewing. The other upright, glaring at him.

No horns. Females.

Hardin stretched his arms out as he back-peddled, relieved they weren't bull elk.

"It's all cool. Mean no harm."

The standing elk's head dipped in defensive pose.

"Easy there, momma. Juuust passin' through."

The moment she charged, Hardin realized what he'd stepped into— *its calving season, their newborns are near.*

"Oh shit!" He pivoted to run but tripped over his swollen feet.

The last thing he saw was the elk's cloven hoof filling the pink sky as it stomped, blotting out everything.

57.
We've been given every tool except one

"Hmm... hmm."
Someone hummed faintly in a far corner of Jim's mind. A deep, tremulous purr.

He woke in twilight, chilled. He lay on top of a sleeping bag he'd pulled from The John's tent.

"Hmm..." the voice resounded.

He sat up fast, jerking his head toward Christy's tree.

"Hmm." There it was again.

He pulled the headset off his ears and heard nothing. A silent forest. The source of the humming was coming from the wireless microphone he'd clipped to the rim of the hollow to record Christy.

Jim scrambled to the opening. "Christy?" He peered in, clamping the headset back onto his ears.

"Hmm."

"I'm here, Christy. I'm still here."

"We are here... too." Her voice sounded deeper, a lower register.

Jim couldn't believe his ears. "We? Christy?"

"We are now... a we."

It was Christy, only not just Christy. The tree was speaking with her, through her.

Oh, god, it's it! The interval she and Kip talked about!

"I am an old tree by your measure, but there are much older, much larger ones near here."

"I'm listening."

"The larger the tree the more it is being connected to through the roots by other trees. My roots touch other roots of this forest all the time. Our root systems are most precious to us. They can live for hmm… more than ten thousand years because we are so united."

This was too incredible. Although stunned, Jim moved into interview mode.

"May I ask a question?'

"Hmm."

"Will Christy live on through you?"

"Yes. We are sharing our lives. She is a feisty one, and oh, so much heart."

"That's really good to hear."

"We are showing her what it is to be a forest."

"Oh… okay." Jim gently pressed the record button on the camera.

"How we connect to each other. How our young, baby trees have all the survival information they need to grow."

"Yes?"

"I see your young don't have this. They once did. Hmm… long ago. Our seeds carry all the planetary information for a tree to live. No matter what the age, the tree knows how to survive because it knows how to connect with the community. That's not something we learn. We are born with this… this knowing."

"I understand."

"Your kind doesn't have that. I would call that a shortcoming. Our shortcoming is possibly that we cannot walk around like you do. Your shortcoming is you are born without survival instincts."

"That is true."

"And without caring."

"Did you say, 'caring'?"

"You are born not knowing how to care. You have to be taught it. Shown how to care. Hmm… and many, many of you never learn that."

There was a long silence. Jim didn't let it linger.

"I have another question. How did this come to happen? This transmutation with humans?"

"We called for help."

"You called who for help?"

"Five hundred years ago we stood strong. Two hundred years ago we began to hear the cutting. A hundred years ago we knew it would be taking us. We feel rushed away… far too soon. We called out to the winds to help find a way."

"The winds?"

"The outer winds."

Jim's mind fumbled, trying to compute what the tree described.

"One of your kind must have been listening," the tree said.

Jim was about to ask about that, but held back, not wanting to interrupt.

"We've been given every tool except one. We cannot fight the uncaring ones. We can ward off anything natural because of who we are as life bearers. We bring in a great deal of water from the universe, always. This is why fire cannot consume us. We do not die in fire. It never harms us because our waters never cease."

Jim considered what it said. Before he could ask another question, the tree continued.

"And now this uncaring is taking our lives. It is forcing us to leave, and it will in time force you to leave. It seeks to bring everything down to its level. And it is succeeding with us."

The voice went silent. Jim listened, waited, hoping the interval would not end.

"Will this work?" he finally asked. "The tree people... inside you. Will they help stop the cutting?"

The voice returned, its speech slowing down.

"We... hope. It may not be enough. We grieve for those of you who will lose us because we are so much a part of your life... and the life force of the planet.

"What else can we do?"

"Hmm... what I tell you is from what I know as a tree."

"Okay."

"Speak to others. Touch their roots, like a forest. And..."

"And?"

"Never... never let... your waters... cease."

"How do we do that?"

There was no response.

"Hello?"

Nothing. That was it. The interval was over.

"Whooooh!" Jim yanked the headset off his ears, howling with elation. Then he slapped a hand to his mouth, surprised at how loud he'd let loose.

He shut off the record button on the camera, leaned his back against the tree and sat there in the stillness. As he pondered what just took place, a realization jolted his senses. He could now feel the presence of another intelligence— the redwood trees, not simply as things, or immense plants, but as great sentient beings sensing him, conscious of his actions, his emotions.

He lifted his head to the surrounding ring of trees. "Hello there. I see you better now."

Jim woke the next day eager to hear more from the trees. The interval ended too abruptly. Unprepared, he'd fumbled with the exchange. He had more questions to ask. Questions about their perception. How they came to be on this planet. Do they sleep? Do they dream? What was that it said about humans once being born with survival instincts? When was that? How'd we lose it? And what will happen to the planet when the forests are gone?

Jim stayed near Christy most of the day, holding the shotgun Kip had left, ready to take the necessary steps should some murderous intruder invade Sweetwater. He found food in the cabin. Took short walks around Christy's grove, looking at her tree from different vantage points to help him remember where it stood, noting distinguishing features, its large collar burl, a high snag arching overhead, and the direction he needed to take from the cabin to reach her.

Walking around he came upon a monstrous fallen tree in slow decay, long as a football field, wrapped in bright green moss with a sapling growing straight up out of it.

"There's no death here," Jim mumbled. "It's all one continuous chain of creation."

The time had come to think about going back to work on the documentary. He'd stay one more night, wanting to be there when people returned— *if* they returned. What happened to them, anyway? What happened to all the big talkers they planned to bring in to confirm the authenticity of this phenomenon?

Then again, no one came storming in wielding firearms either.

Jim set up his camera intending to tell the whole story as he experienced it. He planted the monopod so he'd be in the foreground with a clear view of Christy's tree behind him. Her body now a soft cloud inside the trunk. Around the rim of the goosepen, new buddings sprouted through the twists of ragged bark. How many years it would take to enclose the opening completely he could only guess.

It hadn't taken long for the process to stiffen Christy's body. Inside the growing net of fibers, he watched her fingers lock up, her torso solidify, her flesh discolor and shrink into the bones of her face, making her features skeletal.

At first it was disturbing to see the changes, but knowing Christy lived to make the shift, Jim stayed with her, neither turning away, nor submitting to revulsion. He documented the minute by minute changes in his mind lovingly.

As he checked the framing through the view finder, a question surfaced: What if this is just the beginning of the metamorphosis? What if the petrification of her body is like the larval stage for some other form to be hatched from the tree… later? Given what's happened, the idea was not preposterous. Jim let it go. Guess, time will tell. He hit the record button only to discover the camera battery was dead.

Just as well. Not sure I'd come across very convincing.

Jim remained close by the rest of the day, speaking to Christy every once in a while, imparting random thoughts, as well as the words of sages he'd memorized. The solace they offered when he lay emaciated in that hospital close to death was replaced by a new sense of wonder. He could still hear the voice of the tree telling him, "Our roots are most precious to us."

He imagined them spreading beneath his feet, pushing through the earth, fibrous fingers reaching outward to touch another tree's roots— more than touch, to share nutrients and support. He thought of UC Davis's project and realized it was about measuring how far the blood of tree people would carry through the redwood forest.

And to think, right now Christy's blood is being received by other trees. Not just her blood, her spirit.

That evening he lay at the base of her tree and spoke to her in a stream of consciousness. "I'm still here," he said in a half-whisper. "Just want to say you picked a lovely place to be reborn. A medicine place." He looked up at the lofty heights. "The setting sun is shining high in the treetops. It reminds me of being with you that day inside Grace Cathedral. You took me there. And you took me here. Only, this is different. You can't build this. You can't build anything like this. Nobody can. No vaulted ceiling or stained glass compares. This is alive."

58.
Never let your waters cease

The call of a bird woke Jim. His eyes opened stubbornly to sunbeams lending a luminous aura to the morning vapors lifting off the forest floor.

He unzipped the dew damp sleeping bag, wiggled out, and turned to check on Christy inside the cavity of the tree. Her wooden body was swathed in a lacy, white robe. But she was no longer there. Her radiant field of light gone, passed over to the tree, to its roots.

"So be it," he nodded.

Time to go.

He dismantled the lean-to and went about clearing the area, spreading needles and duff to erase all signs of footprints and human activity. He made plans to come back and camouflage all the tree people with branches and bark.

"I'm taking the maps with me until I return," he announced.

Before setting off, Jim orbited the circle of trees in the grove, guitar case in hand. He touched the shaggy bark of each trunk and said, "Never let your waters cease." Then he hiked to the old Weaver homestead where he gathered a baggie of fungus and a baggie of the paste to show people at *News Bang*, stuffed them into the front pockets of his pants, hid the shotgun under the loose floor plank, and shut the cabin door behind him.

As he ambled through the woods, he pictured Kip in San Francisco showing the video to Bryce Wiley and Gomez, their jaws on the floor.

The stream rang like tiny chimes. Minnows flashed in the silken water. A stranger's reflection startled him— his own face, gaunt with sunken, glassy eyes, a scruffy beard and scraggly hair.

He washed the dirt off his face and moved on, winding around the ferns that lined the rivulet. He stopped at the waterfall where he and Christy filtered water. The day of their vows. The day of the killers.

I can find my way back to her tree from this spot. Now to find my way out.

"We follow the stream for a mile or so." He recalled Christy saying. "It will bend around the dead end of an old fire road."

Jim started across the stream, only to hold back midway. He stood there, wavering, staring trance-like as cool water eddied around his ankles. His eyes misted. His mouth soured. He could no longer contain the mix of emotions he'd been packing around. He gushed a short, agonized eruption, his shoulders pitching forward, rattling the handle of the guitar case.

After his outburst, Jim ran a forearm across his eyes. The light had shifted, and something else. He dipped his head and patted his pockets. The baggies of fungus and paste made a splotchy sound.

Yes.

His heartbeat accelerated.

He stepped out of the water and walked back into the redwoods.

"One in every grove."

Acknowledgments

Redwood trees are life-bearing masters, breath-makers who create habitat for innumerable forest creatures. I have vivid childhood memories of family trips camping among groves along the Eel River, and later years living under their graceful branches. Writing about them only begins to touch the awe and gratitude I feel for these gentle giants.

I am thankful for the heartfelt support of Veronica, my wife and companion, and for all the help I received from Alta Engstrom, Gretchen Alford, Donna Sarah Taylor, Claire Whitehead, and the generous counsel and surgical editing of Jeffrey Smith.

I also wish to thank and applaud the environmental activists for their selfless, unrelenting efforts to save the redwoods and other old growth forests from extermination.

About the Author

T his is M. St. Croix's second book of fiction. His sto-
rytelling ideas come from life experiences as a painter,
sculptor, carpenter, actor, playwright, educational TV producer, Earth energy practitioner and world traveler.

www.mstcroix.com

CPSIA information can be obtained
at www.ICGtesting.com
Printed in the USA
FFOW01n2136260418
46379338-48104FF

9 781545 622421